A TRUE GENTLEMAN

Jena Leigh's head snapped up, and her gaze collided with smoldering silver eyes. Her throat closed off, and she could not utter a word. He was everything she'd ever fantasized that a man should be. Why did he have to be the enemy?

"Dare I hope that your true motive in coming here was to see me?" He touched her hand and her fingers instinctively curled around his; then she jerked her hand away.

It took a moment for his meaning to penetrate Jena Leigh's thoughts. When it did, she quickly stepped out the door and onto the stoop. "You're out of your mind! Apologize right now!"

A quick smile curved his mouth. Most women would act indignant, pretend to misunderstand his meaning, or pretend to be faint and call for smelling salts. But this little hellion was demanding an apology. "What is a gentleman to think when a lady shows up at his place without a proper chaperone?"

She backed toward the stairs, a shocked look on her face. "I would never confuse you with a gentleman."

HAWK'S PURSUIT

Constance O'Banyon

LEISURE BOOKS   NEW YORK CITY

A LEISURE BOOK®

October 2006

Published by

Dorchester Publishing Co., Inc.
200 Madison Avenue
New York, NY 10016

ISBN 0-8439-5636-4

The name "Leisure Books" and the stylized "L" with design are
trademarks of Dorchester Publishing Co., Inc.

Printed in the United States of America.

Visit us on the web at www.dorchesterpub.com.

HAWK'S PURSUIT

Prologue

Kingsley's Home for Children
El Paso, Texas, 1858

"A drink ... please. Water," ten-year-old Jena Leigh Hawk whispered weakly, wondering if anyone could hear her. Her lips were dry and cracked, and she moistened them with a sweep of her tongue. She felt a tightening in her throat and arched her back in pain when a bout of coughing shook her entire body. With an effort born of desperation, she tried to take a deep breath, but that attempt only resulted in her choking and gasping for air.

She tossed restlessly on the cot in the infirmary where she had been quarantined with three other children. In one of her bouts of consciousness she'd heard voices describing her condition, and someone said that she had diphtheria. She didn't know what diphtheria was and wondered if she was dying. She thought she might be, since she had to fight for every breath.

Shivering with cold, Jena Leigh pulled the covers to her chin one minute, only to throw them off when she felt as if her body were on fire. In a fever-induced state she moaned, wishing she had the strength to draw someone's attention. She was so thirsty, she hurt all over, and she wanted her sister, Laura Anne, to comfort her.

Jena Leigh drifted off to sleep, but a short time later she woke in panic. There was heat everywhere, not just from her fever, but enveloping her and pressing in on her. Smoke parched her throat, making it even harder to breathe.

It was hot—so hot. She tossed her head back and forth and tried to fight against the deep lethargy that kept pulling her down. Something was terribly wrong—even in her fever-induced delirium she sensed it. Her eyes felt heavy, as if weights were holding them down, but she forced them open a crack, and came fully awake. She couldn't understand what the red glow near the door was, or why it shimmered, climbing up the walls to the rafters.

Jena Leigh heard shouting, and there was a roar that made her head ache. Using all her strength, she focused on the red glow, not certain whether it was real or one of the nightmares that had plagued her since she'd become ill.

"Fire!" someone shouted.

"The whole place is on fire!" someone else screamed.

Jena Leigh was horrified when she saw fire licking at

2

the rafters over her bed. She heard something that sounded like a loud explosion and watched as the inner wall of the infirmary collapsed into flaming rubble. She tried to raise her head, but it was like a heavy weight, and she fell helplessly back against her pillow. In alarm, she saw sparks from the rafters fall onto her bed, and she tried to move, but she was too weak. She doubled over, choking from the smoke. She became desperate when her blanket ignited, sending flames toward her body.

Through a haze of agonizing pain she looked for her sister. Jena Leigh wanted Laura Anne, and she silently called to her as the flames leaped higher; the whole roof was on fire. The empty bed next to Jena Leigh's was already engulfed in flames—it seemed as if the whole world were on fire.

Just when she had resigned herself to the fact that she was going to die, she saw Laura Anne fighting her way through the wall of fire that separated them. Jena Leigh tried to scream, to tell Laura Anne to go back, but her throat closed up; she could do no more than whimper. She was horrified as the east side of the building caved in. Jena Leigh reached out her small hand as she watched Laura Anne disappear behind a wall of flames!

She fought the overwhelming weakness that swamped her, wanting to go to her sister. Then strong arms lifted her. In confusion and aching pain, Jena Leigh stared into a blackened face that was unrecognizable: the person's hair had been singed, and angry red welts marred the face. Tears swam in Jena Leigh's eyes when she recognized the matron's voice. Mrs. Kingsley had been a mother to the Hawk children since the day they had arrived at the orphanage. The sweet lady was already horribly burned, and still she fought to save her children.

Mrs. Kingsley's voice seemed to come to Jena Leigh from far away. "Don't worry, sweetness—I'll get you safely out of here."

With sobs choking her, Jena Leigh attempted to tell the matron about Laura Anne, but the only sound she could make was a keening moan. She struggled, pointing in the direction of where she'd seen Laura Anne go down, but the matron wasn't listening. She was too busy dodging falling timbers and licking flames. Soon they reached the door, and Jena Leigh was able to take a cleansing breath. Mrs. Kingsley carried her away from the inferno and laid her gently on the grass beneath the elm tree that had once sheltered the playground, now blackened and twisted. Helplessly, Jena Leigh watched Mrs. Kingsley hurry back into the burning building. She clutched at the rough tree trunk until she was able to pull herself into a sitting position. Her sister was dead—she knew that—and so were many other children. Her ears started ringing, and dizziness swamped her, taking her down into a deep darkness where there was no pain, no fear, no sorrow.

In spite of the havoc going on around her, Irene Prescott kept a cool head. Flames spiraled upward, illuminating the night sky. A bucket brigade stretched from the water well behind the hotel to the burning two-story building. She knew it was a hopeless task—the second floor had already collapsed onto the first floor. There would be nothing identifiable when the ashes cooled. Dazed children, many with blackened faces and scorched hair, wandered aimlessly about while several adults tried to herd them to safety.

Irene hiked her skirt up and tucked it into her waistband so she could kneel beside one of the children who had been rescued and left on the grass. The poor girl's hair had been singed down to her scalp, and her face was blackened by smoke. Sadly, Irene lifted the skeletally thin child in her arms with the intention of placing her with the critically burned bodies. But when the little fist closed over her hand, pain stabbed her heart as she stared down at the child. She found she was reluctant to relinquish the girl.

"God," she prayed, "so many children have died here tonight. Please let this one live." Tears of anguish filled her eyes, and she lowered her head in total devastation. The smells of death and smoke clogged her throat. Pity slammed into her like a fist when Irene gently touched a sprig of charred hair, unable to tell what color it had been.

"Just put the body over there," a grim-faced undertaker informed her, pointing to a tent where a makeshift morgue had been erected.

"This one's not dead," she told him. "Not just yet, anyway."

She touched the small hand, and her eyes widened when she discovered the fingers were hot. This child had a fever.

"She's very ill," Irene said, turning away from the scene of death. The light from the fire fell on the small face, and she watched the lashes flutter open. A pair of amber eyes stared back at her in bewilderment. With a rush of relief, Irene saw the slight rise and fall of the girl's chest as she struggled for each breath. A soft moan escaped the child's lips, and Irene grasped her tightly against her chest, feeling as if a miracle had just occurred.

"I'll not be placing this girl among the dead," she said, striding hurriedly across the street and away from the fire. She rushed into the hotel lobby and, with renewed hope, climbed the stairs to her rented room. Once inside, she gently placed the child on her bed. She had already learned there was only one doctor in El Paso, and he would be busy with the injured. Irene rolled up her sleeves, determined to do everything within her power to save the young girl.

Jena Leigh rolled her head back and forth, battling fear and sadness. She shivered with dread—there was something she needed to remember … something that was going to hurt her badly. But she couldn't think, couldn't grasp a single thought.

As she slowly opened her eyes, a lone tear trailed down her cheek. Everything was coming back to her now—at first in bits and pieces, and then like a flood, hitting her with a force that left her heartsick and frightened.

Laura Anne had died in the fire!

Her eyelids were just too heavy to hold open, so she closed them again. It couldn't be true—Laura Anne couldn't be dead. *Please, God, no,* she prayed silently, hoping she was only having another nightmare, and her sister would greet her with a smile in the morning. What would she do without her sister?

Jena Leigh felt a cool cloth on her forehead, and she heard the mumble of voices—a man and a woman, but she couldn't quite grasp their words, and she didn't want to fight against the darkness that hovered over her. Finally it took her again.

Irene studied Dr. Randolph's ruddy complexion and shook her head. "You're telling me that this child had diphtheria before the fire?"

The tall, angular man nodded his head. "I treated her and three others for the disease only two days ago." His gray eyes became guarded as he looked at the woman who was a legend in Texas. "You shouldn't have brought her here to this hotel, you know." There was accusation in his tone. "By doing so you've not only exposed yourself to the disease, but others as well."

"Don't worry about me—I've already had diphtheria." Irene glared angrily at the doctor. "What was I supposed to do? Leave her in the street to die alone? What would you have done?"

"It might have been kinder if you had just left her with the others." He snapped his bag shut, his eyes on the girl, who was laboring for every breath. "You know I'll have to quarantine this hotel now."

"Then do it and be done with it!" Irene snapped. "The girl stays here."

He placed a tube of ointment and a bottle of liquid on a bedside table and shook his head, leveling a censorious glance at Irene. "The damage is already done." He nodded at the medicine. "The liquid is to ease her breathing—give her a teaspoon every three hours. The ointment is for her burns—rub it on her as often as you think she needs it. Especially on her face and head." He rubbed the back of his neck as if it ached. "She probably won't survive the night."

Irene turned her back on the doctor, dipped the cloth in water, and reapplied it to the child's forehead. "Oh, yes, she will," she vowed. "I don't want to hear any more of your gloomy predictions. Take your defeatist attitude with you and get out of here!"

Dr. Randolph was not surprised by Irene Prescott's anger or her stubbornness. Somewhere in her early forties, she was one of the most respected newspaperwomen in the state. Tall and slender, she had deep brown eyes that could cut through a person like a razor—just like they were cutting through him at the moment. Her dark red hair had been clipped short, more for practicality, he imagined, than from an attempt at stylishness. Her starched white blouse fit high against her neck. Beneath her plain blue broadcloth skirt, he spotted a pair of scuffed, brown Western boots. Irene dressed for comfort and not to impress anyone—she was definitely a force to be reckoned with. She lived in Altamesa Springs, Texas, and was owner and editor of a small but prestigious newspaper. As a reporter she never avoided controversy, and she was not afraid to plant dissent in the minds of her readers. Her bold style gave new meaning to the phrase "The pen is mightier than the sword."

Irene's husband, Garland Prescott, had been a worldwide correspondent for several New York newspapers, including the *New York Times*. He and Irene had traveled the world and sent back stories from distant places, which the ravenous American public devoured. After Garland had been killed in a hunting accident in India a few years back, Irene had returned to her roots in Altamesa Springs and started the newspaper that soon became so popular it was distributed throughout Texas. Dr. Randolph himself subscribed to the *Altamesa Springs Gazette*. He liked the way Irene Prescott challenged the daily complacency of the general public and fired people's minds—made them think. This slight woman could take any issue and make an editorial out of it.

"How long you plan on staying in El Paso?" he asked, picking up his bag and moving to the door.

Irene cast him such a hard gaze, he was sure it could have driven a nail straight through a two-by-four plank. "I don't intend to go anywhere until this child has recovered. And then," she said, rubbing ointment on the child's smudged face, "if no family claims this girl, I intend to take her home with me." That admission surprised Irene as much as it seemed to shock the doctor. As an only child, Irene knew nothing about children. She and Garland had never had any.

As a matter of fact, she had always felt uncomfortable around youngsters, not knowing how to communicate with them—she didn't even particularly like them, and had never wanted any of her own.

The doctor shook his head. "I don't know this particular child. But the fact that she was living at the orphanage probably means she doesn't have parents. However, you might want to consider that she could have siblings." He ran a blunt finger over the catch on his worn black bag. "There is also the possibility that if she had brothers or sisters, they might have died in the fire."

Irene nodded slowly. "I've already considered that. I'll make inquiries tomorrow and find out what I can about her."

The doctor's eyes filled with regret. "If she's still with us tomorrow."

"Quit saying that!" Irene berated him.

"Suit yourself," he said wearily. Today had been a hard day for him. So many lives lost. "I do hope she makes it."

"When I held this little girl," Irene confessed, "I was hit with the first real emotions I've felt since Garland's death. This child has gone through too much to lose her life now." Irene touched the girl's hand, feeling the small bones. "You're a fighter, aren't you, little one?"

Jena Leigh's eyelashes fluttered, and Irene stared into the saddest amber eyes she'd ever seen. The small hands slipped out of her grasp and formed into fists, as if she were holding on to her sanity by a thin thread.

"It's all right. You can go back to sleep. I won't leave you."

* * *

10

Irene glanced in the mirror and quickly ran a brush through her short hair. She paused to look at the lines of exhaustion around her mouth and the dark circles underneath her eyes. She hadn't had much sleep in the last four days and nights. With a weary sigh, she turned to the girl, who had just awakened, then dropped onto a chair and smiled at the child.

"I'm glad you're awake. I'd like you to eat some of this broth if you feel up to it," she said, holding a spoon to the child's mouth.

Jena Leigh clamped her mouth together tightly and rolled her head to the side.

"If you will take one spoonful," Irene cajoled, "I'll explain to you about the fire."

The amber eyes filled with tears as Jena Leigh turned back to the woman and took a sip from the spoon. It took her a moment to swallow the liquid because her stomach protested at the thought of food, and she felt as though she were going to be sick.

"There now—that wasn't so bad, was it?"

Jena Leigh frowned, wondering who the woman was. She stared into brown eyes that were softened by compassion.

"Take a little more. You haven't had anything to eat in days. You need nourishment."

"How long?" Jena Leigh asked in an almost inaudible whisper, causing Irene to lean closer to hear her words.

"I brought you here four nights ago. The sheriff told me the fire started on the second floor, where someone must have knocked over a lamp." Irene reached for a glass of water and lifted it to the child's lips. She watched her take a sip before pushing the glass away.

Singed lashes swept upward, and the girl regarded Irene with tear-filled eyes. It was difficult for Irene to tell much about the child's features because of the pasty white ointment she'd smeared on her face. She watched as the small body shook with anguish, and pity hit her so hard she had to break eye contact. Instinct warned her this child was proud and would not want anyone's pity, and that she would want to know the truth.

"Can you tell me about my sister?"

Irene tried to think how she could lighten the blow, but there was no way to lessen the pain. "I talked to the sheriff." Her hand closed over the small one lying limply against the patchwork quilt. "Your sister was not listed among the survivors."

Tears of devastation trailed down Jena Leigh's cheeks, and her fingers dug into the quilt. "I saw her die." She licked her dry lips and glanced into the woman's eyes. "She ... she was trying to get to me—to save me."

Tears gathered behind Irene's eyes, but she refused to let the child see her cry. "Do you feel like taking a little more broth?" she asked, holding the spoon to the girl's lips.

Jena Leigh turned her head into the pillow, refusing to take another bite. "Where am I?"

"At the Broadrick Hotel."

"I ... need to know what happened to Mrs. Kingsley."

Irene realized she was about to deliver another devastating blow to the child. She would liked to have kept the news from her until she was stronger, but the wise little eyes were probing hers for answers.

"I'm sorry. She didn't make it."

Fresh tears flooded Jena Leigh's eyes. "Oh. She … she saved me from the fire. Then she went back inside to … to save others."

Irene felt inadequate to comfort a child who had already faced so much sorrow. She watched helplessly while the small body shook with sobs.

She patted the small hand, and it clamped around her fingers. "From what I heard about Mrs. Kingsley, she would not have left the burning building until she was sure all the children were safe."

After a while Jena Leigh managed to control her sobs and glanced back at the woman. "Who are you?"

Irene stood, stretching the cramps out of her shoulders. "I'm Irene Prescott. I brought you here the night of the fire. You were very ill. What is your name?"

"Jena Leigh Hawk," she replied. Fighting back tears, she had to know what had happened. "Mrs. Prescott—"

"Just call me Irene."

"Is it permitted for me to use your Christian name?"

Jena Leigh was polite in spite of her sorrow, Irene noted, and there was decided intelligence reflected in those amber eyes. "I would like it if you would."

Jena Leigh thought that over and decided not to call the woman anything at the moment. She asked the question that was tearing at her mind. "Why did I live while so many others died? Why did my sister and Mrs. Kingsley have to die?"

Irene took the small hand in hers. Diphtheria had ravaged the frail little body until the girl was little more than skin and bones. Although the child's face and head were smeared with ointment, Irene could still see the angry burns on her right cheek and across her forehead. "The only answer I can give you is that you're still here because God intended you to live."

Jena Leigh asked in a broken voice, "Why couldn't I have died with my ... sister? I don't want to be left alone."

Irene was a battle-hardened reporter who had seen many tragedies in her lifetime, but this small girl's plight hit her like a blow to the heart. "I don't know why such things happen," she said, knowing the child was seeking answers she didn't have. "But I do know that you're not alone. I'll be with you."

Now Jena Leigh really looked at the woman who had tended her throughout the darkest time of her life. "Why should you care what happens to me?"

Irene looked into the questioning eyes that were now flaring with anger. "Because you and I have something in common. You see, I'm alone, too. And I figure if we stay together, we'll have each other. What do you think?"

"About what?" the child asked with little real interest. Her eyelids drifted over her eyes.

"When I leave El Paso," Irene explained, still thinking she had lost her mind for taking on the responsibility

14

of this girl, "I want you to go with me. Would you like that?"

The tiny fingers picked at the frayed quilt while her other hand clasped Irene's as if it were a lifeline. "It doesn't matter," she answered without bothering to open her eyes. "Nothing matters anymore."

By taking on this child, Irene knew her life was about to undergo a drastic change. She'd lived alone for years, and she liked it that way. When Irene attempted to withdraw her hand, the child's grip tightened, so she remained still until the small fingers relaxed and fell away. Irene had learned only that morning that the children who had survived the fire were being transferred to a facility in Dallas. She was not going to allow this girl to join that group.

She watched the steady rise and fall of the girl's chest, noticing that she was breathing easier now. The burn on her cheek wasn't deep, so it probably wouldn't leave a scar, but the one on Jena Leigh's forehead might. It was the scars on the inside that Irene was worried about—they would take much longer to heal. The little one needed something to believe in—her spirit was broken, but Irene intended to do everything she could to help her recapture her will to live.

Night had fallen before the child awoke again. Irene had been to the dining room and ordered everything she thought a child might like to eat. She saw it as an encouraging sign when the girl ate a few bites of chicken breast and had two spoonfuls of lemon pudding.

Jena Leigh was propped up on the pillow watching Irene. "Tell me about your home, Irene."

"I live in Altamesa Springs in a big house where I was born. I think you'll like the town. The weather isn't as hot as it is in El Paso, and we have snow in the wintertime."

"Do you mean real snow? The cold white stuff?"

"The genuine article."

"Mrs. Kingsley told me about snow, and I've read about it in books. I've always wanted to see it for myself."

"And so you shall."

Jena Leigh's small fist closed around the pendant she wore about her neck, as if it brought her comfort.

"What's the story on that?" Irene asked, thinking it was a very fine piece of jewelry for a child to have—especially an orphan.

"I can only tell you what my brother Whit told me. I was too young at the time to understand everything he said." Beads of sweat had popped out on the child's face, and she took a sip of water.

She was still so fragile, and Irene wondered if it was wise to question her about her past at this time. "Why don't you just rest for now, and tell me about it later?"

"I want to tell you now. I don't remember my mother or my father."

"Why don't you tell me what you do remember?" Irene said, deciding it might help Jena Leigh look toward the future if she put the past behind her.

Her eyes clouded. "There were four of us Hawk children: two brothers, Whit and Drew, then Laura Anne and myself. I was the youngest."

"Do you know what happened to your parents?"

The child took a deep breath before she continued. "Whit told me we once lived in Galveston. He said we had a very fine house there, and our father owned a shipping company."

"Of course!" Irene said in amazement. "I've heard of Hawk Shipping in Galveston. That was some years back, though."

"Whit said our father had a bad habit of gambling and lost the company and our home. My brother thought our father just didn't care much about anything after our mother left."

"Your mother died?"

"No. She left us all and went away with some man. Whit didn't tell me that, but I overheard him and Drew talking about it when they thought I was asleep."

Irene shook her head. "You don't have to talk about this any more if you'd rather not."

The child drew in a shaky breath. "It's all right. I'd like to tell you what I know, which isn't much."

Irene was impressed with how smart Jena Leigh was for such a young child. Her enunciation of each word was perfect—someone had taught her well. "You don't know where your mother or father is?"

"None of us have heard from our mother since she left. Our father went to California, and when Whit was old enough, he went west to find him." Jena Leigh's gaze settled on her hands, which were clutched in her lap. "Whit never came back, and neither did our father. I know my brother would have returned if he could have—that's why I'm worried about him."

Irene was careful not to mention the sister who had died in the fire. "That would leave your brother Drew. Do you know where he is?"

Tears gathered in the child's eyes. "He left as soon as he was old enough. He went to find my brother and my father." She raised her head as if she were studying the ceiling. "They are all gone but for me."

Once again Irene felt an unfamiliar sensation—tears. She fought them back before she spoke. "Jena Leigh, I own a newspaper that is read all over Texas. My promise to you is that I will write an article inquiring whether anyone knows the whereabouts of your brothers, and ask them to contact me if they do. You can never tell—perhaps your brothers may even read the article themselves."

Jena Leigh laid her head back against the pillow. "Irene, you remind me of Mrs. Kingsley. She was kind like you."

A lump formed in Irene's throat. No one had ever accused her of being kind. "Tell me about the pendant," she said, edging the conversation in a different direction. "What does it represent?"

Jena Leigh held it out for Irene's inspection. The most prominent feature on the pendant was a tall ship with a hawk flying above it. Irene assumed the bird represented the girl's last name.

"The Latin on the banner means 'To four I give the

world.' It means our father gave his four children the world." She lowered her head. "Of course, that did not turn out to be true."

"Do you read Latin?" Irene asked, thinking the girl had merely memorized what she had been told by her brother.

"Yes. Latin, Spanish, and ancient Greek."

Irene was stunned. "Ancient Greek!"

"Yes, ma'am."

This child *was* special—she was a genius. "Jena Leigh, who taught you those languages?"

"Mrs. Kingsley. She thought that girls deserved to have the same education as boys. She was very intelligent, and it was a ..." Jena Leigh's voice faltered. "She made learning fun."

"How old are you, Jena Leigh?"

"I will be eleven on the twenty-third of next month."

"Incredible! Did the other children learn languages, too?"

"Only the ones who wanted to. Mrs. Kingsley was strict about not putting more on the children than they could handle."

"And you could handle it all, couldn't you?"

Jena Leigh blushed. "Mrs. Kingsley said I had an active mind. She ... she let me read her personal copy of *The Iliad*. She treasured the book because her father had given it to her when she was a child. It must have been destroyed in the fire."

"Was it written in Greek?"

"Yes. I liked it very well."

19

"Your Mrs. Kingsley was a treasure. I would have been honored to meet her."

Jena Leigh moved her head to look out the window and said nothing.

Irene's mind was still reeling. "So you were given this pendant by your father," she said, taking the child's mind back to the past.

"Papa had rings with the same design made for himself and my brothers, and pendants made for our mother, Laura Anne, and me." Her eyes filled with sudden tears. "I wonder where Laura Anne's pendant is now?"

Irene tried to distract the child. God only knew she wasn't good with children, and she had no idea what she was going to do with this one. But she was going to try to give Jena Leigh a good life, whatever that entailed. "Allow me to tell you about your new home." Irene went on to describe Altamesa Springs. "The people there are nice, and you'll like them. I know they'll like you."

Jena Leigh's gaze went back to the window. Her first childhood memories were of the orphanage; it hadn't been a bad place to live. Mrs. Kingsley had once told Whit that his two sisters were her brightest students, and Jena Leigh had loved every subject the matron taught, especially history and geography. But most of all she liked to read. She had devoured all the books in Mrs. Kingsley's library—some she had read many times. Those memories were too painful to think about now, so she turned back to Irene. "Will you tell me about your life?"

Irene smiled. The little scamp had artfully turned the tables on her, but Irene nodded. "Jena Leigh, I have traveled to far-off places. I have buried most of my family members with the exception of two cousins who live in Tennessee. I don't know them, and I probably wouldn't like them if I did. I lost my husband, who was my other half, some years ago, and have lived alone since his death."

"You like being alone, don't you?"

"I'm used to my own company, and I would like to ask you to be patient with me if I sometimes do or say the wrong thing. I don't know anything about children."

She saw the child smile for the first time. "I'll teach you."

A week later Dr. Randolph pronounced Jena Leigh well enough to travel. As the child stood before the oval mirror that hung on the wall, she stared at the two red scars on her face. She touched her head, where there was fuzz instead of hair. Horrified, she drew away from her reflection, squeezing her eyes tightly together. "Will I always look this frightful?"

Irene had no idea how Jena Leigh had looked before. "Your hair will grow back, and your face will heal."

Jena Leigh reached for the straw bonnet Irene had given her and slipped it on her head. "I would like see the ruins of the orphanage before we leave, if you don't mind."

* * *

Later that afternoon Jena Leigh stood before the charred ruins of the only home she remembered, her head bowed and tears washing down her cheeks. A sudden dust devil picked up the ashes and whirled them around, stinging her face.

Irene sensed the child's need to be comforted, but she didn't know what to do. She slid her arms around the frail shoulders and felt the child lean against her. A heavy lump formed in her throat, and Irene allowed herself to cry.

After a long moment of silence, Jena Leigh glanced up at her benefactress. "I'm ready to leave now."

Chapter One

Col. Clay Madison shoved his hand through his thick hair, wondering what had ever possessed him to reenlist after the war. A friend of his family, Brigadier General Townsend, was the assistant adjutant of the United States Army, and after the war, Townsend had bumped Clay up in rank and convinced him to take the position of adjutant in Galveston. There had been a successful law practice waiting for Clay in Baltimore, but he'd turned his back on it and accepted Townsend's offer.

There was no woman in his life—not since Paula. He frowned when he remembered how close he'd come to marrying her, and how fortunate he had been to discover her deceitfulness just before the wedding.

Paula Granville had seemed like every man's dream, with black hair, sky blue eyes, and a face that caused men to make fools of themselves; and Clay had been no different from the other poor devils who vied for a smile from her ripe lips. But it was Clay she had chosen to marry. At the time he'd thought of himself as the luckiest man alive, and he'd treated her with the greatest respect, taking only a few stolen kisses from her sweet lips. She'd been the epitome of purity and gentility, and he would be the man who would introduce her to lovemaking on their wedding night.

He shook his head in disgust. How wrong he'd been about her.

Clay thought of the note he'd received just three days before his wedding, which had stated merely, *Meet me in the summerhouse at midnight*. He had thought Paula had sent the note, and he'd envisioned spending a few moments alone with her. How eagerly he'd watched the clock, even leaving his house early to meet her. Their two estates adjoined, and he'd walked the short distance to the summerhouse on the Granville property.

But the meeting hadn't turned out the way he'd expected it to. When he had neared the summerhouse, the light from a full moon outlined two silhouettes—a man and a woman embracing. He had been puzzled at first, thinking it was someone else. He'd started to retrace his steps when he heard the woman speak—it was Paula's voice. he would remember her words until his dying day: "Touch me, Hollis; kiss my breasts. Make love to me."

When Clay had realized that Paula had been in the arms of his best friend, something had slammed into his heart. He didn't know how long he'd stood there feeling sick inside, but it hadn't taken long for rage to drive him up the steps to the summerhouse.

He closed his eyes, still feeling the pain of betrayal. He wasn't sure which had hurt more: the treachery of the friend he'd known since boyhood, or the faithlessness of the woman he'd wanted to marry.

Paula had been the first to see him, and her face had been stricken as she pulled her bodice together and shoved Hollis away, trying to convince Clay that Hollis had taken advantage of her innocence and forced himself on her. But he had known better. Hollis had immediately confessed to sending the note to Clay with the intention of preventing him from making a grave mistake in marrying a woman who was as promiscuous as she was cunning. He'd tried to explain to Clay that Paula had already been intimate with several of their friends.

As far as Clay was concerned, Baltimore held nothing for him. If he was being honest with himself, he'd have to admit he'd come to Texas to escape his past. Of course, he hadn't known when he'd accepted this post that he would be taking on a passel of trouble.

Clay's department had the luckless assignment of seeking out and apprehending anyone bent on disturbing the fragile peace that existed in Galveston—meaning Union soldiers as well as any of the local citizens who caused trouble. His office had to investigate every complaint brought before him—a task that usually kept the lamps in his office burning long into the night.

The citizens of Galveston were still chafing from the

blockade that had closed off the port for most of the war, and they now had to contend with martial law. Every day brought new fractious incidents, and the makeshift stockades were overcrowded with men waiting to be brought to trial.

Clay glanced up when Sergeant Walker handed him a document.

"Here's the list of newspapers you asked to see, sir. As you might expect, there are quite a lot of them."

Clay scanned down the list of hostile newspapers that had been targeted by his office for printing inflammatory articles. There had been too many incidents of harassment from both the Union Army and the local citizens, and they had to stop. "We're sitting on a virtual powder keg, Walker, and it would take very little for the locals to revolt. I'm determined to defuse the situation before that happens."

Walker looked worried as he said, "It won't be an easy task to ferret out all the troublemakers, sir."

Clay flipped through the pages, reading the names of reporters who were bent on causing trouble. "They will either follow the rules of this office, or I'll see their presses shut down and their offices closed."

"Texas is a big state, sir."

"It's my belief that when the worst of the lot have been yanked into line, the rest will be easy to control." Clay frowned when the same reporter's name was mentioned several times on the list. "Take this one, for instance—this J. L. Rebel. He doesn't know it yet, but he's about to hear from me."

* * *

Byron Arnold helped Jena Leigh from the train, his gaze troubled. "I don't like leaving you here alone like this."

Jena Leigh smiled at the man who had worked for Irene for twenty years. There was no one in the business better than Byron. It would have been difficult to have survived the last year without his help. He had made sure the presses kept rolling in those dark days after Irene's death.

"The return train to Altamesa Springs leaves in fifteen minutes, but I can always take a later one so I can see you settled," he told her.

She shook her head. "I'll be fine, Byron." She looked into his worried gray eyes. Although he was in his fifties, there was very little gray in his thick brown hair, and he still stood as straight as a ramrod. "I appreciate your accompanying me here. But you're needed back at the *Gazette*."

"I still feel like I should stay until Mrs. Marsh comes after you."

She patted his arm. "She is probably waiting for me right now."

He nodded. "I suppose." Another crush of people surged forward as Byron's train arrived. He nodded gravely toward two men in blue Yankee uniforms, then turned his gaze back to Jena Leigh. "Are you sure?"

"I am." She pressed a quick kiss on his rough cheek and pushed him forward. "If you don't hurry, you'll miss your train."

He boarded the train and stuck his head out the window. "If you run into the least bit of trouble, you come on home right away," he told her decisively.

She nodded and waved, feeling the heat press in on her. Despite the fact that it was early morning and the sun had barely touched the eastern horizon, the weather was sweltering. Jena Leigh watched people greeting their arriving family members with warmth and enthusiasm. Her welcoming committee would be a stranger, her new landlady.

She watched Byron's train until it was out of sight before her composure crumbled, and she wondered how she would ever make it on her own. Since those awful days after the fire in El Paso, Jena Leigh had become Irene's fledgling—she hardly knew how to go on without her. Her dear, sweet mentor had lost her life last spring. If Irene had been able to choose her own manner of death, it would probably have been in pursuit of a story like the flood she had been covering in San Antonio. Jena Leigh missed Irene every day, and she probably always would.

Well aware of her own rash nature, Jena Leigh knew she was impulsive and often acted before she considered the consequences. Irene had gently guided her when she would have floundered. Now she would have to depend on her own judgment, and that could be dangerous.

Jena Leigh didn't have to worry about money. Irene had left everything to her, including the *Gazette*. Jena Leigh intended to remain in Galveston for some duration. The newspaper would continue to thrive under Byron's capable custodianship.

Over the years Jena Leigh had finally come to terms with her sister's death, but she hadn't given up hope of finding Whit and Drew. The main reason she had come to Galveston was the hope of finding her brothers. Since she'd received no response to the article she had placed in the Galveston newspapers, she didn't expect Whit or Drew to be in town at the moment—but she hoped they would eventually arrive, and she intended to be waiting for them when they did.

She took a deep breath and let it out slowly, trying to concentrate on what was going on around her. A loud hiss announced the train's departure, and heavy iron wheels turned on the rails, gathering momentum—black vapor puffed from the smokestack to curl skyward and dissipate into the low clouds.

The smell of sea air assailed her, but it invoked no memory of her childhood in this place. Of course, there was no reason she should remember—she'd been a baby when her father had taken the family to live with his sister in west Texas. Everything within her view was alien to her, and she resisted the urge to take the next train back to Altamesa Springs, where everything was dear and familiar.

She stepped around her trunk and peered at the clock inside the depot. She'd been waiting for forty-five minutes. Perhaps Mrs. Marsh had the wrong date for her arrival. The sun was climbing higher in the sky, and the temperature was climbing with it. Jena Leigh opened her sunshade, hoping it would give her some relief from the heat. Glancing at the palm trees down the way reminded her that Galveston was a tropical island; she should have expected it to be hot. For some reason, the heat was reminiscent of the year she turned thirteen, when Irene had taken her to Egypt for her birthday. Jena Leigh smiled at the memory of Irene on a camel, holding on for dear life, but determined she was going to ride the beast. She remembered the two days they had spent at the great pyramids and shopping in quaint little marketplaces. Although there had been a war raging in the States at the time, Irene had taken her to London and Paris for her fifteenth birthday. It had been Irene's belief that traveling abroad would give her ward a well-rounded education. But no matter where they traveled, Jena Leigh had always been glad to return to Altamesa Springs. She wished she were there right now.

She glanced up at two seabirds circling above her and watched them swoop and land on the branch of a mimosa tree. Would she find Whit and Drew here in Galveston? If they were alive, they had to know she would be searching for them. Maybe they didn't know Laura Anne had lost her life in the fire. She dreaded being the one to tell them about that.

A sudden breeze struck, but did nothing to dispel the heat. She fanned herself with her handkerchief and wished she dared loosen the top button of her traveling gown, then decided against it. If only she'd thought to wear a lighter-weight gown. Removing her bonnet, she dangled it by the ribbon and felt some relief.

Suddenly a feeling of unease crept over her, and she discovered four men standing across the street watching her—she could tell by the way they nodded in her direction that she was the subject of their conversation. One of them was actually gawking at her. She descended the wooden steps, deciding she'd just walk a little way down the street, maybe around the corner, to get away from their unwanted attention.

Jena Leigh soon became absorbed in the quaintness of a house built high off the ground, probably to keep it from flooding when a storm came ashore. As she stepped over a crack in the sidewalk, she caught a whiff of bread baking and followed her nose to a delightful little bakeshop with wide windows and blue shutters. Glancing though the window, she watched a woman remove a pan of muffins from a brick oven, and the scent of cinnamon and raisins permeated the air. Her stomach rumbled with hunger, and she had just decided to go inside the shop when she noticed a man in a Yankee uniform strolling toward her. His face was half-hidden by his wide-brimmed hat, but as he drew close enough for her to see his eyes, they seemed to burn with a lascivious expression. She quickly crossed the street, wondering what was the matter with the men in this town. Hadn't they ever seen a woman before?

To Jena Leigh's dismay the man also crossed the street and stalked in her direction. Instinct warned her that she was about to have an unpleasant encounter with that Yankee. She glanced at his hands—they were large and hairy, and he was missing a finger on his right hand.

Now that he stood in front of her, she could see a deep scar that ran down the right side of his face, as if he'd been slashed by something sharp.

When Jena Leigh tried to step around him, he took a step sideways, blocking her path.

Snapping her sunshade shut, she aimed the pointed tip at him. "Get out of my way, Yankee." Her words were brave, but she cringed inside as his gaze swept her from head to toe in the most insulting manner. There was lust in his brown eyes and something more—pure hatred radiated from him. Jena Leigh took another step backward.

"What makes you think you're so high an' mighty?" he asked, his voice deep and raspy. "Underneath all them petticoats, you're the same as any other gal. You think you're too good for the likes of me."

Something deep and horrible crept into her heart and mind, and she took another quick step backward. But that was a mistake, because he countered with a move of his own that brought him within inches of her. She attempted to move in the other direction, but once more he stepped in front of her.

Fury burned inside as she cast him a heated glance. "Get out of my way!" Brave words, but she had no way to back them up.

Before she could react, the man bumped against her with such force that it sent her careening backward, her body slamming painfully against the brick building.

"Maybe you'd like to go in that alley with me and let me show you a few things."

She glanced around, hoping someone would come to help her. "Are you out of your mind?"

"If you walk the streets alone, lady, you'll find yourself in trouble." His threat was so malevolent that it turned her fury to fear. But Jena Leigh was always at her best when cornered. She straightened away from the wall, rubbing her arm, knowing it would be bruised. "I told you to get out of my way and allow me to pass!"

"Now why would I do that?"

She could feel her heart beating in her throat. This man wanted to hurt her, and she didn't understand why.

Clay paused at Sergeant Walker's desk and placed a file in front of him. "Review this list to make sure everything is in order before you dispatch it to the quartermaster's office."

Walker's gaze was already tracking down the list of armaments the colonel had requested. "Yes, sir."

Clay moved to the front window and stared at the weed-infested vacant lot across the street. He'd have someone out there tomorrow to clean it up so tents could be erected as temporary housing for the reinforcements that arrived daily.

Clay frowned, and his mouth compressed in displeasure as he witnessed a young woman being harassed by a soldier. With anger boiling inside him, Clay nodded toward the window and spoke to the sergeant. "Did you see that?"

Walker followed his colonel's gaze, but saw nothing.

"Begging your pardon, sir, but what was I supposed to see?"

Colonel Madison stalked to the door and flung it open while Sergeant Walker jerked to his feet and lumbered after him. By the time they reached the walkway the young woman was running down the street, and the soldier who had been with her was watching, as if deciding whether or not to follow.

"Sergeant," Clay said, his anger deepening, "take that soldier into custody and have him wait for me in my office. I'm going after the young woman. Incidents like this only add to the unrest in Galveston. I will not tolerate this insult to a woman from any of our soldiers."

"Yes, sir," Walker said, still not clear about what had happened.

When Clay turned the corner, the young woman was still running, and he crossed the street in pursuit of her.

"Madam, wait!"

His actions only made her run faster.

Jena Leigh heard the bootsteps hurrying behind her and assumed her pursuer was the man who had given her such a fright. She was relieved when she finally reached the depot, where there were people around. Pausing to catch her breath, she leaned against the building. But she jerked her head up when a shadow fell across her face.

The sun was blinding her and she couldn't make out the man's features, but she did see his blue uniform. "I told you to leave me alone. If you don't go away, I'll call for help."

"Madam, I'm not the man you were running from. I saw what happened, and I just wanted to make sure you're all right. With the greatest courtesy, I ask your pardon, and apologize for what happened."

Bringing her hand up to shade her eyes, Jena Leigh could see him more clearly. No, this was certainly not the man who had accosted her. This was a high-ranking soldier with eagle epaulets on each shoulder—he was an officer. The other Yankee had been base and crude; this man's manners were polite. His frock coat was buttoned according to regulation. His jaw was square, and his hair as black as midnight. There was a troubled expression in those blue eyes. She turned away from him—he was a Yankee, and deserved none of her time or her consideration.

"Madam—"

"I don't want anything from you except your absence," she stated, positioning her sunshade between the two of them.

Clay circled her so he could see her face. "Please allow me to introduce myself."

She twirled her sunshade in obvious irritation. "I don't care who you are. I don't want to know you."

He was exasperated, but not enough to miss noting that this woman was probably the most beautiful female he'd ever seen. Her skin was unblemished, her bone structure delicate and fine. Those marvelous gold-flecked eyes were framed by long, silken lashes. His gaze flickered to her hair and he saw that it was golden, like her eyes. With considerable effort, Clay pulled his thoughts back to the problem at hand. "I can't tell you how sorry I am about what happened."

She was still shaken. "You have apologized prettily, so be content that you have satisfied your obligation. Just go away."

Clay watched her glance down the street as if she were expecting someone. "You know, you really shouldn't be out alone without an escort. A lone woman is only asking for trouble." There was a mild reprimand in his tone, and he saw her eyes widen.

Jena Leigh swirled around to face him. "Let me see if I have this right. You are blaming me for what that man did?"

"That isn't what I meant, and you know it."

Jena Leigh shook her head. "I just arrived by train, and I had a companion with me. I'm now waiting for someone to come for me. Does that satisfy your sense of propriety?"

"I ..." He saw the anger in her eyes. "Yes, I see." He hadn't meant to ask, but the words just slipped out. "Are you are waiting for your husband?"

"Not that it's any of your concern, but no, I'm not. I see your intended meaning. You think an unmarried woman should stay locked in her home while your soldiers are afforded the freedom of our city. You blame me for what your man did." She drew in her breath. "That's exactly what I would expect from a Yankee."

Clay was becoming more frustrated by the moment. "That's not what I meant at all. You completely misunderstood me."

"Shouldn't you be questioning your own man—he is the wrongdoer here, isn't he? You're wasting your time with me."

He noticed how pale she looked—the incident had upset her more than a little. "What he did was wrong, but if you don't accompany me to my office and lodge a complaint against him, there is very little I can do about it."

"You are a stranger to me. I'm not going anywhere with you. But I'll leave you with this warning—you're in Texas now, sir. Here we don't suffer insults lightly, and we don't ask anyone in a blue uniform for help. You'd better know that about us if you are going to stay around for long."

Clay bowed slightly to her. He'd done all he could to make amends, but she wasn't listening. "Good day to you, madam."

She turned away from him, and he paused a moment, staring at her rigid back. He didn't blame her for not trusting him after what had happened to her.

She snapped her sunshade backward and almost hit him the face. With measured steps, and trying to bury his anger at her, Clay started back to his office.

If she wouldn't come with him to face the man who'd harassed her, there wasn't much he could do about the incident.

He wondered if all Texas women were as stubborn as that one, or even half as beautiful.

Chapter Two

Sergeant Walker lumbered through the door and brusquely motioned the soldier to follow him inside the building. "Button your uniform, and remember to stand up straight when Colonel Madison questions you," he reprimanded. "I don't know what you did, but you have plenty of reason to worry. What's your name?"

"McIntyre. Sgt. Wayne McIntyre."

"What outfit you with, Sergeant?" Walker barked in a commanding tone.

The man hesitated a moment while he buttoned his jacket and pointed to the insignia on the sleeve. "The Rhode Island Fifty-fourth Rifle," he said, feeling no guilt about taking a dead man's identity. He eyed the heavyset man disdainfully—he would be in trouble if someone started checking into his background and discovered that the real McIntyre was dead, but he doubted anyone would.

"I never heard of your unit," Walker said, not surprised, since new regiments arrived almost every day.

"We only got here yesterday," the man lied. "And about that young lady ... it wasn't what it seemed. She encouraged me, and then when I got close to her she rebuffed me. It was just a little misunderstanding. I didn't do anything she didn't ask for," he said belligerently.

"I wouldn't try that speech on Colonel Madison if I were you. He saw with his own eyes what you did. It was brainless of you to accost a lady in the first place, but to do it in front of the adjutant general's office is something only an idiot would do."

The man glared at Walker. "Who is this Colonel Madison who thinks he can tell me what to do? I'm not connected to this unit."

"You'll find out who he is," Walker warned. "Come with me. You are about to feel the full force of this office; if I were you, I'd be plenty worried. I warn you, this officer doesn't suffer fools."

Sergeant Walker had been with Colonel Madison for three years, but he didn't really know much about the officer's personal life because the colonel was a private man. It was common knowledge that the colonel had been born into money and power and had high connections in Washington, D.C. While most officers had been demoted in rank after the war, Colonel Madison had gone from the rank of major to colonel, and he was only twenty-seven years old. Walker respected his superior's dedication to duty, and he liked him well enough. Of course, they never met socially, so he didn't know how the colonel acted when he was among fellow officers. Madison treated his subordinates with respect and asked for their opinions, and often acted on their advice. One of the things Walker liked most about the colonel was how he listened when someone talked to him—no matter their rank, he really listened.

Harman Parnell braced himself for trouble. Anger raged in his brain, and he tried to think how he could get out of this predicament. It was that woman who was to blame, not him.

Walker ushered the soldier into Madison's office and saluted. "This is Sergeant McIntyre, the man you wanted to see, sir."

The soldier snapped to attention and saluted. "Sir."

Clay was seated behind his desk, and rolled a pencil between his fingers, his gaze riveted on the man he was about to interrogate. "That will be all," he told Walker, and waited for him to leave before he spoke to McIntyre. He didn't say anything for a few moments, just watched as the soldier squirmed uncomfortably.

"Are you aware that our relationship with the people on this island hangs by a thread, McIntyre?" he asked at last.

"No, sir," he snarled under his breath. "I didn't know that."

Clay was disgusted. "Do you think you helped our cause any by pushing your unwanted attentions on one of their women? Suppose you tell me what happened— I've already spoken to the lady."

Harman Parnell's face reddened with anger, but he pretended he was embarrassed. "I didn't do anything wrong. I was just teasing her."

"I saw you, and it didn't look like teasing to me. We are an occupational force in this town, and we have to be extra careful that we don't insult these folks. Do I make myself clear?"

Parnell's back stiffened; he had a sullen twist to his lips, and rage swirled in his mind. He didn't like being talked to as if he were a nobody. But this officer would prod and search until he found out his real name if he didn't act as if he were sorry. He hid his anger behind an attitude of subservience. "Yes, sir. Very clear, sir. It won't happen again."

Clay imagined the man had seen a pretty girl, tried to talk to her, and then been rebuffed. It was easy to imagine such a scenario, especially with that little beauty. He had a stack of important papers that needed his attention. He decided to let the man go with a reprimand. This was an office governed by laws—there wasn't much Clay could do, since the young lady had refused to lodge a complaint. "See that you conduct yourself in a manner befitting the uniform you wear, soldier. I'd stay clear of the local ladies, if I were you." His mind was already on the stack of documents he had to go through. "You are dismissed. But if you're ever brought before me again, you will regret the day you were born."

Parnell lowered his gaze as he saluted. "Yes, sir. I understand what's expected of me now."

Clay would have liked to detain the man, but he still

wasn't quite sure what had happened. Only one thing was clear—the young woman was very upset.

His job wasn't an easy one, and he imagined it was going to get a lot worse before long.

Glancing at the clock, Jena Leigh was still angry as she stalked from her trunk back to the depot door. Judging by the position of the sun, she decided it must be past midday: the clock showed twelve thirty. Finally, too weary to stand, she dropped down on her trunk, thinking Mrs. Marsh had surely forgotten about her. It was blisteringly hot, and she was hungry.

She had a difficult task ahead of her just settling into a strange town, trying to find her brothers, and finding a job on one of the local newspapers. Not that she needed the money, but she had built a reputation as a reporter under the name of J. L. Rebel. People would probably accept a lady reporter living by herself. But a young lady of fortune living alone was another matter, and would probably garner attention of the worst kind. Like the kind she had encountered today from that Yankee. Well, both Yankees.

As often happened, Jena Leigh's thoughts shifted to her brothers. She had considered the possibility that Whit or Drew could have fought in the war—if so, they might still be making their way back to Texas. If they had joined the Confederate Army, they might not have seen the numerous notices Irene had distributed statewide, searching for them. Jena Leigh wouldn't ever allow herself to consider that either of them had been wounded or even ... killed in the war.

She was so distracted by her troubled thoughts, she hadn't noticed the slightly built man who stood before her, hat in hand. "Yes," she said stingingly, finally giving him her full attention. She was not ready to be accosted by another man. "What do you want?"

"Begging your pardon, ma'am; would you be Miss Rebel?"

She felt a rush of relief as she looked into inquiring brown eyes. "Yes, I am."

"I'm Mrs. Marsh's hired man, Ethan. She's sent me to fetch you. I'd have been here sooner, but one of the team horses picked up a stone, so I stopped off at the smithy. I hope you ain't been waiting long, ma'am."

She had, but she didn't see any reason to lambaste this poor man for what had happened to her. "Not at all."

When Jena Leigh was settled in the buggy, she was still troubled by the incident with the Yankee soldier. She supposed the women in town should expect such treatment—Texans were the vanquished, and she discovered today that the Union officers would only blame the lady if their own soldiers acted in an ungentlemanly fashion. Although that officer had made a faint attempt to apologize to her, he hadn't seemed completely sincere.

Ethan guided the buggy down a wide tree-lined boulevard, and Jena Leigh wondered if any of the houses they passed could have once belonged to her family. Several structures showed signs of destruction, and even more were deserted—one house was little more than rubble, and she imagined it had been blasted by a Yankee cannon during the heat of the siege. Several fine old trees had been uprooted, and the grass was dry and dying. But there were also signs of rebuilding; it seemed Galveston was coming back to life. What troubled her most was the sight of Yankee soldiers—they seemed to be everywhere she looked.

A short time later Ethan pulled into a curved driveway and halted the team before a huge two-story redbrick house. Jena Leigh took in a deep breath to fortify herself. The white trim on the doors and windows was chipped and in need of painting, and the vast grounds were overgrown with weeds. But she found the place enchanting, and imagined the house must have been very grand in its day; the opulence of twelve sets of dormer windows stretched across the entire edifice, reflecting sunlight like mirrors. Steep steps led directly to wide double doors. Jena Leigh, feeling apprehensive, retied her bonnet in a smooth bow. Taking Ethan's proffered hand, she allowed him to assist her to the ground. She swallowed her nervousness when a matronly woman dressed in a fine blue hoop gown appeared in the doorway and flashed Jena Leigh a welcoming smile.

"Miss Rebel, my dear, I'm happy you have arrived at last," Henrietta Marsh exclaimed. "Come inside out of this heat," she said, guiding Jena Leigh into the house. Before she closed the door, she turned her attention to Ethan and said in an authoritative voice, "Take Miss Rebel's trunks directly to the cottage."

Jena Leigh anxiously observed Mrs. Marsh. The woman was small in stature, her white hair pulled back in a neat chignon, her gray eyes watchful and alert. "It's exceedingly kind of you to send Ethan to the station to meet me, Mrs. Marsh."

"Nonsense!" Henrietta remarked. "For what you pay for the use of the cottage, that was the least I could do. You will understand why I charge such a price when you see the place. It is completely furnished, from bedding to kitchen utensils." She frowned, carefully scrutinizing Jena Leigh's features. "You're much younger than I imagined, Miss Rebel. You can't be twenty."

"No, ma'am, I won't be twenty for two more years."

The older woman looked shocked for a moment and then compressed her mouth. "Well, maybe you can be a friend to my daughter, Grace, who is in dire need of proper companionship." She paused for breath. "I can tell you that most of our finer families moved away from Galveston during the war, and only a few of them have returned. The social life in Galveston is not what it used to be, what with all the Yankees lurking about, watching us as if we were fish in a bowl. I tell you, it isn't safe for a woman to be out alone."

Jena Leigh agreed wholeheartedly with Mrs. Marsh; however, she saw no reason to mention what had happened to her when she arrived. She removed her bonnet and looked about the room with interest. The dark pine floor was scattered with cream and green rugs. She noticed that the worn green silk couch and chairs matched the tattered draperies at the window. Fine large mirrors hung on the four walls, giving the illusion that the room went on without end.

"Your home is lovely, Mrs. Marsh."

The older woman shook her head. "It isn't what it once was. I'm sure you've noticed we no longer keep a gardener. The house needs painting inside and out, and ..." She clicked her tongue. "But enough of my chatter—you must be weary from your journey. I thought you might like to go upstairs and refresh yourself and have something to eat before I have the maid show you the cottage."

"That would be most kind of you, Mrs. Marsh."

"I must ask you something to satisfy my own curiosity: What sort of name is J. L. Rebel? Surely your mother couldn't have given you such a name."

"The initials stand for Jena Leigh, ma'am." She decided not to mention her last name. "J. L. is my professional name," she went on to explain.

"Humph. So you use a professional name instead of your own. That seems very strange to me."

Jena Leigh was tiring of the continual prodding. "I find it necessary, Mrs. Marsh."

"I suppose you are right, since you'll be living alone," she admitted grudgingly. The woman looked distracted for a moment before she spoke. "You do understand that you'll be responsible for your own meals. The cottage has a small kitchen. I know you sent money so we could stock it, and I believe my daughter did an admirable job there, but your money didn't quite cover all expenses, such as sheets and quilts. I'll just attach the

additional amount to your next month's rent if you'd like."
A calculating expression wrinkled the older woman's
mouth. "Unless, of course, you'd would like to pay me
now. I find myself in need of funds at the moment."

Stunned by an overload of babbling from her landlady, Jena Leigh opened the drawstring of her green
velvet purse. "How much is the amount?"

"Seventeen dollars even will cover it very well."

Jena Leigh was shocked, wondering how much bed
linens for one person could cost. As she placed the bills
in Mrs. Marsh's outstretched hand, the landlady counted
along with her and then closed her fist on them.

"You're a good girl, paying your bills so promptly."
Her gaze suddenly probed Jena Leigh's. "You know I'll
expect the rent to be paid on the fifteenth of each month
and not a day past."

Jena Leigh met Henrietta Marsh's greedy gaze, unsure how to converse with her. "Be assured I will place
the money in your hand on the appointed day."

The older woman's eyes hardened just a bit, and her
mouth settled in a disapproving frown. "You failed to
mention in your letters that you are so pretty."

Jena Leigh recognized the accusing note in the
woman's tone, but before she could think how to answer, she heard movement at the door and was relieved
to turn her attention to the young woman who had entered the room.

"This," Mrs. Marsh said with pride, "is my daughter,
Grace. She has been in a dither to meet you. She reads
your column whenever she gets the chance, although I

try to discourage her, since your notions are a bit controversial at times. There is never any good news in our newspapers anyway since the war ended, or even several years before, for that matter."

Grace Marsh was petite like her mother, and Jena Leigh towered several inches above both of them. The young woman's mahogany-colored hair was piled on top of her head, drawing attention to her delicate heart-shaped face. Her eyes were gray, and she shyly dropped her head.

"You are close in age," Henrietta informed Jena Leigh. "Of course, you are tall for a woman, aren't you? And your eyes are rather strange-looking, aren't they? I'm sure you've already discovered that men don't like oddly colored cat eyes." She prattled on without giving Jena Leigh time to answer. "I understand you've traveled abroad. As for myself, I could never see any reason to go rubbing shoulders with foreigners. You will have to understand that Grace has lived a protected and sheltered life." There was a guarded look in the older woman's eyes. "I wouldn't like you filling her head with this and that."

"I hardly know what to say," Jena Leigh answered, and she didn't. Mrs. Marsh was certainly plainspoken, verging on being insulting. Jena Leigh had never met anyone like her, and she didn't know whether to be mad or to laugh—the woman was rather silly in her nonsensical rambles. She clearly needed to be enlightened, but Jena Leigh decided she wouldn't want that task.

"I'm glad you're here," Grace said, her cheeks flushed.

She was clearly embarrassed by her mother's outspoken-ness. "Ever since Mama told me you were going to be living at the cottage, I've been looking forward to meeting you."

Though they might be nearly the same age, Jena Leigh felt as if years separated her and Grace. The older girl seemed to be such an innocent. "It's a pleasure to meet you, Grace."

Mrs. Marsh glared at her daughter. "Show Miss Rebel upstairs to your room so she can freshen up and have a bit of lunch before she begins unpacking. I'm expecting guests this afternoon, and there is much to be done before they start arriving."

"Thank you, ma'am," Jena Leigh said, forcing a smile. In truth, she was glad for the chance to escape her new landlady. She followed Grace out of the room and up the staircase. They had reached the top step, out of Mrs. Marsh's earshot, before Grace spoke. "I can hardly believe you're here! I read your column faithfully, although Mama doesn't know it. I wish more than anything I could be like you."

Jena Leigh smiled. "It isn't always easy to be me. I get myself into lots of trouble. You would do well to be who you are."

"But your life is so exciting, and you can say what you want to, and think how you want to think. Just look at you now—out on your own at such a young age."

"I would prefer to have a family, as you do."

Grace lowered her head. "I'm dull as dishwater, while you write words that everyone wants to read."

"And that, Grace, is the very reason I'm always getting myself into trouble."

Grace led the way down a wide hallway where portraits of grim-looking Marsh ancestors stared down at them. "My room is just here," she said, opening the door and allowing Jena Leigh to precede her inside.

The room was beautiful, but the decor would have been more appropriate for a young girl than one of Grace's age. The lace curtains and bedcoverings were pink and cream, and the color scheme was carried out in the scatter rugs that covered the polished floor. A cream-colored chair faced a vanity with pink lace around the mirror. At the moment the bed looked very inviting to Jena Leigh.

"Would you like me to leave you alone?"

"Why don't you stay and talk to me?" Jena Leigh suggested, removing her jacket and unbuttoning the top button of her blouse. She poured water from a pitcher into a basin and washed her face and hands, drying them on a pink linen towel, while Grace settled on the edge of the bed, watching her.

"I hope you will be comfortable in the cottage." Grace nervously twisted a strand of hair around her finger. "Please forgive some of the things Mama said to you." She dropped her head. "She isn't really unkind— it's just that we've gone through hard times. Mama doesn't want her friends to know we need the money she gets from renting the cottage."

Jena Leigh nodded, understanding why Mrs. Marsh

had behaved so defensively. "It seemed to me that your mother doesn't approve of my profession."

For a moment Grace hesitated, and then she decided to be honest with Jena Leigh. "Mama disapproves of a woman working at any kind of job outside the home. She thinks a lady should only look after a house and have children. Please don't think badly of her. It's just the way she is."

A servant girl entered, carrying a tray, and placed it on a low table. Jena Leigh pulled out a chair and sat down, nodding her thanks to the departing servant. "I feel obliged to your mother for allowing me to rent the cottage. If I'm fortunate enough to acquire a position with a local newspaper, I might be coming and going at all times of the day and night, and that would have been difficult if I had been forced to live in a boardinghouse or a hotel."

"Do you miss your home?"

Jena Leigh spread butter on a biscuit. "Yes. Very much."

"Is there ... do you have a beau back in Altamesa Springs?"

Jena Leigh poured herself a glass of water and drank half of it before she answered. "No. I don't. Do you?"

Grace's cheeks flushed, and she lowered her head. "There is someone I like very much. But Mama doesn't approve of him." She raised her gaze and met Jena Leigh's. "Mama has someone else in mind for me." Grace twisted her fingers in her lap. "I despise the man she expects me to marry."

51

Jena Leigh tried to disguise her shock. "Surely you aren't being forced to marry a man you don't like!"

"Mama is ... she usually gets her way in everything." Realizing she had spoken too plainly to someone she had just met, Grace suddenly changed the subject. "Are you afraid to be out on your own?"

Jena Leigh took a drink of tea and set her cup back in the saucer. "Somewhat," she admitted. "But I have felt alone ever since Irene died."

"It must have been exciting growing up with someone like Irene Prescott to guide you. Everyone respected her—even Mama." She shook her head. "Mama likes anyone who is a success at anything, and uses success and wealth to measure a person's character." She raised inquiring eyes to Jena Leigh. "That isn't right— I know it isn't."

Jena Leigh frowned, not wanting to be drawn into the middle of a family squabble. "I can't speak for your mother."

Grace nodded, knowing she'd said too much. "You won't have any trouble finding a position on any of the local newspapers," she said, changing the subject.

"I hope you are right."

"As J. L. Rebel you have been widely read across Texas. Surely any editor would be happy to hire you."

"Actually, that may be the very reason no one will hire me. Irene allowed me a free hand that I can't expect from anyone else. And sometimes my articles are controversial, a fact that may hurt my chances."

"Galveston is crawling with Yankee troops who don't

necessarily want anyone riling up the public." She suddenly giggled. "But wouldn't it be fun to tromp on Yankee boots just a bit?"

"It might not be wise, but I refuse to write anything but the truth." Jena Leigh took a deep breath. "At least, the truth as I see it."

"I probably shouldn't tell you this, but Mama says your articles encourage dissent. She says now that the war is over, we should all try to look to the future."

"There are many who believe the same thing. I just don't happen to be one of them." She remembered the man who had harassed her only a few hours ago, and felt angry again. "I never approved of the war, but while our men were fighting I supported their cause. Now that the war is over, I don't like seeing Yankee soldiers on every street corner in Galveston."

"Did you have Yankees in Altamesa Springs?"

"No. We were too small for them to be concerned about—we aren't an important seaport like Galveston."

Grace smiled, and her whole face lit up. "What you said, and the passion with which you said it, is the very reason I wish I could be more like you. Your articles make me examine my way of thinking, and they've given me an interest in politics that I never had before."

Jena Leigh smiled. "It's good to know I have one reader in town."

Grace stood. "I have to go downstairs now. I'll send the maid to you, and she can take you to the cottage." She paused at the door. "I think you'll like the place.

Mama made sure you would be comfortable and had some repair work done on it."

"She is most thoughtful."

Grace smiled hesitatingly. "I wish I didn't have to attend Mama's supper tonight—I'd much rather help you get settled. Simon Gault will be here, and mama will be fawning all over him, trying to impress him."

Jena Leigh saw the shudder that shook Grace's slight frame. "And you don't like Simon Gault."

"No. I don't. But Mama wants me to be nice to him. He's the man she's chosen for me to marry."

Grace left suddenly, and Jena Leigh stood in stunned silence, knowing the young woman had barely been holding back tears. What kind of a situation had she gotten herself into? It was clear Mrs. Marsh wasn't happy about renting her the cottage and had done it only because she needed the money. And Grace was the unhappiest young woman she'd ever seen. She shrugged. It was none of her affair. She had troubles of her own.

The maid interrupted her musing. "My name's Nancy, miss, and I'm to show you to the cottage."

Jena Leigh followed the tall, slender woman down the back staircase and through the kitchen. Once outside, they made their way along a pathway, past a small pond where the water had turned moss green from neglect. The grounds were vast and beautiful in spite of their derelict state. There was a rose garden that needed weeding, and palm trees that needed trimming.

Her eyes widened when she saw the cottage. It was hidden from the main house by trees and hedges. It was built of rustic white brick with ivy growing up the sides. There were green shutters and a thatched roof. "This place is enchanting, Nancy."

"I think so too, miss." The maid pushed the door open and stepped back so Jena Leigh could enter first. "I've unpacked your trunks and put everything away for you."

"You are very kind. Thank you, Nancy."

"This is called the library, because there is no formal sitting room," Nancy volunteered. "Madam says the books are here for you to read if you'd like. They belonged to Mr. Marsh, who was a great reader."

Jena Leigh evaluated the room; it had a decidedly masculine air about it. Maroon curtains hung at the windows, and the chairs were brown leather. There was a huge green ottoman that served as a couch. The bookshelves were built in such a way that the books were flush with the wall, and she couldn't wait to explore every title. She walked into a bedroom that had also been decorated with a man in mind. A dark hunter green quilt covered a brass bed, and matching curtains hung at the windows. "Lovely," she told Nancy, pressing down on the mattress. "I think I shall be very comfortable here."

"There is a small kitchen through there." Nancy pointed past the library. "And there is a modern bathtub that the master had built before he died."

"Who used this cottage last, Nancy?"

"Mr. Marsh, miss. In his last years he spent most of his time here. He'd disappear from the main house for days, and we'd always find him here reading, as pretty as you please, as if he didn't have a care in the world. Which suited both him and—" The maid broke off her speech, realizing she was being indiscreet.

"Thank you, Nancy," Jena Leigh said, dismissing the servant. She could imagine why Mr. Marsh had used this cottage as a retreat. Mrs. Marsh was an overbearing woman. She would put anyone's nerves on edge.

Jena Leigh moved to the window and stared toward a small dirt lane that led to a major thoroughfare, and loneliness slammed into her like a fist. "Whit, Drew, where are you?"

Chapter Three

The office of the *Daily Galveston* was humming with activity as the presses churned out the afternoon edition. The premises were three times larger than the ones at the *Altamesa Springs Gazette*. Jena Leigh was in the private office of Noah Dickerson, the owner and editor. She sat stiffly on a cane-bottomed chair, her hands folded in her lap, her anxious gaze on the man's face. The door was ajar, and she counted six men rushing about, performing their jobs.

The whole situation was somewhat intimidating, and so was Mr. Dickerson.

Jena Leigh had worn her plainest gown, a gray broadcloth without trim of any kind. Her gray bonnet had slipped a bit, and she resisted the urge to straighten it. Her hair had been drawn tightly to the back of her head, and her wire-rimmed glasses, which she wore to make herself look older, were securely in place. She hoped

Mr. Dickerson didn't suspect how nervous she was as she clasped and unclasped her white-gloved hands.

Dickerson was a bear of a man, somewhere around six-foot-four, not fat but huge, with muscled arms and a thick neck. It was hard to tell what color his eyes were behind his thick glasses, or to judge his age. She surmised after taking a closer look at him that he must be past his forties, because there was a mixture of gray in his sandy-colored hair and beard.

He suddenly focused his attention on Jena Leigh, and she cringed inwardly. "I've read your column on occasion. I have to say I've yet to meet a female who can handle the day-to-day stress of working at a newspaper. Aside from that, if a woman is a looker, she can be a disruption for the men. Would you agree with that?"

"You have my assurance that I'll go out of my way not to disrupt the gentlemen who work for you. And even though I am a woman, I'm a good reporter. If you'll give me the chance, I'll prove it to you." She moved forward, bracing her hands on his desk. "I'm not boasting when I tell you that I know the newspaper business backward and forward. I can set type or write an editorial."

He looked thoughtful for a moment. "Irene Prescott was a remarkable woman. I've respected her for years— hell, who wouldn't?" He made no apology for his colorful language. To his way of thinking, if a woman chose to invade a man's world, she shouldn't expect special privileges. When she made no comment, he continued. "So she was your teacher?"

"Yes. I can never hope to be as good as she was."

"Hmm," he mused. "Irene Prescott sometimes published articles that no reasonable newspaper would touch. She would rush headlong into trouble without fear of reprisal," he said accusingly. "She courted danger and, to my knowledge, was never intimidated by printing the truth, no matter the consequences." He glanced at her over the rim of his glasses. "Would you agree with that assessment?"

His peremptory tone deflated Jena Leigh. He wasn't even going to give her a chance. "Well, yes—"

"Irene Prescott trod on politicians' toes and sliced up city council members in almost every county in Texas with a tenaciousness that sometimes made her very unpopular—am I right?"

"That's true, but only if—"

"In short, Irene Prescott liked to stir the pot and see what she could cook up, and that's the woman who taught you the newspaper business."

Squelching her annoyance and feeling the need to defend her dear Irene, she said, "She was one of the best newspaper reporters in Texas—or any other state, for that matter. She taught me some of what she knew, although I'll never come up to her standards—I only wish I could."

He tapped a blunt finger against the scarred desk. "So you'd like to walk in her footsteps—is that what you're saying?"

Her temper flared. "No one, not even you, could walk in Irene Prescott's footsteps."

His eyes became piercing. "For the most part, I like what I've seen of your work. Although I always assumed that you were a man—most people do; you know that."

"Not many people outside Altamesa Springs know my true identity. Is my being a woman a problem for you?"

Instead of answering her, he posed another question. "Do you share Irene's radical views on politics?"

Jena Leigh met his gaze without flinching. "Irene wasn't a radical. She merely believed that politicians who make the laws that govern the rest of us should be answerable to the people who put them in office. And you might as well know right now, my philosophy is very much the same," she stated. "If those aren't the qualities you respect in a reporter, then I wouldn't want to work for you."

"I think—"

In anger she held up a trembling hand to stop him. "I've heard enough," she said, jerking to her feet. She was almost out the door when his voice stopped her.

"How soon can you report to work, J. L. Rebel?"

She turned slowly back, sending him a quelling glance while she watched him tap his pencil against his desk. "What did you say?"

"You heard me. You have a job, if you think you can handle it."

Relief washed over her, and she smiled— hesitantly at first, and then brightly. "I think I can. I know I can!"

"You're too pretty for anyone to take seriously, and that might be a problem," Dickerson observed.

She came back and dropped down onto the chair she had just vacated. "I can't do anything about how I look."

He gave a big belly laugh. Most women he knew, when told they were pretty, would deny it and wait for a man to convince them otherwise. There was something refreshing about J. L. Rebel's attitude, and he found himself admiring her truthfulness. His gaze swept from her prim bonnet to her glasses, and then to her white gloves. She seemed totally unconcerned that she was beautiful. "No. You can't help how you look, but you're sure trying to make yourself look plain, aren't you?"

"I have to live with the face God gave me, Mr. Dickerson. And it hasn't been easy in my profession. You don't know how many times I've wished that I *were* plain-looking."

Loud laughter rolled out of him again. "If only all women were similarly endowed and as unaffected by their beauty." His laughter subsided, and he merely grinned. "It's like you're trying to hide the sun under a bucket. It can't be done." He studied her closer. "You don't really need those glasses, do you?"

She slowly removed her glasses and clutched them in her fingers. "No, sir, I don't. The lenses are just clear glass."

"That's kinda what I thought. But you're fighting a losing battle, you know."

"What job do you expect me to do?" she asked, ignoring his backhanded compliment. "I am willing to set the print or clean the offices, or anything you say."

He smiled slightly. "I wouldn't waste your talent by making you a cleaning woman." He looked speculative for a moment. "I don't suppose you'd be interested in taking on the society page? You could get into houses and mix with the upper classes better than Don Parkins does. He usually asks all the wrong questions and gets himself tossed out."

Her heart sank. "I wouldn't care to write that kind of column."

"No. I didn't suppose you would." He leaned back in his chair and watched her with a speculative gaze. "J. L. Rebel isn't your real name, is it?"

"J. L. are the initials for my two first names, but Rebel isn't my last name, no. Does that bother you?"

"Not if it doesn't bother you. As J. L. Rebel you have already established a name and a following. I'm a businessman who will shamelessly capitalize on the fact that your name is well-known. Does *that* bother *you?*"

"Not at all." She hesitated for only a moment. "You see, the real reason I came to Galveston is to look for my family."

"You have family here?"

"Have you ever heard of Whit or Drew Hawk?"

He looked thoughtful for a moment—so her last name was Hawk. "No. Can't say as I have."

"They are my brothers. Some years back we lost touch with one another, and I hope to locate them here in Galveston, since my family lived here at one time. I hope they are also searching for me."

"I only moved to Galveston seven years ago, but in

that time I've never heard of anyone by the last name of Hawk." He shoved his glasses back on the bridge of his nose. "I'd be interested in hearing the story of how you misplaced your family."

"It's not anything I want to talk about. I hope you understand."

"And here I thought you came to Galveston just to work for me," he stated blandly, but with a grin.

"That, too. I am on my own since Irene died. I need to know if I can make it in the publishing world without her guiding hand."

"I don't think I've ever met a woman with that kind of attitude. Most of your gender are looking for a man to take care of them."

"Not me."

"How do I know you won't leave me if you find your brothers, or if some man comes along and snaps you up?"

"Because I give you my word that I'll stay with you for six months, no matter what. If you'd like, I'll sign a contract to that effect."

"I don't think that'll be necessary. I think you're a woman who gives her word and keeps it."

"I can't thank you enough for this opportunity, Mr. Dickerson."

She was a damned good reporter, and he knew he was lucky to have her—but he wouldn't be telling her that or she might demand more money. So far she hadn't even asked about salary. He noticed the expensive cut of her gown. He doubted that money was a worry for her.

"I wonder," he asked with the bluntness of a longtime

reporter, "have you thought of looking in the graveyard for your brothers?"

Her breath closed off. "No, I haven't. But I should have thought of that first." She lowered her head. "It will be difficult to search for them in such a place."

He waved a dismissive hand, realizing he'd just struck a nerve. "This is Friday. I'll expect you to be here Monday morning by seven thirty. I believe in punctuality, so don't be late."

Jena Leigh stood, straightened her bonnet, and stuck out her hand, and he gave it a firm shake. "Thank you, Mr. Dickerson. You won't be sorry you hired me."

He watched her walk away, thinking what a striking beauty she was. She had talent that would take her a long way, if some man didn't come along and insist she be his wife and give birth to his children. She had been honed and groomed by the best. He stared into the distance. He would have to quell her exuberance a bit or they might both find themselves in trouble with the Yankees. He shook his head and let out a low whistle. It was hard for him to believe he'd just hired the infamous J. L. Rebel.

Gary Armstrong, one of Dickerson's reporters, strolled into the office, eaten up with curiosity. "I suppose that little beauty was here to place an ad or to have us print something about a social she's giving?"

"No." Dickerson grinned. "That, my friend, was J. L. Rebel, and I just hired her. Watch out or she'll have your job."

Armstrong looked astounded. "Rebel is a woman?"

"That's right."

"Hell, I'll gladly give her my job if she'll let me hold her hand."

Dickerson frowned. "I'll expect you and the others to treat her with the respect she deserves. If I hear of anyone getting out of line with her, they'll be told to hit the door."

Armstrong wasn't worried about losing his job. His boss knew he'd never insult a woman—he was a married man with three children, and he loved his wife. "Imagine that," he said in amazement. "J. L. Rebel—a female."

Chapter Four

Jena Leigh had been invited to have dinner with the Marshes, and she was so excited about her new job she could hardly contain her joy throughout the meal. But she managed to hold off telling Grace and her mother until they gathered in the sitting room after dinner. Mrs. Marsh was working on a tapestry, and Grace was embroidering a long table runner.

"Miss Rebel, you're welcome to get your sewing if you want to join us," her landlady said. "You know idle hands are the devil's workplace."

Jena Leigh sat with her hands folded in her lap. "I'm sorry, Mrs. Marsh, I never learned to sew. I'm not sure Irene ever learned the craft either."

"I would imagine she was taught to be a proper lady, but evidently she didn't pass the skills on to you. There was some neglect in that. I can't imagine what she was thinking not to teach you to do the finer things expected of a young lady."

Jena Leigh clamped her lips together to keep from defending Irene. She met Grace's gaze and saw the compassion in her eyes—Grace understood very well that her mother had insulted Jena Leigh.

"I assume," Mrs. March continued, "because you have not mentioned it, that you didn't get the position with the *Daily Galveston*."

Jena Leigh smiled, still unable to grasp the fact that she had the job. "Actually I did. I'm to report to work on Monday."

Grace giggled with delight. "How wonderful for you! I imagine you are the only woman reporter in Galveston."

Mrs. Marsh took a different view. "I never thought anything would come of it," she said, frowning. "You mark my word, it will cause nothing but trouble, your working with a bunch of men—and none of them gentlemen, except maybe Mr. Dickerson. And I'm not sure about him, although Mr. Gault seems to think highly of him."

Jena Leigh's spirits were not dampened by the haughty look Mrs. Marsh cast her way. "I have worked at a newspaper for much of my life. Even when I was young, Irene allowed me to write short stories for children at Christmas and Easter. I wouldn't know how to do anything else."

"Hmph. You'll never catch a husband if you don't abandon your independent ways."

Jena Leigh drew in a steadying breath, trying not to show how offended she was by the older woman's criticism. "I'm not looking for a husband."

"Every woman wants a husband, whether she admits it or not," Mrs. Marsh said piously. "When I met Mr. Marsh, he knew immediately that I was a proper lady," she added with an air of superiority.

"I would never marry without love, and I realized a long time ago that no man will ever accept me for who I am. Irene was fortunate that she found a husband who was proud of her accomplishments."

"Don't speak to me about love," Mrs. Marsh said, sending her daughter a quelling glance. "Whether a woman loves her husband or not, it's her duty to care for him and provide him with a comfortable place to come home to after a hard day's work. A woman's love is best saved for her child." Her hard gaze bored into Grace. "A young girl might fancy herself in love with the first handsome gentleman who comes along, but it never lasts," she scoffed. "Marriage and love seldom go hand in hand. And you might benefit by what I always tell Grace—men don't like their women to be so bookish."

"From all the books I saw in the cottage, I suspect that your husband was a great reader," Jena Leigh stated.

"My husband had the good sense to keep his books in the cottage and didn't bother me with such nonsense. Grace fancies herself a reader, but I try to discourage that flaw in her character."

Jena Leigh couldn't imagine a mother discouraging her daughter from reading. "Perhaps if I am lucky, I'll meet a man with Garland Prescott's attitude—he knew Irene was special," Jena Leigh pointed out, her anger rising. "Irene had a wonderful life with him. A life most women can only dream about."

"Yes, well, there was that. But she would have ended up an old maid if Prescott hadn't come along. From what I've heard of him, he was a man of some wealth and stature—well-thought-of."

"Then," Jena Leigh said with pointed candor, "I can only hope I will someday meet a man like him."

"I have to warn you, my dear, that's highly unlikely. Grace, here, had some silly romantic notion that she'd lost her heart to a shopkeeper from a family with no social standing and little prospects of ever having any." She shook her head, and her curls bobbed back and forth. "It near breaks my heart to imagine my daughter marrying into the Taylor family." She looked thoroughly disgusted. "But I've managed to direct her attentions in a different direction, and she'll thank me for it someday. Simon Gault is very well respected in Galveston. He's the most eligible bachelor in town, and he has his eye on my Grace."

Grace could not hide the shudder that shook her body. "But, Mama, Mr. Gault is old. I don't even like him."

Jena Leigh watched the exchange between mother and daughter, grateful that Mrs. Marsh's attention had been turned from her—until she saw that Grace was devastated, and there was real fear in her eyes. Couldn't that woman see her daughter was terrified of Mr. Gault? She decided to rescue Grace by changing the subject.

"Mrs. Marsh, I want to thank you again for allowing me to stay in your cottage."

"Nonsense," Henrietta exclaimed. "You pay good money for the privilege." Henrietta sighed. "Although what my friends will think of my renting the cottage to a woman of your profession, I can hardly guess."

"I wouldn't want to put you in an awkward position," Jena Leigh stated, wanting to weigh Mrs. Marsh's need for money against her desire for social standing in town. "Would you rather I seek lodging elsewhere?"

The woman's face actually whitened. "I won't hear of you moving elsewhere! Don't even think about it."

"Please stay," Grace said, shoving her embroidery frame aside and dropping down beside Jena Leigh. "I love having you here."

Mrs. Marsh frowned. "Perhaps Mr. Gault will be impressed that we have an established reporter living on our grounds." Her eyes suddenly sparkled with warmth. "Yes, I think he might. He's a reader, like my husband was."

"Mrs. Marsh, I'd like your advice. I will be needing a horse and a place to stable it. Can you recommend someone who might help me?"

"Of course I can, my dear," she said, sounding pleased that she'd been asked. "I keep a stable, and you can use one of our horses. There will be a small fee, of course."

"I would expect to pay."

"But, Mama, she can use my horse, and she needn't pay for the privilege," Grace insisted, her cheeks tinged by humiliation.

Looking pensive, Mrs. Marsh said, "Of course. Your horse is the very one for her. But with the cost of feed going higher since the Yankees are grabbing up most of the grain for their stock, there's little to be had for our use." She actually smiled. "Ethan will be happy to help you with tack."

"Thank you. You are very kind."

"My horse, Buttermilk, is a fine animal. She is in need of exercise, because Mama won't allow me to ride her off the grounds since the Yankees came ashore," Grace said softly. "I would be pleased if you would use her as your own."

Grace looked miserable, and Jena Leigh could only imagine what must be going through her mind. She was such a gentle young woman, and to have such a mercenary mother seemed difficult for her. Jena Leigh stood. "It's settled then. I'll wish you both a good night. Mrs. Marsh, thank you for the lovely dinner. The roast was delicious—I particularly liked the lemon ice."

"Good night," Grace said, walking her to the parlor door. "I hope you are comfortable in the cottage."

"Who wouldn't be? It's wonderful." She lowered her voice. "You can always come visit me when you want to read one of your father's books. Even if I am not there, go in anyway."

Grace squeezed her hand. "Thank you. I will if I can sneak away from Mama."

Jena Leigh turned away, grateful that she had been raised by Irene, who allowed her to think and do for herself. As she walked down the path to the cottage, a cool breeze touched her cheek, and a bout of homesickness hit her. "I'm going to make it, Irene," she whispered. "If my brothers are still alive, I'm going to find them."

Jena Leigh dismounted and rubbed the neck of Grace's dapple-gray mare. The horse had a spirited gait, and she longed to ride it in open country to see what it could do. But that was not possible today. Already it was past noon, and she had many things to do before dark. She'd spent most of the morning searching through old records at the county registrar's office until she had located the house that had once belonged to her family.

With a tightening in her heart, she looped the reins through a rusted lion's-head hitching post. Her father must have tied his horse to the same hitching ring, since it was on the property that had once belonged to her family.

She walked past an untended oleander hedge that was blooming despite neglect. But she came to an abrupt halt when she saw that the house was in complete ruin. She stared in horror at the three white columns that had collapsed to the ground and noticed that three others were badly listing, held in place only by the remnant of a splintered roof. It was still possible to recognize that the house had been built in the Greek Revival design, and it must have been very grand at one time. Whit had once told her that the family had been wealthy when they lived in Galveston. It was sad to see the front of the house caved in, the wood rotting in this damp climate. She supposed it was possible that the house had taken some damage from cannon fire from one of the Yankee gunboats that had blockaded the island during the war.

She moved forward carefully, heading for what had once been a veranda; it was now warped and splintered like the rest of the house. Her riding boots crunched on broken glass, and she bent to pick up a blue shard, examined it closely, and realized it had once been a bowl made of hand-blown glass. An ache started around her heart and spread through her body as she dropped it back on the ground. With the intention of getting closer to the house, she stepped over a collapsed iron railing, careful to avoid rusted nails that stuck out of the warped boards.

Although she had no memory of ever living in the house, she was still hit by a wave of nostalgia. As she looked at the ruins, her mind put the pieces back together like a fragmented puzzle. There must have been a time when her family had been happy in this house. She could almost see her brother Whit running down the steps to see the new pony their father had bought him for his eighth birthday. She knew about that incident because her brother had described it in great detail. She could also imagine sweet, serious Drew asking their father when he could have a pony of his own, and their father explaining he would get one on his next birthday.

Sadness pelted her with such force that she grabbed onto a rusted pole and lowered her head. Her heart actually hurt as she reached for a life she had lived but had been too young to remember. Over the years she hadn't given much thought to her mother or father because she couldn't put a face to either one of them, but she thought about them now.

What had they been like?

What had been their dreams?

Why had both of them deserted their children and split up the family?

Since she had no answers to her questions and never would, she dismissed them from her mind. Her thoughts turned to Laura Anne. Even after all these years, she still missed her sister. She smiled, remembering how Laura Anne had tried to mother her, although they had been only a year apart in age. And Whit had been just a young boy of ten when he'd taken over responsibility for their family. She thought of Drew, who had always tried to bolster her spirits and make her laugh when times were hard. It was difficult to think she might never see any of them again.

Picking her way carefully through rotted planks, she finally reached the back of the house. Her foot struck something solid, and she bent down and picked up a model ship. The mast had long ago rotted away, but the rest of it was still very well preserved. She turned it over in her hand and read the faint markings on the side. It was a model of the *Sarah Jane*, the very ship that was on her pendant. She clasped the broken treasure to her as a part of her past. Jena Leigh walked about, trying to catch fragments of that past, but it was not to be found in these ruins. She settled on a warped bench and remained there until dark clouds rolled in from the gulf, and the daylight began to fade beneath a darkened sky. After a while she mounted her horse and rode to the Strand, where she went from store to store asking everyone if they had heard of her brothers. She fanned out on side streets and asked the same questions, but no one had ever heard of Whit or Drew. One woman at a leather goods shop thought she recalled someone by the name of Hawk who had once owned a shipping company that had been bought by Simon Gault. But she informed Jena Leigh that Mr. Gault had bought the company long after Mr. Hawk had gone away.

For some reason Jena Leigh didn't care to speak to Mr. Gault. She doubted he would know anything about her father, since he'd come to town long after the man had left.

The last place she stopped was the blacksmith shop. The gray-headed man said he'd never heard the Hawk name.

She was weary, and the humidity was so heavy she could hardly breathe. Jena Leigh glanced worriedly at the gathering storm, hoping it would hold off for a few more hours, because she still had one more place to go. The next stop was going to be the hardest one yet. She reached inside the neck of her blouse and clasped her pendant, hoping it would give her courage.

Shaking off the heavy feelings of despair, she mounted the horse and rode away with no more information than she'd had when she'd arrived in Galveston. Just as she guided her horse into the flow of traffic, she heard a rider behind her. When he drew even with her, she spotted a blue-clad leg with a yellow stripe down the side. A Yankee.

"Hello, madam," the rider said. "I never thought to see you again."

Jena Leigh whirled her horse away from the Yankee officer, glaring at him. "I remember you," she said, meeting his amused gaze. "You're the officer who blames a woman if a man insults her."

"You chose to misunderstand me, madam," Clay told her, touching the brim of his hat.

Jena Leigh watched the officer control his spirited mount with a firm hand on the reins, and she imagined he controlled his men with the same ease. Staring after him as he rode away, Jean Leigh hoped she'd seen the last of him.

Chapter Five

Half an hour later Jena Leigh dismounted at the grave-yard, drawing her collar up around her neck. The gusting wind was strong, and she had to keep her hand on her bonnet to keep it from being torn off her head. With a watchful eye, she walked past crumbling tombstones where the names had been weathered away, as well as some that had decayed with time. If either of her brothers was buried in this place, their tombstones would be newer, and she would have no trouble reading the engraved names. Each time she approached a new tombstone her body tensed, and her heart lurched inside her breast.

It started to rain as she trudged on in her sad task until she had examined every grave site and read every name that was carved into stone. At last she raised her head while tears of relief mingled with the rain. As long as there was no proof of her brothers' deaths, she had hope that they were alive.

On her ride back to the cottage, the sky opened up and rain fell heavily, soaking her through to the skin. She had to think Whit and Drew were still alive and out there somewhere, looking for her.

Later, after taking a warm bath and eating a bit of supper, she fell asleep to the sound of rain hammering against the windows, her pendant clutched in her hand.

It wasn't yet dawn Monday morning when Jena Leigh slid out of bed, yawning. Today was to be her first day at work, and she had been too excited to sleep much. She quickly dressed in her dark blue skirt with a white blouse and matching blue jacket and was pinning her long braid to the nape of her neck on her way to the kitchen. She was actually humming as she placed the coffeepot on the stove and then turned to slice the loaf of apple bread Grace had left for her. Still humming, she buttered it and took a bite. Her mind rushed ahead to what her first assignment might be. She didn't expect it to be anything exciting, but she was looking forward to it anyway.

The last two days had been difficult. She had revisited a past she didn't remember. And if Whit and Drew were still alive they were certainly making it hard for her to find them. As she took a sip of coffee, she glanced at the clock. After taking another bite of buttered bread, she rushed out the door and down the path to the stable.

Jena Leigh arrived at the *Daily Galveston* twenty minutes early to find the front door locked. She caught the attention of a man sitting at one of the desks, and he admitted her.

"Morning, ma'am. I saw you the other day when you were in here, but we weren't introduced. I'm Bob Steiner—I work the presses. And you'd be J. L. Rebel."

Jena Leigh smiled at the elderly man with stooped shoulders and shining brown eyes. He had a shock of white hair and bushy eyebrows that met across the bridge of his nose. "It's a pleasure to know you, Mr. Steiner. I look forward to working with you."

"I've been reading your column, and I can tell you with all honesty, I'm one of your admirers."

She was warmed by his praise. "You are very kind."

He shook his head. "Not really. I just know good journalism when I read it—and you're good."

"I don't mind telling you I'm nervous this morning."

Before Steiner could answer, a second gentleman sauntered in from one of the back rooms with a grin on his face. He was tall and lanky and wore wide black suspenders. His eyes were a nondescript gray, but his smile seemed genuine. "I'm Jeff Rowland, and you're J. L. Rebel, in person."

She offered him her hand, and he shook it firmly. "I'm supposed to tell you that Dickerson asked to see you in his office as soon as you arrived."

Jena Leigh nodded and walked purposefully across the office as excitement battled with nervousness inside her. The door to Mr. Dickerson's office was closed, and she knocked lightly.

"Come on in."

When she opened the door, he nodded at a chair. "You're early."

"I usually am."

"Are you ready to go to work, J. L. Rebel?"

She opened her leather case and held a notepad of paper on her lap. "Yes, sir. I'm ready."

"Good." He had been scanning a file before handing it to her. Then he leaned back in his chair so he could see her reaction. "Since you are a seasoned reporter, I'm going to skip the preliminary easy assignment I usually give to an apprentice and hand you a case worthy of your abilities. You might say this one is an investigative assignment. Do you feel up to it?"

She felt excited at the prospect and flattered by his praise. "Yes, sir, I am—I do."

"Good, good." He nodded at the file she clutched in her hand. "Included there is all the information we gathered on the case, and the article Gary Armstrong wrote about the murder. There aren't many facts, and I'm hoping you can find out more than my other reporter was able to."

She quickly scanned the file and then read the newspaper article:

On Friday, the seventeenth of this month, the body of Goldie Neville was found on a deserted stretch of beach. It was apparent she had been strangled and had been dead for some time before her body was discovered. Miss Neville was one of the women employed at Chantalle Beauchamp's

establishment. On questioning Mrs. Beauchamp,
reporters were told that the young woman had
been missing for two days before her body was
discovered. Mrs. Beauchamp informed the au-
thorities that Miss Neville had no enemies that
she was aware of. Col. Clay Madison, who is with
the adjutant general's office, is working on the
case. He has assured the press he is looking into
the matter personally.

Jena Leigh was stunned. This assignment was beyond her usual probing into politics. Mr. Dickerson was
watching her intently, and she got an inkling that he was
testing her in some way.

"It seems to me," she said at last, meeting his gaze
with a steady one of her own, "that I should begin by
speaking to Mrs. Beauchamp and then to this Colonel
Madison."

"You're right. I've already arranged both interviews."

"Can you tell me anything more?" she asked, poising
her pencil above her notepad.

"The murder happened last week. No one, not even
the authorities, can find out much about it. Since you're
a woman, I'm thinking you might be able to ask questions none of us have thought about." His eyes grew
cunning. "First you'll go on over to Chantalle Beauchamp's place and question her—see what she'll be
willing to share with you."

Jena Leigh jotted down the information and then

glanced up at Dickerson. "What time do I see Mrs. Beauchamp?"

He leaned his elbows on his desk. "Most everyone calls her Chantalle, and she was just told you'd be stopping by her place sometime this morning. Of course, I made a specific appointment for you to question Colonel Madison." He smiled. "Your radical articles about Yankees in general may have escaped his notice. Let us hope so. I've had some dealings with him, and he can be like an itch you can't scratch. He's cold, intelligent, and out to quash any trouble that comes his way. If I were you, I'd tread lightly around him, Miss Rebel."

"Why should I?"

"Nothing seems to escape his notice. He's focused on his job, and he gets it done one way or another, or so I hear. The last reporter I sent to his office lasted for only five minutes."

She was scribbling notes, taking down anything Mr. Dickerson could tell her about the people she was going to question. "What is Colonel Madison's job?"

"He's attached to the adjutant general's office. As far as I can tell, his function is to ferret out dissenters and keep the peace in Galveston. And apparently to investigate murders."

She nodded and made more notes. "Can you tell me anything more about the dead woman?"

He looked her straight in the eyes. "Only that Goldie Neville was a prostitute."

Jena Leigh's hand wavered a bit, but she still managed to add to her notes. "I see."

Noah Dickerson tried not to smile, wondering what her reaction would be at his next bit of information. "Chantalle will be of more help to you in that regard." He laced his fingers together with a placid expression on his rugged face. "You see, she's the madam and owner of a house of pleasure where the dead woman worked. You do know what a madam is, don't you?"

"Of course." She refused to meet his gaze and hoped he hadn't heard the tremor in her voice. She scribbled on her notepad.

Dickerson stood. "I'll have someone drive you to Chantalle's place and wait around so he can take you on over to the adjutant general's office for your appointment with Colonel Madison," he said. "I'd be on time for the appointment with him if I were you. I don't think he'll give you much information, but you never know what a pretty woman can wrangle out of a man."

Jena Leigh hoped her face didn't show the turmoil she was feeling. To suggest that she could get the officer to talk to her just because she was pretty was an insult, and Dickerson knew it. However, she thought it was better to ignore his little barb. "Can you tell me anything more about this Chantalle woman?"

"She runs a first-rate place." He smiled sheepishly. "Or so I'm told. Nothing cheap about her establishment. As for Chantalle Beauchamp, she's a mystery. No one knows much about her past, and she was certainly tight-lipped with the reporter I sent over. I'm hoping she'll open up and talk to you."

Jena Leigh heard movement behind her as one of the

men sniggered while another laughed out loud. She was definitely being tested; possibly Mr. Dickerson was trying to see if she could stand up under the pressure. She tucked the information he'd given her neatly inside her leather case, trying to still her trembling hands.

"You haven't changed your mind, have you?" her new boss asked.

Although her face flushed with embarrassment at the thought of conversing with a ... a soiled dove, she gave a brief shake of her head. "Why should you think I'd change my mind? I'm a reporter, and I take whatever assignment I'm handed." She squared her shoulders, stood, and moved to the door. Wordlessly, the others watched her cross the outer room.

"She's something," Bob Steiner stated, as he watched her climb into the buggy that waited out front.

"I thought she'd refuse to go," Armstrong admitted. "She looks so prim and proper."

"I knew she would do it," Dickerson told them. "That little miss has a will of iron. I think she could do anything she set her mind to."

Jena Leigh studied her scant notes as the buggy moved into the flow of traffic. She dreaded the task ahead, especially her interview with a real madam. She squared her shoulders and raised her head, determined to show Mr. Dickerson that she was capable of taking on this assignment.

Chapter Six

Reluctant to meet with the madam, Chantalle, Jena Leigh forced one foot in front of the other. A heady breeze stirred the foliage on the oak trees as she walked beneath their shade toward the front door of the brothel. There was nothing that would set the two-story red-brick mansion apart from one of the finer residential homes in Galveston. Moss, like filmy lace, clung to the branches of the oaks, while pink petals from an olean-der hedge were scattered across her path. With heavy dread she glanced back at the buggy she had arrived in to make sure the driver was still waiting for her.

He was.

When she reached the door, she knocked lightly and waited apprehensively for someone to answer. When no one came she knocked again, this time louder.

Moments later the door was whisked open by a dark-headed woman who looked startled and then curious. "Well, well, if you aren't the prim and proper schoolmarm," the woman stated with a spiteful twist to her painted lips. "Have you lost your way, honey?"

The woman had long black hair and wore only a filmy pink robe over her corset. Although the color on her face had been artfully applied, it was easy to tell it wasn't natural. Jena Leigh needed no artificial means to add color to her cheeks; embarrassment did that for her. "I'm here on business." She stared into cunning blue eyes and asked, "Are you Madame Chantalle?"

"Do I look like I could afford to own a place like this?" The woman snorted, moving back from the door so Jena Leigh could step inside.

Impressed by the lavish decorations, Jena Leigh took in the red velvet draperies that reflected in the gilded mirrors. There were several red and white couches scattered about the large room, and a bar in the corner.

Jena Leigh was stunned as she stared at a stained-glass window that depicted a scantily clad image of some Grecian goddess.

Angie frowned as she assessed the icy beauty, who looked uncomfortable and out of place. She felt a prickle of jealousy. The woman was young, probably not yet twenty, and Angie was pushing thirty-one. While Angie had to cover her blemishes with paint, this woman's complexion needed no help—it was perfect. In fact, everything about her was perfect. But, Angie mused spitefully, someone should help the visitor choose a proper wardrobe—she wore clothing fit for someone twice her age. It was a hot day, so why was the woman wearing a jacket? Angie reminded herself that she was not unattractive, and most men who frequented the place asked for her. She knew just how to entice them and keep them coming back to be with her.

"I suppose you work for Madam Beauchamp," Jena Leigh remarked, not knowing what to say to the woman.

Angie couldn't resist baiting the young lady. "Would you like me to describe what I do?"

"I ... No. That won't be necessary."

Although Angie worked for Chantalle, she now considered her real boss to be Simon Gault. She had agreed to spy for him, and he paid her well for it. Simon kept a room here where he could easily sneak up the back stairs unseen so the good people of Galveston wouldn't know about his habits. Simon liked his sex rough, and so did Angie. The boss lady had an aversion to her girls getting batted around, so Angie was always the one sent to Simon's room. Chantalle and Simon hated each other, and Angie couldn't understand why Chantalle still allowed him to keep a room in her establishment. There was a story there, and maybe if she found out what it was, she could use it to her advantage.

Angie smiled tightly. "A word of advice, honey— Chantalle doesn't like to be called a madam. And by the way, I'm Angie. You didn't give me your name."

"I'm J. L. Rebel."

"Well, J. L. Rebel, why don't you tell me why you're here, and I'll tell Chantalle?"

"Thank you, but what I have to talk about with Mrs. ... Chantalle is private. She's expecting me, so if you'd just let her know I've arrived, I'd appreciate it."

Angie was irritated because the woman was so discreet. She tossed her head and her dark hair caressed her shoulders. "You can tell her yourself," she said peevishly. "Her office is at the top of the stairs. You can find your own way, I'm sure."

Jena Leigh nodded, knowing the woman was irritated about something, but for the life of her she couldn't think what. At the top of the stairs the hallway veered off in two directions. She decided the room with the open door must be Mrs. Beauchamp's office. Standing just outside the door, she waited to be acknowledged. The woman behind the desk was not at all what Jena Leigh had expected. She had dark red hair, and Jena Leigh assumed it wasn't natural. Her face was scrubbed clean, and Jena Leigh thought she would look like an ordinary housewife if it hadn't been for her bright red dressing gown, which plunged in front to display how well-endowed she was. Jena Leigh placed her age at somewhere in the late forties or early fifties. She had good features; in fact, she was attractive, so she must have once been quite beautiful. Jena Leigh couldn't help wondering what set of circumstances had caused this woman to choose such a sordid way of life.

She cleared her throat to make her presence known and the woman jerked her head up, staring at her.

"Forgive me for interrupting you, but the woman who answered the door told me it would be all right if I announced myself. Are you Chantalle Beauchamp?"

Chantalle nodded at the primly dressed young woman. She was beyond pretty—she was stunning. She took in the blond curls that had escaped from beneath her bonnet and the stunning, amber-colored eyes. Even though her clothes would have been more appropriate for a much older woman they were obviously expensive. This person certainly hadn't come to her in search of a job.

Chantalle said, "We have established who I am, but you failed to give me your name. And please call me Chantalle."

Jena Leigh balanced her leather satchel and stepped forward, holding out her hand. "Forgive me, ma'am. I am J. L. Rebel. I work for the *Daily Galveston*, and I believe you are expecting me. I wonder if I might ask you a few questions?"

Chantalle smiled and shook the young woman's hand. "I've read your columns, but I had no idea you were a woman."

Jena Leigh withdrew her hand. "May I sit?"

Chantalle nodded. "Yes, please do."

She lowered her body onto the edge of a chair and opened her leather case, removing a pad and pencil. "I'm here because Mr. Dickerson has asked me to investigate the death of Goldie Neville. I was hoping you could help me." She saw the displeasure reflected in the woman's eyes, and Jena Leigh wondered why.

"The local authorities, as well as Colonel Madison, who is with the Union Army, have already questioned me, and I told them everything I know, which wasn't much."

Jena Leigh balanced her pad on her lap. "Can you tell me what kind of person Miss Neville was? Did she have family? Was there a special man in her life? Do you know of anyone who had a grudge against her?"

Chantalle stared at the young woman, thinking she had seen someone with the same unusual eyes—but who and when? "Goldie was just what her name implied, bright and happy." Chantalle's eyes filled with sadness. "She had no family that I know of, and I can't think of anyone who would have wanted to do her harm. She was like sunshine, and always kind to everyone." She frowned. "Wait a minute. I just recalled something she once told me. I'd forgotten all about it until just now, when your question prodded my memory. She once expressed an interest in someone she'd met on the Strand one night when I'd sent her after supplies." Searching her mind, Chantalle tapped her desk with manicured nails. "Yes. I remember now—he was a soldier with the occupying force—a sergeant, I think. I never met him, so I can't tell you anything about him. I believe he and Goldie met several times away from here."

"Did you tell Colonel"—she glanced down at her notes—"Colonel Madison about this man?"

"No. As I just said, I didn't remember him until now. But I doubt the man had anything to do with her death."

Jena Leigh wasn't so sure. "Someone did. And it could have been him. As you say, you never met the man."

"True. But, if you will pardon me for saying so, the authorities and the army did nothing when there was a similar murder last month. So I doubt they will do anything about this one."

Jena Leigh's investigative instincts were triggered,

and she became alert. This was something she hadn't been told about. "What murder is that?"

"The body of a young woman who worked at the Lucky Dollar Saloon was found near the railroad tracks. She was strangled in the same way Goldie was."

"Were you acquainted with her?"

Chantalle could not get over the feeling that she had seen eyes like Miss Rebel's before. She dragged her mind back to the question the young woman had posed. "Her name was Betsy Wilson, and she was probably somewhere around your age. To my knowledge the authorities paid no attention to her death at all. Last year she came to me for a job, and I hired her. It didn't take long for us both to realize she didn't like my strict rules, and she left. That was when she went to work for the Lucky Dollar, I suppose."

"Can you tell me whom I should speak to at the Lucky Dollar?"

"The owner of the place is Max Calhoun. I don't know him at all. But I've heard he doesn't water his whiskey. That says something about his character."

Jena Leigh looked startled. "Is it a practice for saloon keepers to water their drinks?"

Chantalle shook her head at Miss Rebel's naïveté. "It's a practice more widespread than you can imagine."

Jena Leigh refrained from asking the madam if she watered her drinks. "Is there anything else you can tell me about Miss Neville?"

Chantalle shook her head. "Why? So you can smear her personal life in the newspaper?"

Jena Leigh had never used her articles to smear anyone—well, maybe a crooked official. "I don't work that way, ma'am. I have never dragged a person's name through the mud just to get a story. And I won't do that to Miss Neville either."

"I've read some of your articles, and you never struck me as a person who was short on descriptions. I suppose you came here with some preconceived attitude about Goldie. Is she nothing but another story to you? I said this to the other reporter Dickerson sent around, and I'm repeating it to you: I won't help you crucify Goldie in print. She had a life; she was a friend."

Jena Leigh suddenly felt guilt settle on her shoulders, because she had not thought of the dead woman as a real person. It was apparent that Mrs. Beauchamp had cared a great deal about Goldie Neville. "Be assured that anything I write will be handled with sensitivity and with an eye for the truth. It's not my way to shred a person's reputation. But," she warned, looking into the madam's eyes, "I will not dance around the truth either."

Chantalle saw that the young woman had polished manners and a way of making a person want to tell her everything. "I want satisfaction for Goldie. I want whoever did this to her to be brought to justice."

"And so do I."

Chantalle saw determination in the young woman's eyes, and she started to soften her attitude and to trust her. "I believe you. But I'm the wrong person to talk to if you want to know any of the particulars. You'll have to see Colonel Madison for that. I was told his office was put in charge of Goldie's case."

Jena Leigh stood. "If you hear anything or think of anything that might help find this monster who killed Miss Neville, will you let me know?"

Chantalle stood, belting her dressing gown. "Where will I find you?"

"I'm staying at a cottage on the Marsh estate. Do you know where that is?"

Chantalle nodded and smiled. "I knew Mr. Marsh quite well before he died." She grinned, daring to go further. "I believe he came here for sympathy and to get away from his wife's nagging—at least, that's what he told my girls. However, I can't say for sure, because I haven't had the pleasure of meeting Mrs. Marsh."

Before she could stop herself, Jena Leigh laughed ruefully. "Believe me, it is not always a pleasure to speak to Mrs. Marsh."

"Tell me," Chantalle said, "have you and I ever met before? Something about you seems familiar."

Jena Leigh lifted her eyebrow. "I seriously doubt it, ma'am. I only recently arrived in Galveston from Altamesa Springs. Have you ever been there?"

"No." Chantalle looked at the small upturned nose and then back to those golden eyes framed behind rounded glasses. "Not that I recall. But still ..." She shook her head. "I just have this strange feeling that we've met somewhere."

"I haven't been to Galveston since I was a baby; therefore, we could not have met."

"You worked for Irene Prescott in Altamesa Springs, didn't you?"

"Yes. Irene raised me. Did you know her?"

"I have not had that pleasure, but I was a faithful reader of her newspaper. I was sorry to hear about her death."

Jena Leigh lowered her gaze. "It was hard. I miss her."

"Have you no other family?"

Jena Leigh couldn't imagine this woman knowing Whit or Drew. At least, she didn't want to think of her brothers frequenting a place like this one. "None to speak of."

"Good luck to you in Galveston, although I believe your reputation has already preceded you here. I think you will garner many more readers for Mr. Dickerson's newspaper."

"You are very kind." Jena Leigh hadn't expected to like Chantalle Beauchamp, but she could feel the warmth in her, and her honest grief for Goldie Neville. "I won't take up any more of your time. Thank you for your help."

"Good day to you." Chantalle smiled. "And good luck when you speak to that Yankee colonel. You'll need it. He's one cold gentleman. I can tell you he's never had any interest in any of my girls." She shrugged and smiled. "Of course, you are young and pretty—that might work in your favor."

"I don't want him to like me," Jena Leigh snapped with more anger than she'd intended. "I have no love for any Yankee. I only want answers from him." She slid her pad and pencil into her satchel, her mind already racing ahead to the interview with Colonel Madison. She was also trying to sift through what little information Mrs. Beauchamp had shared with her. She hoped Colonel Madison would be more forthcoming with what he knew about the murder.

As her foot landed on the first step, she caught a movement out of the corner of her eye and turned to watch Angie slink down the hallway. If she didn't know better, she'd have thought the woman had been listening to her conversation with Mrs. Beauchamp. But why would she do such a thing?

She reminded herself, as Irene used to do, that she had an overactive imagination. She saw shadows where there were none and chased them, hoping they would turn into a story for the next day's edition.

Chapter Seven

Jena Leigh arrived several minutes early for her appointment with Colonel Madison. The heavyset soldier who greeted her introduced himself as Sergeant Walker. He briskly informed her that she'd have to wait a bit because the colonel was busy at the moment. When Jena Leigh had arrived, she'd recognized the office as being in the same vicinity as the spot where she had encountered that horrid man her first day in Galveston.

She dropped down on a hard, straight-backed chair, observing the activity in the office. The outer office was larger than the one at the *Daily Galveston*, and everyone seemed busy working on documents. She supposed it took a lot of paperwork to take over a city the size of Galveston. She counted seven desks, but only four of them were occupied at the moment. There were four private offices off the main room—one of them had Colonel Madison's name on the door. Soldiers were coming and going from one office to another, and she heard the scraping of chairs and the shuffling of papers. She was surrounded by men dressed in the hated blue Yankee uniform. It struck her as odd that she was actually observing an occupying army at work.

Anger flushed her face as one of the men glanced up from his desk and winked at her. Indignant, she turned her face away from him. She stood up and stalked to the door. As she looked down the street, her gaze settled on the same bakery shop she'd seen on the day of her arrival. Her anger rose by degrees when she realized it had been in front of this very office that she'd been accosted. If she hadn't been scribbling notes when she'd arrived, she would have recognized the place immediately. She turned to study the face of each man in the room. The man who had insulted her wasn't there—she would have recognized him if he had been.

She returned to her chair and tried to dismiss the incident; there were more important matters to attend to today. She was reading the file Dickerson had given her on Colonel Madison. Irene had taught her that it was good to know as much as possible about the person one was going to be interviewing. He was from Baltimore, Maryland, and had been stationed in Washington, D.C., at the beginning of the war. Later he'd worked for then Vice President Johnson, who had since become president after the assassination of Abraham Lincoln. Colonel Madison had seen action toward the end of the war when he'd joined the Maryland Calvary.

To Jena Leigh's way of thinking, such a high-ranking officer would be an older man. But if he was so important, why had he been stationed at Galveston? Although Texas was proud of her port city, it certainly wasn't the hub of the state.

As time passed she became bored, but resisted the urge to get up and pace the room, knowing that would only call attention to herself. By her calculations Colonel Madison had kept her waiting for over an hour beyond their appointed time. To keep from making eye contact with any of the men in the room, she searched through other files Mr. Dickerson had given her. Then she studied the notes she'd taken about the first murdered woman and frowned. Was it just a coincidence that both women had been prostitutes and had been murdered and left in a deserted area, or was there more to it than that? A shudder shook her body; there must be a connection between the two deaths.

Concentrating on the few facts, Jena Leigh tried to put the pieces together. Staring into space, she was almost sure the two women had been murdered by the same man. She wondered why Mr. Dickerson hadn't told her about the other woman. Perhaps it had been another test to see if she'd put the pieces together by herself.

The heavyset sergeant glanced up at her and smiled. "It shouldn't be much longer, miss." Several other soldiers were watching her, but she managed to look right through them. She squirmed in her chair as another hour passed. Before, she had been only mildly irritated; now she was irate. She carefully weighed her options: What she should do was walk out, but that was probably what Colonel Madison wanted her to do. No, she wouldn't give him that satisfaction. And, if she left, Mr. Dickerson certainly wouldn't like it.

It was stifling in the building, and Jena Leigh fanned herself with her handkerchief. She even moved to the chair nearest the window, but that didn't help much, since there wasn't a breeze stirring. Just when her temper was about to drive her into action and she was preparing to storm out of the place, the sergeant approached and motioned for her to follow him.

Jena Leigh's footsteps were measured as she crossed the room. What she wanted to do was give Colonel Madison a piece of her mind, but if she gave in to that impulse, he might refuse to answer her questions, or even have her thrown out of the place.

"Sir," Sergeant Walker said as they entered the room, "the reporter from the *Daily Galveston* is here."

The colonel had his head bent over whatever he was working on and didn't bother to glance up at Jena Leigh. He waved the sergeant out of the room while he scribbled notes on a ledger. There was a chair in front of his desk, but Jena Leigh preferred to stand until the man acknowledged her.

She studied him carefully—his hair was black; his face, what she could see of it, was—

Jena Leigh backed against the wall, grasping the door handle to steady herself. It was the same officer she'd encountered the day she'd been accosted—the one who'd chased her down the street and had made a half-hearted attempt at apologizing.

He was insufferable!

There was no end to his rudeness. She hadn't liked his high-handedness that day, and she liked him even less now that he'd kept her waiting so long.

Her gaze rested on his hands; his fingers were long and tapered and without calluses—the hands of a gentleman. Again she considered leaving, but decided against it for all the same reasons.

Jena Leigh's pride took over, and she levered herself away from the wall, firmly clasping her gloved hands around her satchel and trying to paste a demure expression on her face. If she had to, she would stand there all day, or however long it took for him to acknowledge her.

Clay heard movement and glanced up, confused to find a woman standing before him. It took him a moment to recognize her because she was wearing eyeglasses. "Madam ... so, our paths cross once again. I never expected to find you here."

She stared at him with eyes that sparked, and he thought she might still be angry from their first encounter. "Neither did I," she replied tersely.

He stood. "What may I do to help you?"

Jena Leigh stared into piercing eyes that were such a light blue color they were almost silver. "I had an appointment with you over two hours ago."

His gaze never wavered from hers. There was the same harsh arrogance she'd noticed in him before, and it put her immediately on guard. Like an officer commanding his troops, he nodded for her to be seated.

Skepticism laced his words, and he stated blandly, "How could I have known we would meet again so soon? You can't be the reporter from the *Daily Galveston*."

"Oh, but I am." She dropped down on the edge of the chair, keeping her back straight and her eyes level with his.

"You were unwilling to give me your name the first time we met. I hope you have changed your mind by now."

Her anger was now directed toward Mr. Dickerson, who obviously had not informed this office to expect a woman reporter. Jena Leigh was not about to allow this Yankee to intimidate her, or Mr. Dickerson to make a fool of her.

"I'm J. L. Rebel. And just for your information, my time is as valuable as yours, and I don't appreciate being kept waiting."

He eased back into his chair, a smile tugging at his lips. Her name had a familiar ring to it, but he couldn't think why while he was staring at the lovely creature. "You are right, of course," he said at last. "It was rude of me to have kept you waiting. I ask your pardon."

She glowered at him. "It seems you're always asking my pardon." She was no more mollified by this apology than the one he'd attempted the other day. "Can you tell me what you've learned about Goldie Neville's murder?"

Clay was so caught up in watching her lush mouth

that he didn't hear her question. He had known she was a beauty the first day they'd met, but seeing her now, here in his office, he was enchanted. He was fascinated by the way her golden eyes sparked with anger, even if that anger was directed at him. "I'm sorry. What was your question?"

She ground her teeth and held on to her forbearance by a thin thread. He was making it clear that nothing she had to say was of any importance to him. "I was speaking of Goldie Neville."

"Oh, yes." His eyelids lowered. "The woman who was murdered. My office is looking into that. If we have anything of interest to your newspaper, I'll have Sergeant Walker dispatch it to your office."

Insufferable man, she thought. "I am doing my own investigation," she informed him. "Were you aware that there was a woman similarly murdered less than a month ago?"

That got his attention. "What are you saying?"

She let out an impatient breath. "I'm saying"—she glanced down at her notes—"that a Betsy Wilson was killed in the same way Goldie Neville was just over three weeks ago. I'm wondering if you've made any connection between the two murders?"

"To my knowledge, this office was never informed of another killing."

"And why is that?"

She was beginning to irritate Clay. "Because, Mrs. … or Miss Rebel, our job is not to investigate local murders unless they involve us directly."

"It's Miss," she informed him. "And if what you say is true, why has this office taken such an interest in Goldie Neville's death?"

God, he thought as he watched her raise her chin and look at him with contempt, he loved her eyes. She was magnificent! He might not like her attitude, but he liked everything else about her. He didn't much care for women who put themselves forward, but she was no novice at her job, and she knew how to hit home with her questions. For some reason, he was glad to learn she wasn't married.

"In the Neville death, we were asked by local authorities to look into the matter because it took place near where one of our ships was docked." He glanced down at his own file. "It says here that this office gave our findings on the Neville death to a Mr. Goodall, thus concluding our part in the investigation."

Jena Leigh glanced back at her notes. "Would it come under your jurisdiction if I told you Miss Neville was secretly meeting one of your own men?"

He was startled. "One of my men?"

"A Yankee, a Federalist, a Union soldier—I don't know if he was from this office. You Yankees are everywhere, aren't you?"

With practiced discipline he let her barb pass unchallenged. "How could you know that? It didn't come out in our investigation."

"Mrs. Beauchamp informed me that Miss Neville was very interested in a Yankee sergeant she was seeing."

He'd talked to the madam, of course, but he was surprised Miss Rebel had. "And you think this figment of Mrs. Beauchamp's imagination killed Miss Neville?"

She let her breath out slowly, trying to hold on to her temper. "Why would you assume Mrs. Beauchamp imagined the man? What would she have to gain by making such an assertion?"

"All I know is, she didn't mention it to me. And I questioned her at some length."

Jena Leigh folded her notes and placed them in her case. Standing, she leaned her hands on the desk so she would be at eye level with him. "I can see you don't care about the death of just one more soiled dove, do you? You only want to protect your own image and not get your hands dirty delving too deeply into such a death."

Instead of being angered by her accusations, he grinned. "A soiled dove—you mean a prostitute, don't you? "

She glared at him. "If you like. But I can tell you, I have no respect for your office. You already know what happened to me the first day I arrived in Galveston. I want to know what you've done about the man who insulted me right in front of this place."

Clay's brows came together in a frown. "If you remember, I did try to apologize to you."

"But what about the man—was he punished?"

"I reprimanded him."

"Is that all you did?" She was really angry now. "If your job is to protect your soldiers when they behave improperly, you have succeeded admirably." She reached for her case and held it in front of herself like a shield. "I'm wasting my time here."

His gaze was steady and probing. "Sit down, Miss Rebel," he said. "It's my job to see that both sides are heard and to prevent trouble before it begins. I can assure you that we, in this office, will do everything in our power to bring peace to the region."

"And where is the man who harassed me?"

"Since you wouldn't talk to me that day, I had only McIntyre's word on what happened between the two of you. He implied that you encouraged him."

She shook her head. "And you believed him?"

"Of course not. But I had nothing to go on but his word. Had you accompanied me back to this office, you could have lodged a complaint."

"I don't trust you or anyone connected with your army."

Jena Leigh watched Colonel Madison frown, and the dark look in his eyes softened a bit. "I am sincerely sorry. On behalf of the Union Army I once again apologize for the actions of one of our soldiers."

She met his steady gaze, and her anger receded enough for her to really look at him. Each feature was perfectly blended to make him one of the most handsome men she'd ever seen. His jaw was strong, his mouth perfect. She stared into his eyes and found him similarly observing her. She tore her gaze from his, reminding herself why she was there. "I'm not impressed by your apology. I imagine that if a man from Galveston dishonored one of your women, you would slap him behind bars fast enough. Is the man who insulted me and shoved me against a wall behind bars, Colonel?"

Clay shifted uneasily, because he realized he should have taken sterner measures with McIntyre. "Not at this moment."

"But you did confine him?"

He took a steadying breath, as if he were trying to be forbearing. "No."

"In what way did you punish the man?"

"I warned him that if he committed another such offense against a woman, he would have to face the full force of this office."

"You did that much," she said critically. "He must have been trembling in his boots." She shook her head in disgust. "Read my column tomorrow and find out how the people of Galveston feel about your attempts to bring harmony to the community."

Sobering, Clay gave her a speculative glance. "You're a rarity, Miss Rebel. I can't decide if you are an idealist or merely a troublemaker."

To Jena Leigh's way of thinking, he had just insulted her. She didn't like him in the least. "I don't know how your Northern women feel about it, but here in Texas we don't like being treated with disrespect by any man."

He was becoming more frustrated by the minute. She was a spunky lady, and she knew how to hit and keep on hitting. "I imagine it's much the same everywhere. No woman should endure such disrespect."

They glared at each other until Jena Leigh finally said, "I have nothing further to ask of you. I'll wish you

a good day, sir. I've taken up enough of your valuable
time."

Before Clay could reply, she turned and swept out of
the office, weaving her way past the desks in the outer
room. He stood with the intention of going after her,
then shook his head, reconsidering. She was a hellion—
a woman who seemed to push her way through life. A
smile touched his lips. He would see J. L. Rebel again;
of that he was certain. She was going to cause him trouble; he felt it in his gut.

He motioned for one of the soldiers in the outer office. The young private hurried forward and snapped to
attention. "Yes, sir," he said, swallowing hard because
he'd been called before the big man himself.

Clay looked into puzzled hazel eyes and wondered if
he'd ever been that young. "What's your name, Private?"

"Nathaniel Ellison, sir."

"Private Ellison, I want you to do something for me."

The young soldier had never been singled out to do
anything for one of the high-ranking officers, especially
not the most important officer in the building. "Yes, sir.
I'd consider it an honor, sir."

"You saw the woman who just left here?"

"Yes, sir." He gulped, wondering if he was in trouble
because he'd winked at her and had been staring at her.
But who wouldn't have? She was like an angel. "The
one wearing glasses. Yes, sir, I saw her leave," he managed to say in a shaky voice.

"Her name is J. L. Rebel, and she works for the *Daily
Galveston*. Find out where she lives. I want you to be-

come her shadow for a couple of days. Note where she goes, and whom she talks to. But be discreet. Don't let her suspect she's being watched."

Ellison wondered what this was all about. But it wasn't his place to question an officer. "I'll be her shadow, sir, and she'll never know I'm there."

"Report back to me if she does anything out of the ordinary."

The young private saluted. "Yes, sir. I will, sir."

Chapter Eight

Jena Leigh paced Noah Dickerson's office, clasping the notes she'd taken earlier in the day. "I can tell you right now," she interjected, "that Yankee officer was insufferable! He has one job and one job only, and that is to keep his own men from being accused of anything outside the law. He wears blinders about the people of this town." She paused to take a breath. "But I suppose that's to be expected." She shook her head in frustration. "Tell me, where do we go for justice? Where?"

Dickerson turned in his swivel chair so he could follow her pacing. "Will you be seated, J.L.? You're making me dizzy."

She dropped onto a chair and, using the toe of her boot, moved her satchel from under her feet. "I'm sorry, but he made me so angry. He knew what happened to me right in front of his office, and all he did was make a half-hearted attempt to apologize. And you know what he told me? He said he'd spoken with the man. What does that mean?"

"What did you expect? The Yankee officers are going to look after their own first. If he said he spoke to the soldier, that's as good as you're going to get from him."

"Unless I'm wrong, he thinks I deserved what happened to me."

Dickerson smiled, thinking that Colonel Madison must have had his hands full with J.L. "He probably didn't know what to think about you."

"Yes, well, I might have been prejudiced against him because of our first meeting, which I found offensive; but under the circumstances, who wouldn't have been?"

The editor glanced down at the notes she'd handed him. Already she had gone farther in her investigation than any of his other reporters. "So Mrs. Beauchamp said Goldie Neville was seeing a Union soldier."

"Yes. The woman wasn't quite what I had expected. She really cares about the people who work for her. She wants Miss Neville's killer brought to justice."

He arched a brow at her. "So you liked her?"

Jena Leigh shook her head. "I don't know her well enough to form an opinion. And she and I hardly travel in the same sphere." She leaned back and let out her breath. "I don't think we will be sharing lifelong secrets with each other."

Dickerson knew that today had been hard for her. He imagined that Irene Prescott had protected J.L. from the seamy side of life, and rightly so. "You may find this hard to understand, but Chantalle is well received by many people in Galveston. She's a successful business-woman."

Jena Leigh nodded. "It's her business that I find objectionable."

"Well," he said, smiling, "I can see how you would."

Jena Leigh decided it might be better to change the subject. She watched Dickerson closely as she asked, "You have already connected the murders of Goldie Neville and Betsy Wilson, haven't you?"

He stared at her, stunned. "What! I hadn't thought ..." He shook his head. "Where did you get such an idea?"

"Surely you know about the death of Betsy Wilson?"

"Of course. But I don't recall that there was much of a fuss made over her death. I believe we had a mention of her in the obituaries. At the time she was just another prostitute, and no one was sure how she died."

Jena Leigh leaned her hands on his desk and stared into his face. "She was a human being, and she had a life until someone took it away from her in a most brutal way."

He rubbed his temples. "Who put you on this track?"

"Mrs. Beauchamp."

"She tied the two deaths together?"

"Not exactly. But I think the deaths are related."

"Not even the authorities made such a connection." The glimmer of triumph heated his blood. He could smell a big story, and it had taken this young woman to dig out what was right before them all. "Maybe I should put Armstrong on this story. He can push hard and batter through obstacles."

"No, you don't!" she said, slamming the palm of her hand against his desk. "This is my story, and I'm going to pursue it."

Dickerson had rarely had his authority challenged, and her defiance raised his hackles. "I say who does what around here."

"Fine," she said, standing up and working her fingers into her gloves. "But Mr. Armstrong had weeks to work on this story, and he didn't come up with anything. It took me one day to put the pieces together."

"Simmer down; simmer down," Dickerson soothed, waving her toward the chair. "I'm not going to take it away from you unless I see you are in over your head."

Jena Leigh dropped down on the edge of the chair. "I can do this." She watched his face carefully as she asked her next question. "How far will you allow me to go as a reporter?"

"What do you mean?"

She shoved a sheet of paper across his desk. "I've written an article, and I was wondering if you would approve it for print."

He held up his hand to silence her while he read what she'd written. She watched him closely but couldn't tell what he was thinking from his bland expression. When he finished, he glanced at her. "The devil sent you to complicate my life, didn't he?"

Hope blossomed inside her. "You'll publish it—as is?"

"You know this could mean trouble for us both?"

"I'm willing to chance it if you are. And should anyone object to the article, I'll take all the blame."

He laughed long and hard. "I'm afraid most of the risk is on my side." He tapped the paper against his palm and then handed it back to her. "Give it to Bob Steiner and tell him to set it in type."

She smiled at him, and even an old married man like Dickerson was not immune to her charms. "You could talk the devil into repenting," he said, waving her out of his office. "Go on, get this thing done." She was going to cause trouble for him—he could feel it in his bones.

"Thank you. You won't regret it."

"Yeah, yeah, yeah," he mused. "Visit me in a Yankee prison when Colonel Madison has me arrested."

Clay heard the sound of shattering glass in the outer office, and rushed out to find out what had happened. He stopped in his tracks just as another stone was hurled through the front window, showering glass everywhere. "What the hell!" he said, unsnapping his scabbard and moving to the door. His men were either huddled behind desks to avoid flying glass or flattened on the floor.

The mob of people consisted of twenty or so men and women—some shaking their fists, others spitting, and still others aiming more stones at the office. Clay's boots crunched shards of glass, and he stepped out the front door.

"What is the meaning of this?" he asked angrily. "Who is responsible here?"

At that moment the crowd fell silent. But then after a short lull, everyone started taking at once, and Clay couldn't understand anything that was said. "Silence!"

He held his up his hand. "Speak one at a time so I can hear your complaints." He looked at one man with broad shoulders and an angry gleam in his eyes and picked him out right away as the leader. He spoke directly to him. "Can you tell me the meaning of this?"

"If you'd read the *Daily Galveston*, you'd know why we're here," the man replied churlishly. "We ain't going to stand around while our women are molested by Yankee soldiers."

By now Clay had been joined by several of his men, who were aiming their rifles at the crowd. Realizing the mob could turn ugly if he didn't defuse the situation, he motioned for his men to lower their rifles. He then moved toward the man he'd singled out as the leader and stopped within inches of him. "What is your name, and what is your complaint?"

"My name's Carl, and me and these good people of Galveston want to know what you're going to do about what happened." He shoved a newspaper into Clay's hand and stepped back. "Read this and say it isn't true."

"Right now," Clay ordered, "I want you all to disperse and leave in an orderly manner. Sergeant Walker will take your names and make appointments with any of you who want to talk about the matter in a calm manner. Otherwise, I'll be forced to take stern measures, and you won't like that."

The man named Carl reluctantly nodded. Clay watched the mob for a moment, then motioned to Sergeant Walker to take each of their names.

Clay was still angry when he entered the building,

clutching the newspaper that had been thrust at him. "Get this glass cleaned up," he told a young corporal who was frozen in place. "And get someone out here to replace that window. Right now."

The corporal turned to his companion, watching in awe as Colonel Madison disappeared into his office. "He's a cool one. I've always thought officers sent men like us to do their grunt work. He faced down that mob single-handedly until our men joined him out there."

"He's got nerves of iron, right enough," the other man replied. "That's why he's an officer, and we're just corporals."

Clay spread the newspaper out on his desk, and his jaw tightened as he read.

The most trying times for mankind are not always when the dragons of war have been unleashed, but sometimes when the dragons have been caged, and the usurpers of peace are turned loose on the populace. Two of Galveston's own, Goldie Neville and Betsy Wilson, were brutally murdered, and no one at the adjutant general's office seems to think their deaths are a priority. I myself spoke to Colonel Madison yesterday, and I got neither respect nor satisfaction from his answers. Another young woman, who shall remain nameless, was accosted by a Yankee soldier right in front of that office. Do we sit back and allow the conquerors to insult our women? I say no! I say Betsy Wilson and Goldie

115

Neville deserve to have their killers brought to justice. We cannot have this kind of monster walking the streets. I say we will not allow Miss Wilson's and Miss Neville's deaths to be ignored. We still have a voice, and I am willing to use mine. Good people of Galveston, are you?

Clay raised his head, fury driving him across the room. "Sergeant Walker, get over to the"—he snapped his fingers, trying to think—"the *Daily Galveston*, and find J. L. Rebel. If she won't come with you willingly, place her under arrest."

"Yes, sir." Walker's eyes widened. "Right away."

It was two hours later before Sergeant Walker reported back to Clay. "The newspaper office was closed by the time I'd arrived, and I spoke to a man called Bob Steiner. He said he didn't know where Miss Rebel lived, but I'm sure he was lying."

"Never mind. The workmen are here to put in the window. Stay until they are finished, and then you can go home. I'm leaving now."

Clay rode home, still fuming about the trouble that woman reporter had caused. He dismounted at the apartment house where he had taken a room. He was so deep in thought he hardly noticed when a young boy came forward and led his horse to the stable behind the boarding-house. His mind was on other matters as he pressed a coin into the young lad's hand. "Give him a good rub-down, and feed and water him."

Clay had access to his apartment by the back stairs, and his tread was angry and heavy on each step. He closed the door and stood for a moment, hands on hips, staring out the window. He still carried the image of flashing amber eyes. God, that woman was going to drive him to distraction. What had she been thinking to write such an article? For that matter, what had her editor been thinking to publish it? Galveston was explosive at the moment, and it wouldn't take much to ignite the fuse. Today they had narrowly escaped disaster. Next time they might not be so fortunate.

He unbuckled his gun belt and placed it on the dresser, then removed his crimson sash, unbuttoned his jacket, and draped it over a chair with his sash. After unfastening his shirt to the waist he rolled up his sleeves, all the while contemplating just how he'd like to strangle Miss J. L. Rebel. The first thing he'd do when he saw her again would be to demand to know her real name. Obviously she was going by an alias. It was also obvious why she'd chosen the last name of Rebel.

A soft knock fell on his door, and he moved to open it. It was sundown, and the small stoop outside his room was in shadows, but he could see the slender silhouette of a woman, although he could not see her features. "What can I do for you?"

"I had heard you wanted to see me. Sergeant Walker told me where you live, and here I am."

"J. L. Rebel." He opened the door wider and leaned against it. "You're the last person I expected to find outside my door." When she said nothing, he stepped aside and swept his hand forward for her to move past him.

Jena Leigh was reluctant to enter his apartment, but she did; however, when he would have closed the door, she stalled him. "Please leave it open. I don't want anyone to think ... I would prefer you don't close the door."

"As if it would matter now, after the fact. If anyone saw you come here, they will already have drawn their own conclusions. But you are a young woman who throws caution to the wind, aren't you?"

Jena Leigh heard the bite to his tone. "I know it looks that way to you," she said nervously. She watched him light a kerosene lamp and turn up the wick, casting soft light across the floor. The room was not at all what she'd expected. It was sparsely furnished with a bed, dresser, two chairs, and a desk piled high with paperwork. The wooden floors glistened in the lamplight, and she stepped across a green braided rug. She raised her gaze to Clay and found him watching her closely. "I know it wasn't proper for me to come here tonight, but I just wanted to ... to ... "

"To?" he prodded.

"I heard about the riot today, and I never thought anyone would—"

"Riots," he corrected. "There were three. One at my office, one where several units are garrisoned, and a third at the quartermaster's offices."

She lowered her gaze, feeling like a child being reprimanded by a grown-up. "I never intended that to happen."

He swept his hand forward, offering her a chair. "What did you expect?"

She remained standing. "I don't know—not that."

Clay's gaze swept across her face. She looked so young—she couldn't be more than eighteen or nineteen. His jaw tightened. "If you aren't going to sit down, would you mind if I do? It's been a long day."

She noticed the tired lines in his face, and she couldn't help seeing him as a man and not the enemy. He had been dressed formally the last time she'd seen him, and that had made him seem more formidable. He wasn't wearing his jacket now, and his scarlet sash was thrown over a chair. He was unrolling his sleeves and buttoning them, and her gaze went to his bare chest before he buttoned his shirt. She jerked her gaze back to his face. "I shouldn't have come here."

Clay could feel her unease. "Forgive me," he said, reaching for his jacket and pulling it on. "I wasn't expecting a guest tonight, or I wouldn't have been dressed so informally." He sat down on a chair and crossed his legs, his hand resting on his highly polished boot. "I'm afraid I can't offer you refreshments. These are only temporary quarters until I can find a suitable house, and as you see, I have only the bare minimum here."

"Think nothing of it. My only reason for coming is to make you understand that inciting a riot was not what I had in mind. And I want you to know that Mr. Dickerson had nothing to do with it at all."

"Ah, the truth comes out—you want to rescue your boss." He folded his arms across his chest. "But the hour is late, and I think we could talk about this at a more opportune time—say, at my office tomorrow. Be there at nine o'clock in the morning, and we will discuss this in more detail."

"Yes," she said glancing over her shoulder. "I must leave. But before I go, I would urge you to recognize that Mr. Dickerson had nothing to do with my column. If you must punish someone, the blame is all mine."

Clay stood, moving toward her and staring down into her face. "What should your punishment be, Miss Rebel?" His voice deepened. "Tell me, and I'll see to it."

She took a step backward, not liking the gleam in his eyes. "Don't expect me to write a retraction, because I won't do that. Everything I said was true."

He stepped closer. "You don't intend to write a retraction?" His gaze dipped to her trembling lips, and his voice lowered even more. "Are you sure?" Her mouth was so inviting, he could hardly concentrate on what he was saying. "Very sure?"

She took another step toward the door. "Yes, I am."

He took another step, bringing him within inches of her. She smelled of some sweet, exotic scent that he found enticing. Her skin looked smooth, like silk, and he resisted the temptation to touch her. "I see you aren't wearing your glasses."

"I ... No. I forgot them."

"I suspect you don't even need them."

Jena Leigh's head snapped up, and her gaze collided with smoldering silver-blue eyes. Her throat closed off, and she could not utter a word. He was everything she'd ever fantasized that a man should be. Why did he have to be the enemy?

"Dare I hope that your true motive in coming here was to see me?" He touched her hand, and her fingers instinctively curled around his; then she jerked her hand away.

It took a moment for his meaning to penetrate Jena Leigh's thoughts. When it did, she quickly stepped out the door and onto the stoop. "You're out of your mind! Apologize right now!"

A quick smile curved his mouth. Most women would act indignant, pretend to misunderstand his meaning, or claim to feel faint and call for smelling salts. But this little hellion was demanding an apology. "What is a gentleman to think when a lady shows up at his place without a proper chaperone?"

She backed toward the stairs, a shocked look on her face. "I would never confuse you with a gentleman." Instantly, she wished she could retract her rash words. She was already in trouble with this man, and insulting him was not the way to gain his goodwill. She thought carefully, considering each word before she spoke again. "I suppose any man might draw the wrong conclusion under the same circumstances." She felt her cheeks burn because he had misunderstood why she had come to see him. "I shouldn't be here." She turned to leave, but his voice stopped her.

"I will want to see you in my office tomorrow morning. Be there on time."

She turned back to him. "Why can't you just tell me what you want to say now? That way I won't need to go to your office."

Clay didn't know what motivated him to do it, but he reached out and cupped her chin, tilting it up to him. "What if I told you I can't think of anything but you when you are this near?" He watched her lips part in surprise and dipped his head so his mouth was near hers.

Jena Leigh stared into his eyes, feeling a faint fluttering around her heart. She couldn't move, couldn't even speak as his breath touched her lips. She took a deep breath, trying to find her voice.

Clay straightened away from her. "No, Miss Rebel, we can't talk here."

She was so stunned by what had just happened to her that she blurted out the first thing that came to her mind. "You have no right to make demands on my time. When last we had an appointment, you kept me waiting for two hours. How do I know you won't do it again?"

"Nine o'clock," he reiterated.

She nodded. "I'll be there, but if you don't see me at that time, I'll leave."

"Miss Rebel, that wasn't a request. It was an order."

She nodded and moved to the steps.

Clay watched her descend the stairs and disappear into the shadows. He could still smell the lingering scent of her sweetness as he listened to the sound of her horse racing away. He braced his hands on the railing, still unsure about what had just happened. He was suspicious, and he supposed it came from the nature of his job. He was particularly mistrustful of beautiful women and their motives. He thought of Paula, whose treachery was the rod by which he now measured every female. All women had a motive for what they did, and Miss Rebel's was probably the worst of the lot. She hadn't gained a name as a reporter without pushing the boundaries of propriety.

That little beauty would mean trouble for any man, or many men, if she took it into her head to turn on her charms. Tonight she had seemed nervous and embarrassed. It had been a pretty act, because the other times he'd seen her she'd been angry.

She had disrupted his office, incited the citizens of Galveston, and he couldn't allow her to get away with that.

Tomorrow he would see her dance to his tune.

Chapter Nine

Whitford Hawk dismounted and led his horse into the barn, where Mort, the old cowhand who looked after the animals, took the reins and unsaddled the animal.

"Those three new fillies arrived this morning. Since the best grazing's in the east pasture, we drove 'em there until you let me know what you want done with 'em, boss."

"Let's leave them there for now," Whit said, knowing Ortega, the foreman of La Posada, would decide which of the hands should break the horses.

Whit glanced out the barn doorway, watching the setting sun paint the sky crimson and purple. Life was good—the price of beef was up, and the ranch was thriving. It was hard for him to believe that only two short months ago the ranch had been on the auction block.

"Has Ortega returned from Galveston?"

"Nope. He sent word by Sam that he'd be another few

days. The bull wasn't on the train when it got into Galveston. Sam said it'll be there Wednesday."

"I wonder what that's all about?"

"Don't know," Mort stated. "Sam said something about the rancher missing the train connection in Mexico."

"Well, good night, Mort," Whit said, moving out of the barn and making his way toward the house, where his spunky redheaded wife would be waiting for him. Before his boots touched the porch the door opened, and Jackie smiled at him. She was his world, his reason for being. Her love had pulled him out of the depths of despair and saved his soul.

She moved aside for him to enter, her hair falling over her shoulders like red velvet. "Gram made your favorite dessert tonight—chocolate cake."

He gathered her close. "You're my favorite dessert."

Jackie nestled her head against his chest, loving him so much it hurt. "That comes later tonight," she said, pressing her face against the rough material of his shirt.

His deep laughter rang through the house. "That," he said, tilting her chin up so he could look into her glorious eyes, "is something I'm looking forward to. I can't wait."

She searched his face, sensing he was troubled about something. "We have a few minutes before the biscuits are done. Why don't you tell me what's troubling you?"

Whit shook his head. "I can't hide anything from you, can I?"

"I seem to know when you are troubled about something, just like you can always guess when I'm worried.

It comes from loving someone so much, you know what's inside them."

He lifted her into his arms and sat down with her on his lap. "I sent inquiries out three weeks ago, trying to locate Drew."

Jackie nodded. "I know."

"I just got a letter." He reached into his pocket and withdrew it, handing it to Jackie. "I'd written to Colonel Briggs, who was garrisoned in Galveston during the war, inquiring whether he had any records on Drew." He nodded at the letter Jackie was reading. "As you see, Drew didn't serve under him, and he has no knowledge of him at all."

Jackie folded the letter and handed it back to him. Looking into his golden eyes, she ached for the pain she saw reflected there. He carried a heavy load of guilt, thinking he was responsible for the death of his two sisters, Laura Anne and Jena Leigh. He reasoned that if he'd been with them when the orphanage burned, he could have saved their lives. He also blamed himself because he couldn't find Drew. She touched his cheek. "If Drew is alive—and I believe he is—his path will one day lead him to you. We just need to have faith."

He leaned his dark head back against the chair and took a deep breath. "I have faith, Jackie. I just don't have much hope left."

She took his face between her hands. "Whatever comes, we'll meet it together."

His arms went around her and he lowered his head, grateful that this woman had come into his life.

"Supper's ready," Jackie's grandmother called from the kitchen. "Come and get it while it's hot."

After Jena Leigh had stabled the horse, she walked down the path toward the cottage, berating herself for going to Colonel Madison's apartment. How could he help but imagine the worst about her?

What had she been thinking?

She hadn't been thinking; that was the trouble. She had been at the leather shop, buying a saddle, when she heard about the riot at the adjutant general's office. She had gone directly to the newspaper office to talk to Mr. Dickerson, but he had already gone home. Mr. Steiner had told Jena Leigh that a Yankee by the name of Sergeant Walker from Colonel Madison's office had just left. And he'd been looking for her.

She had panicked, thinking Mr. Dickerson would be in trouble because of her rash article. Colonel Madison had thought she'd gone to his place to . . . so he would . . . It was just too humiliating to think about.

She moved down the path that gave her a full view of the veranda at the back of the Marsh house. Music filled the air, and she realized her landlady was entertaining. To avoid running into any of the guests, Jena Leigh stepped off the path with the intention of walking through the grass to get to the cottage. She had just stepped into the shadows when she saw two people on the veranda.

The man's voice sounded insistent. "What does a kiss matter when you're going to be my wife anyway? That gives me the right to take liberties."

Constance O'Banyon

"Please don't. You're hurting me, Mr. Gault!"

Jena Leigh recognized Grace's voice, and it was clear that she was frightened. She moved back toward the house and up the steps. "Grace," she called out, watching the man jerk his head in her direction and step back. Jena Leigh forced a smile. "Please forgive me. I didn't know you had guests tonight, or I never would have disturbed you."

Grace reached out and clutched Jena Leigh's hand, and there was desperation in her voice. "Please don't go. I'm sure Mama would want you to join our guests."

Jena Leigh moved between the man and Grace. "As you see, I'm not dressed for the occasion." She turned her attention to Grace's fiancé. Light was spilling through the window, and he was studying her intently. "I am J. L. Rebel," she said, offering him her hand. "I live in the guest cottage."

"I'm Simon Gault," he replied, unable to disguise the anger in his voice as he took her hand. "I've heard of you. I also read your column today, the one that started several riots in town."

Jena Leigh withdrew her hand, resisting the urge to wipe it on her skirt. "Three riots, I'm told." She observed him closely. Grace had said he was too old for her, and she was right. He had to be at least twenty years older. He was well-groomed and wasn't a bad-looking man. But he had black, predatory eyes that swept her from head to toe, making her cringe inside. She could understand why Grace was afraid of Mr. Gault.

128

"Mrs. Marsh didn't tell me how pretty you were, Miss Rebel."

Jena Leigh frowned at his lascivious tone, and he made no attempt to hide the fact that he was staring at the swell of her breasts. Grace couldn't marry such a man. "You flatter me, Mr. Gault." She turned back to Grace. "The wind has kicked up a bit. You might want to go inside to keep from spoiling your beautifully arranged hair."

"Yes," Grace said, grabbing any excuse to escape Simon. "Mama will be wondering where I am. I must go inside."

Jena Leigh waited until Grace moved to the door and opened it. "Good night." She turned to Mr. Gault. "And good night to you, sir."

He smiled, but instead of softening those black eyes, his smile deepened them to dark pits. "Clever, Miss Rebel. But your act didn't fool me. Your little friend will come around to my way of thinking. As for you, I'm sure we'll meet again under different circumstances."

She gave him a cold glare and turned away, forcing herself to take slow steps when instinct warned her to flee from something evil. She could feel Mr. Gault's gaze on her even when she reached the path, and she moved into the shadows so he could no longer watch her.

Simon's breath hissed through his teeth. Miss Rebel was graceful and quite a beauty. But her manner was cold, and he liked his women warm and willing. Maybe the little reporter just didn't know what an important man he was. In irritation, he turned toward the door. He was having a hard time getting Grace alone. He'd marry the little socialite, but he would soon tire of her innocence. She feared him, but he didn't mind that. He liked a woman to be afraid of him—it heated his blood and made lovemaking more exciting.

He paused in the doorway and glanced into the night. J. L. Rebel had known exactly what she was doing tonight. But there would be other times he would have Grace to himself. He didn't relish the thought of marrying a woman before he sampled the goods, but with her he might have to. He needed sons to inherit his name and the fortune he'd amassed. And Grace would be their mother, and a pretty trinket on his arm.

It was after midnight when Jena Leigh heard the light knock on her door. She was still dressed, because she'd been working at the small desk in the library. When she opened the door she wasn't surprised to see Grace standing on the step—she'd half expected her to come tonight.

"J.L., if Mama learns I sneaked out of the house, she will be so angry, but I just had to talk to you."

Jena Leigh took Grace's hand and led her to a chair. "I have water heating on the stove. Would you like a cup of tea?"

"No." Her eyes were brimming with tears. "You saw Mr. Gault, and you had to know he was touching me improperly. I can't marry him. You do see that, don't you?"

"Yes, I do. Did you tell your mother about Mr. Gault's behavior?"

"Yes." She lowered her head. "Mama said that when men are in love, they often become too amorous." She shivered. "I hate it when he touches me."

"Then you must refuse to marry him."

Grace shook her head. "If I were strong like you are, I would do just that. But Mama can be very demanding, and she always gets her way in everything."

Jena Leigh sat down in a chair near her guest. "That first day we met, you spoke of a man you cared for. Tell me about him."

Her teary eyes shone in the dim lamplight. "His name is David. David Taylor. His papa died, and his mama was sick for a long time. He'd wanted to go to war with his friends, but he had to stay and take care of her. His store took a direct hit from Yankee cannons during the blockade. He's doing his best to build it back, and business is good, he tells me. David will never be wealthy like Simon, but he is an honorable, hardworking man." She gave a hopeless shrug. "I want more than anything to be his wife."

"And he loves you?"

She smiled through her tears. "He is afraid of admitting how he feels about me, because he doesn't think he's good enough for me. Mama has helped further that notion by giving him a cold stare whenever they meet." She suddenly started giggling. "When I'm near David, he suddenly becomes clumsy, drops things, stumbles. He can't put three words together, and he's not that way around anyone else. He's the dearest man, and I love him so much."

"What's the name of his store?"

"Taylor's General Store. It's just off the Strand toward the docks. He owns the store outright."

"Grace, from here on out you must avoid being alone with Mr. Gault. I don't trust him after what I witnessed tonight. Be careful around him. Only see him when someone else is with you."

"Mama thinks Simon can do no wrong."

"There's something cold and malevolent in his eyes—and I don't like the way he treated you, or the way he looked at me. How can your mother want you to marry such a man?"

"She will have her way in this. She is set on my marrying him."

"But you won't, Grace. You can refuse. No one can make you marry a man against your will."

There was hope in Grace's eyes. "Truly?"

"Absolutely."

"I'm twenty years old, and Simon Gault is in his fifties. He could be my grandfather."

It was strange; Grace was two years older than Jena Leigh, and yet she seemed so young and helpless. "He's shameful, wanting such a young wife. Grace, you must refuse to marry him."

"I … I am going to tell Mama that tomorrow." She frowned. "If I have the courage."

"Wait until I talk to your David. I'll try to see him tomorrow if I can."

Grace's eyes filled with tears. "You would do that for me?"

"Certainly. What are friends for?"

"You are the truest friend I've ever had."

"Go home now before your mother discovers you missing. If you get the chance tomorrow night, sneak out of the house and come here. I'll let you know if I spoke to David and what he had to say."

"I'll find a way to get out," Grace said with more assurance than Jena Leigh had ever heard in her voice. "I'll be here; don't worry." She smiled. "I have to go now. I wouldn't want Mama to miss me."

Jena Leigh watched Grace move out the door and heard her footsteps disappear down the lane. What had she gotten herself into, mixing in Grace's love life? But when she thought of Simon Gault as Grace's husband, it made her sick inside. She had to do something to help the girl, or her mother would have her married to that lecherous man.

She gathered the notes she'd been working on and neatly filed them in her satchel. Tomorrow wasn't going to be easy—she had to meet with Colonel Madison, and she didn't know what he had in mind for her. She gritted her teeth. That Yankee officer was certainly tyrannical, and he probably had the right to exert his power over her. She sat down and lowered her chin to her open palm. He was handsome, though. And she had felt warmth in him tonight, or had she only imagined it? She remembered his silver-blue eyes and felt her heart beat faster. She had to be careful around him. He had a way of making her think about things that had never entered her mind before she'd met him. Like how it would feel to have his lips on hers.

What would it feel like to have him touch her?

Would her heart flutter again if he smiled at her?

She stood up, disgusted with herself. He was the enemy, a Yankee, and not worthy of her notice.

Chapter Ten

Clay was at his desk early. He'd whittled down by half the stack of files that needed his attention. A thought kept nagging at him: Somewhere—he couldn't quite recall where—he'd heard the name J. L. Rebel before. Suddenly he opened the bottom drawer of his desk and removed a file, thinking he remembered now. Flipping a page, he scanned down the list of rogue reporters—of course, her name jumped out at him several times. He recalled reading the list and thinking he would have to rein this reporter in. And he'd been right. Miss Rebel was about to feel the power of his office come down hard on her.

He leaned back in his chair and stared into the outer office, where people were just beginning to gather. Sergeant Walker appeared in the door with a cup of coffee. "You're early, sir. How long have you been here?"

"Since before sunup. Something had been nagging at me, and I found my answer." He took a sip of coffee before he continued. "Do you recall that a while ago we were discussing rogue reporters?"

"Yes, sir. I do."

"And do you recall the name of J. L. Rebel?"

"Yes, sir, the young lady who was here Monday, the one who caused the riots."

He shoved the list at Walker. "Look at this."

Walker hunched over the desk, his finger following the names on the list. "Miss Rebel's on here several times." He straightened up and shook his head. "She's a real hell-raiser, sir."

Clay got a faraway look in his eyes. "Yes. She is that."

"What are you going to do with her, sir?"

Clay ran his hands through his hair. "Damned if I know. But If I don't tread softly where she's concerned, I'll likely have the whole of Galveston at my front door. Yet I have to get my point across to her somehow."

Walker walked out, mumbling, "A real hell-raiser."

Jena Leigh was escorted directly to Clay's office, and he watched her shove her glasses tighter against the bridge of her nose. He gave her a humorless smile. "My compliments. You're early." The look she gave him could have shattered stone, and he had to look away to keep from laughing out loud.

"I'm always punctual." She had decided to behave in a prim and proper manner because of the way she had acted the night before. "Am I here to be lectured or punished?"

He slid a page across his desk for her to view. "I want to know the meaning of this insanity."

She glanced down at her article. "I might have gone a bit too far. I admitted that to you last night."

He sat forward, examining a document in front of him. "According to our findings," he said, "you and trouble are old friends. It seems you like to stir things up a bit."

Jena Leigh looked at the list, seeing her name, along with those of several other newspapermen she knew. Irene's name was on the list as well. "I'm quite sure you have your own reasons for such a listing."

Clay's dark eyebrows swept upward, and he regarded her with displeasure. "I can assure you that my only motive in having you here is to warn you that this office will not tolerate your instigating unrest among the citizens of Galveston. Is that understood?"

"No, it's not understood." She seated herself on the edge of the chair and leaned toward his desk. "I didn't set out to stir people into a frenzy. But they have a right to express their displeasure, just as I have a right to express my thoughts in the press. You may think I went too far, but I had a reason."

"Yes," he said, impaling her with his silver-blue gaze, "I'm sure you think you do."

"What do you want of me?"

"Humor me, Miss Rebel, and all will be made clear to you in time."

"So far you have said nothing I want to hear." Her resolve wavered as his gaze slammed into hers. Judging from his tone and attitude, he was obviously not accustomed to a woman disagreeing with him.

"You will hear me out—or leave, in which case I'll deal with your boss. I don't care which option you choose," he intoned.

She had been looking at the list as she spoke, and slowly raised her gaze to his. Outwardly he appeared to be at ease; the expression on his face was unruffled, and she would not have known he was affected by what she'd said if it weren't for the tight grip he had on his pencil. She noticed the flicker in his eyes and the cynicism reflected there. She also heard his pencil snap in two, and she watched his calm break as well.

"Miss Rebel, you seem to be under the impression that you can start the war all over again. Let me warn you—and it's a dire warning—the fact that you are a woman will not keep me from bringing the full force of the law down on you."

"Go ahead." She smiled, knowing she had him now. "If you don't think you'll start a riot and have to call in the troops to defend you, try to lock me up—put me in your stockade or whatever you call it."

"Don't think I won't. But I didn't ask you here to exchange insults or to play word games with you. I'm here for answers." His gaze pierced hers. "Let me start at the beginning," he said, trying to be tolerant while he took another pencil and poised it above a clean sheet of paper. "First of all, I feel a bit foolish referring to you as Miss Rebel when we both know that isn't your actual name." His gaze hardened even more. "What is your actual name?"

Declining to answer, she merely looked at him.

Polar silence enveloped the room. "I asked you for your true name. Who are you?"

She shook her head, growing angrier by the moment. Then she began enumerating his faults by counting them off on her fingers: "First, I would have given you my name if you had asked for it in a gentlemanly manner. Second, I told you about the man who accosted me in front of this office, and you didn't even seem to care. Am I correct so far?"

"It might be the truth as you see it. But that's not the way it was."

"And third," she continued as if he hadn't spoken, "I resent your—"

"We are not here to discuss my shortcomings, Miss Rebel," he interrupted, his patience stretched to the limit. "You are here because you have broken the law. You are a fairly intelligent female, so you must know what martial law means. Galveston is under martial law. There is no freedom of the press until I say there is." He looked at her inquiringly. "Am I making myself clear?"

"Is it possible you want to dictate what the newspapers print?" she asked, her head held high, her chin at a stubborn angle. "Tell me your law so I can keep it straight in my mind."

Imitating what she'd done earlier, he began counting off on his fingers. "First, martial law means the people of Galveston must act in a reasonable manner. Second, you are in a lot of trouble, Miss J. L. Rebel."

"The way I see it, you are the epitome of what I have come to expect from a Yankee officer." She counted off again on her fingers. "Cold. Efficient. Heartless." She watched his eyes turn glacial and disapproving, and thought she might have gone too far again. He made her so angry!

"What you think of me is of no importance, Miss Rebel."

A curl fell down in her face, and she poked it back underneath her bonnet. "You are here to do a job for your government, and you will crush any of us who dare get in your path. Is that the way it is?"

He gave a half shake of his head. Clay was weary of this little firebrand—he wanted her out of his office and out of his life. "What is your real name? I'll need it for my records. Of course, if you refuse to tell me your name, I can always send a rider to Altamesa Springs and find out. Someone there is bound to know."

She swallowed before she spoke. "How did you know I lived in Altamesa Springs before I came here?"

He nodded at the list before him. "We have our means of finding out what we need to know."

"Very well. Send to Altamesa Springs. That's the only way you'll learn my real name." She stood.

He gritted his teeth and glanced up at her. "Very well, we'll play it your way. You can leave now. But this office will be watching you, so let me just conclude our meeting by warning you to desist from inciting another riot. I won't let you off so easy if there is a next time."

Clay watched her whirl around and walk out the door. She had gotten under his skin, and he couldn't seem to banish her from his mind. J. L. Rebel might be a false name, and she might be attempting to play down the fact that she was a beauty, but she'd failed. Today she'd been wearing glasses, but they only acted as a frame for those beautiful golden eyes. The blond curl that had managed to fall across her forehead had intrigued him, especially when she kept trying to shove it back beneath her bonnet. Her crisp white blouse had not disguised her firm breasts. The plain brown skirt she wore merely emphasized her tiny waist. He smiled at the memory of her scuffed brown boots. He had never met a female like her, and he didn't care to tangle with her again.

He reached for the stack of unread letters and opened the first one. It took him a few moments to realize he'd been scanning down the page without comprehending one word he'd read. His mind was still on a pair of golden eyes belonging to the most fascinating beauty he'd ever crossed swords with.

Chapter Eleven

Jena Leigh chose early afternoon to visit Taylor's General Store, thinking most people would be home for the noon meal, and she was right. When she arrived, there were only two customers in the store: a grandmotherly looking woman and a child. The young boy paid for a stick of hard candy and dashed out the door with a grin on his freckled face. Jena Leigh moved down an aisle toward the front counter and glanced out the back door, where stacks of lumber were piled against a high fence. This was more than a general store—it was also a lumberyard. And to Jena Leigh's way of thinking, there was a lot of building going on in Galveston. She guessed that David Taylor was probably doing quite well.

The gentleman behind the counter was conversing with the elderly woman, and Jena Leigh stood back so she could study him without his being aware of it. He had sandy hair and brown eyes. He was handsome in a boyish way, and she placed him in his early twenties. He had a gentleness about him that she liked, and his smile seemed genuine.

"Mrs. Corsair, how are you this fine day?" he inquired.

"Fair to middling. But, David, I've known you since you were in short pants, and you've always dealt honestly with me until today."

He still smiled at her, and Jena Leigh got the feeling he'd had the same conversation with the lady many times before. "Whatever can you mean this time, Mrs. Corsair?"

"Twenty cents is just too much to pay for a yard of silk, and you very well know it."

"But, ma'am, we couldn't get this silk from the warehouse in Pennsylvania, and it took over two months for it to arrive from New York. And New York charged us more for the bolt."

"I won't pay a penny more than ten cents a yard—so there it is," she said stubbornly. "I don't care if you had to send all the way to China for it."

A smile still lingered on his mouth. "Very well, Mrs. Corsair, I'll let you have it for that price. But if my mother finds out what I've done and takes me to task, I'll tell her to go and talk to you."

She nodded. "Alice knows a fair price when she sees one."

He wrapped her material in brown paper and tied it with twine while the woman counted out her change and slid it across the counter toward him. "You're a good boy, David."

He arched his brow at her. "I'm a man now."

She nodded. "So you are. I don't know what your mama would have done without you after your papa died. I was afraid we were going to lose Alice, too, until you brought in that doctor from Houston to treat her lung sickness. I know you wanted to go away to war with the rest of your friends, but you did the right thing in staying here and taking care of your mama."

Jena Leigh noticed the slight frown that creased his brow. "Sometimes circumstances rule our lives, and we're forced to ride out the storm."

The woman patted his hand. "You are a good *man*, David."

When the woman left, Jena Leigh stepped up to the counter. A gentle brown gaze settled on her. "How may I help you, ma'am?"

"I'm J. L. Rebel, and I'd like to talk to you privately."

His expression brightened. "You live on the Marsh estate, don't you?"

"Yes, I do. And Grace and I have become good friends. She's told me about you."

He lowered his head. "I'm sure she told you our situation is hopeless." He untied his apron and laid it on the counter, then waved to a young boy who was stocking the shelves. "Billy, watch the store. I'm going out back to show this lady our lumber."

His hand touched her elbow as he guided her toward the door. "I'm sorry. This is the only place we can talk privately."

Jena Leigh dodged a stack of galvanized tubs and followed David until they were out of view of the open door. "Mr. Taylor, I would think with all the construction going on, lumber must be a lucrative commodity."

"Yes, ma'am, it is. I have it shipped in from East Texas, and as fast as it arrives, we sell out. The lumber you see here has already been purchased, and I have people begging for more. I have a shipment coming in tomorrow, and it's already sold."

"I guess what I really want to know is how you feel about Grace. Please excuse me for asking such a personal question, but after all, she is my friend, and I care about what happens to her." She watched him study the tip of his shoe, his expression grave.

"I love her more than my life, Miss Rebel. Nothing I do, no matter what success I might obtain, will mean anything to me if I can't share my life with the woman I love."

"You know about Simon Gault?" Jena Leigh saw the misery etched on his face.

"Mr. Gault is probably the most powerful man in Galveston, if you don't count the Yankees. Mrs. Marsh is set on her daughter marrying him." He balled his fists. "Gault is not the upstanding citizen everyone seems to thinks he is. He's evil—truly evil."

"I met him, and though I didn't like him, I wouldn't say he was evil—that's a very serious claim."

"It's true. He sent his henchman, Bruce Carlton, over here to warn me that if I didn't stay away from Grace, he'd burn my business to the ground."

Jena Leigh frowned. "And what did you say to that?"

"I said if Grace would have me, I'd risk everything,

give up everything for her." His voice took on a desperate tone. "Even if Grace doesn't want to be my wife, she can't marry that man. He's too old for her. I've heard from several people that he's started drinking heavily, and he …" He looked away from Jena Leigh. "You are a lady, so I can't tell you the things he does."

"I'm also a reporter, so I've heard it all. Tell me about Simon Gault so I can help Grace escape her mother's clutches."

"He … frequents Madam Chantalle's place. He has his own room there. I'll say no more than that."

"How does your mother feel about your marrying Grace?"

"Mama thinks Grace is sweetness itself. Like me, she's afraid for Grace to marry Gault." He stared into the distance. "Mama lives above the store, and I'm building a house for me and … for me. It's almost finished."

Jena Leigh had heard enough. "I have a favor to ask of you, Mr. Taylor. I would like you to come to the cottage tonight around seven. Will you do that?"

He looked startled. "I have to think about your reputation. What if someone should see me there."

She smiled. "I'll chance it. We have to do something about Grace and Mr. Gault. Will you be there?"

"Yes, ma'am, if you think—"

"Until then, Mr. Taylor."

Jena Leigh made her way back into the store and out the front door. She had one more stop to make, and it wasn't going to be a pleasant one. She moved hastily across the Strand and down a narrow street toward the docks.

She gathered her courage as she stepped into the dark interior of the Lucky Dollar Saloon. She was immediately swamped by the smell of rancid grease and unwashed bodies. When her eyes adjusted to the dim light, she could see twenty or so small tables, a stage with tattered green velvet curtains, and a curved bar that went all along the north side of the building. One man was seated at a table, eating a large steak that hung off the side of his plate. There were other gentlemen bellied up to the bar, talking to the bartender. An elderly man wearing a green felt hat and a matching vest was playing a lively tune on a piano that badly needed tuning.

Suddenly all the men in the place turned their attention to Jena Leigh, and she had to fight down the urge to leave. One of them waved at her, and called out, "Come on over here, you sweet thing, and I'll buy you a drink."

Movement behind her made her spin around to glance at a man who had paused midway down the narrow staircase. His attention was focused on one of the men at the bar, and he snapped his fingers at the bartender. "Take Truman to the back room and let him sleep it off." Only after the bartender had escorted the drunk out did the man's attention fall on Jena Leigh.

Maximilian Calhoun looked the lady over from head to toe and appreciated what he saw. She was dressed in a split leather riding skirt and a yellow blouse. Her hair was gathered at the back of her head with a black scarf,

Constance O'Banyon

and he could tell her blond hair was natural and owed nothing to a bottle of dye. Despite the glasses that were perched on her nose, she was a beauty. "Hello, ma'am," he said, bowing his head slightly. "How can I help you?"

He was tall, with dark hair that came to his shoulders. He wore a gray suit and waistcoat, almost the same shade as his eyes. He was handsome and had a ready smile.

"Would you be Mr. Calhoun?" Jena Leigh asked.

"I'm Max to all my friends. Now that you know who I am, maybe you'll tell me your name."

"Is there somewhere more private where we can talk?"

Max's gaze swept over her, and he could tell she was uncomfortable in these surroundings. He'd bet his last six bits that this was her first time in a saloon. He couldn't imagine why she was there or what she wanted of him. "I'm afraid if I take you upstairs, everyone will draw the wrong conclusion. Let's use one of the tables at the back."

He took her elbow and led her across the room, pulling out a chair for her to be seated. "You've never been in a place like this before, have you?" he asked, taking the chair nearest her.

"I had no reason to until today."

He watched her work her fingers out of her brown leather gloves and clasp them in her hand.

"I'm J. L. Rebel, and I'd like to ask you some questions if I may."

148

He flipped his coat open, withdrew a cigar, and asked, "Do you mind?"

"No. Go right ahead." She watched as he lit the cigar, and blew smoke toward the ceiling.

"I've heard of you." His smile lightened the color of his eyes, and she could see merriment dancing in the gray depths. "You caused quite a stir with your article in the *Daily Galveston*, didn't you?"

She met his gaze without flinching. "I'm afraid so."

He nodded about the room. "This is the place to come if you want to know everything that goes on in Galveston. I can tell you that you were the subject of most conversations hereabouts for the last two days." He grinned. "However, no one mentioned how pretty you are."

She raised her chin just a bit, offended by the thought that she'd been an item of gossip in such a place. And she was getting tired of men telling her she was pretty. She wanted someone to recognize that she had a brain and she knew how to use it. "I don't care much for flattery, Mr. Calhoun. And I don't like having my name bandied about in your saloon."

"I see I have offended you, and that wasn't my intent. You are admired, Miss Rebel—the men of this town look on you as someone who carried the torch for them."

"That's ridiculous."

"You should have heard the heated conversations concerning you. I believe you could run for mayor of the city and win."

She let out an exasperated breath and even smiled.

149

"Don't go on with this nonsense." She sat forward, her gaze on him. "And anyway, I didn't come here to talk about myself. I wanted to ask you some questions about Betsy Wilson."

She watched his eyes narrow.

"What is your interest in her?"

"I'm investigating the death of Goldie Neville, and I'm concerned that the two deaths might be connected in some way."

"I don't see how. I didn't know Miss Neville, but Betsy was a likable young woman. She had a good voice, and she sang for my customers. The authorities came to the conclusion that she was killed by some drifter who rode on to another place. They didn't do much to find the man."

"I discovered that myself—no one seems to really care about Miss Neville or Miss Wilson. Can you tell me any of Betsy's habits? Was there someone she was fond of?"

"I don't know what she did when she wasn't here. But she once mentioned to me that she was seeing a man, and he wanted to marry her. I don't know who he was."

Jena Leigh tensed. "Mr. Calhoun, is there any chance that the man Betsy Wilson was seeing was a sergeant in the Union Army?"

He frowned. "I haven't told anyone about that. How did you know?"

She stared down at her hands. "I'm afraid we have a real problem in this town."

"Why is that?"

She stood up so quickly, the chair she'd been sitting in slid backward. "I have to go. Thank you for the information."

"Wait," he said, following her to the door. "When will I see you again—how will I find you?"

She turned to look into his dancing gray eyes and almost smiled. "Why, just ask any of your customers, Mr. Calhoun. If I am the topic of their conversation, as you intimated, they can tell you everything about me."

He laughed as he watched her walk out the door, thinking that J. L. Rebel was a charmer. He blew a smoke ring and watched until it fanned out and disappeared. That little blond was every man's dream—and smart, too. The memory of her golden eyes lingered long after she'd gone, leaving a lasting impression. He frowned. She was playing a dangerous game if she was searching for a killer. That thought disturbed him more than a little. But he doubted anyone could talk her out of her mission.

Cunning eyes watched Jena Leigh as she walked back to the Strand, where she had left her horse tied to a hitching post.

She paused before she mounted the horse, feeling a strange sensation, as if someone were watching her. Seeing no one about, she shrugged and mounted her horse, turning him toward home.

Harman Parnell stepped back into the shadows, hatred swirling through his brain. Her article was calling attention to the deaths of Betsy Wilson and Goldie Neville, and that could be dangerous for him. She had to be stopped. He'd been surprised to discover she was the same woman who had caused him so much trouble the day she arrived in Galveston. She was no better than the prostitutes he'd killed, and he'd already marked her for death, too. But he was orderly, and he had one more woman to dispose of before he could get to the reporter. Everything had to be just right before he rid the world of another prostitute. He was patient, and she would be worth the wait.

He looked with jaundiced eyes at the beautiful young woman who challenged him. The woman he had wanted to marry had been beautiful, too. Beautiful and faithless. He'd been a good soldier before that day Betty's letter had reached him; the day he'd become a deserter and a killer. Biding his time, he'd waited for just the right chance to desert his unit. He'd burned Betty's letter over a campfire the night he'd fled the battle at Gettysburg, Pennsylvania. But every word she'd written had been seared into his memory. With chaos reigning all about him, he'd slipped past the picket line and eventually made his way to Callas, Virginia. He'd hoped to make Betty see reason, to convince her that she still loved him.

He'd reached her home in the early hours of the morning and found her in bed with the Yankee sergeant she'd professed to love. Anger coiled in his mind like a poisonous snake. He'd shot them both—the enemy first, and then he'd turned his gun on Betty. Before he killed her, she'd fought him, slashing his face with her lover's sword, but later she'd begged for her life. He still carried the scar she'd given him, and he wore it like a badge. He'd taken the identity and rank of the Yankee who had stolen his woman. To his way of thinking, he was still getting his revenge on Sgt. Wayne McIntyre. He had left with the man's discharge papers in his pocket, his money, and his horse. That very same night he'd ridden straight for Texas because no one would know him there. Somewhere on the long ride he'd decided to make it his mission to wipe the world clean of faithless women.

It was nearing dark when Jena Leigh reached the newspaper office. It was imperative that Mr. Dickerson be made aware of the frightening news she'd uncovered. But everyone had gone home for the day. It was just too much of a coincidence that both Miss Neville and Miss Wilson had been seeing a Yankee with the rank of sergeant just before their deaths.

Lingering shadows crept across the street, and she shivered, her stomach tightening in a knot, and a wave of nausea swept through her. If there was a killer on the loose, no woman in this town would be safe until he was captured.

Nudging her mount into a gallop, she remembered inviting David Taylor to her house. She had to get word to Grace to be there as well. She dismounted at the stable, and Ethan was there to take the horse. She thanked him and walked toward the Marsh home. She needed to find a few moments alone with Grace, if Mrs. Marsh would let her daughter out of her sight.

" 'Oh, what a tangled web we weave,' " she quoted, knowing she would have to go against the mother to rescue the daughter. She knew she was interfering in Grace's life, but she couldn't look the other way while Mrs. Marsh married her to a lecherous old man.

Chapter Twelve

Jena Leigh watched the mahogany wall clock tick off the seconds while she lifted her teacup to her lips and took a sip. Thus far she hadn't been able to get Grace alone so she could talk to her about David. As usual Mrs. Marsh was monopolizing the conversation and showing no indication of leaving the room. Grace, on the other hand, seemed even more morose than normal and had hardly said a word. Jena Leigh knew she had to get the mother out of the room, and quickly. It was already quarter to seven, and Mr. Taylor would be arriving at the cottage any minute.

"Mrs. Marsh, I have to compliment you," she said, setting a trap by using the landlady's ego.

The older woman looked pleased. "Whatever for?"

"You told me when I was here last week that you had baked the lemon cookies we had for tea. They were the best I've ever tasted. I wonder if you would give me the recipe. I know I'll never be able to make them as delicious as you did, but I'd like to try."

Mrs. Marsh nodded. "They are good, aren't they? The recipe was handed down from my grandmother, and I'd be happy to share it with you." She stood. "In fact, I'll copy it down for you right away." She went to her desk in the corner and started writing the recipe.

"Thank you. I'd appreciate it." Jena Leigh leaned toward Grace and whispered, "You must come to the cottage as soon as possible."

Grace's eyes widened. "Why?" she whispered back.

"Don't ask questions—just do it." She'd wanted Grace to arrive first, but that wasn't going to happen now.

Mrs. Marsh pushes herself away from her desk and handed Jena Leigh a piece of paper. "The secret is to use thick cream instead of milk. Otherwise, they'll just be ordinary cookies."

Jena Leigh stood, tucking the recipe into her satchel. "You are very kind. I hate to rush, but I have something that needs my attention." She looked pointedly at Grace. "I will see you soon?"

"Why, of course," Mrs. Marsh answered.

Grace nodded, catching Jena Leigh's meaning but looking puzzled.

Jena Leigh hurried out of the house and down the path. A strong breeze was blowing off the gulf, and the moon flickered through the swaying oak branches. She entered the cottage from the back just as someone knocked on the front door, which faced the road. She quickly stowed her satchel and rushed to answer it, thinking that playing matchmaker was not an easy role, and she wasn't enjoying it one bit. David Taylor stood on the doorstep, hat in hand and looking nervous. His hair was smoothed down, and he was wearing a suit.

"I'm a few minutes early, but I couldn't wait. I've been thinking of nothing else all day. Has something happened to Grace?"

She could tell he felt awkward about visiting a female at night. She wasn't sure he entirely trusted her motives. "I can assure you Grace is fine. I saw her just a few minutes ago."

At that moment a soft knock fell on the back door, and Grace entered. Her hand flew to her mouth, and she gasped when she saw David standing there. The two lovers just stared at each other, and Jena Leigh knew she had to take a hand or they'd stand there all night. She spoke to Grace. "Mr. Taylor is here to see you."

"D-David." Grace blushed and lowered her lashes. "I didn't know you would be here."

The young man flicked a quick look of appreciation at Jena Leigh before he took Grace's hand and eased her toward him. Grace had been right: he couldn't seem to utter a word when he was near her, though he hadn't had any trouble conversing with Jena Leigh.

"It's such a nice night out, I find myself wanting to take a long walk," Jena Leigh said, moving to the door. "I should be gone about an hour. I trust the two of you won't miss me too much."

Her guests hardly heard her leave—they were too busy staring into each other's eyes.

"Fate has favored me tonight," David said, pushing his nervousness aside. He loved Grace, and if he didn't tell her tonight she might never know. He slowly pulled her closer to him. She was small, barely coming to his shoulder, and he felt a strong urge to protect her. She was graceful and slender, and her dark hair curled about her pretty face in ringlets. Her eyes were her finest feature—they were soft gray.

David boldly touched his lips to her hand and felt her shiver. "I never dared hope I'd get to see you alone." His mouth moved to her wrist and lingered there.

"Oh," was all Grace could manage to say, because his nearness had made her tremble inside. His eyes were the most marvelous brown, and at the moment they had softened with warmth. Her own eyes fluttered shut, and she hoped he was going to kiss her—oh, how she wanted him to.

"Grace," he said in a trembling voice, "do you know how dear you are to me?"

Her heart quickened. She wanted him to take her in his arms so she could tell him how much she loved him, but she didn't dare. All she could manage was a quiet, "You are dear to me, too, David."

"I think of you all the time," he said, laying his cheek against hers. "Do you ever think of me?"

She wanted him to understand her feelings for him. "There is hardly a time when I'm not thinking of you."

He smiled sadly and touched her cheek. "I can't get you out of my mind. I know that you will soon marry someone else, but that won't stop me from loving you."

She gasped. "You love me?"

"Most desperately."

Her heart pounded, and she wanted to cry. "I wish … I want … If only we could—"

"Will you allow me to kiss you?" he asked in a deep voice.

She turned her face up to his and parted her lips. "Yes, please."

"I've dreamed of how it would feel if I could kiss you." He lowered his head. "Now I'll know." David gently touched his mouth to hers. She was so sweet, and he doubted she had ever been kissed before, because her lips trembled beneath his.

Grace felt as if her heart had just melted. She pressed her lips tighter against his and felt his arms slide about her. At last, breathless, they pulled apart.

"My sweet, sweet Grace. How I wish you were mine."

"David, I want that more than anything." Her eyes brightened with tears. "But Mama will never let us be together."

He looked miserable. "You deserve better than I could ever give you."

She saw anguish in his eyes, and it hurt her. "I don't care about that. If I could be with you, I'd be happy living in a tent."

He smiled. "I don't think it would ever come to that, Grace. I can't bear the thought of you marrying Simon Gault."

She lowered her head. "I hate him!"

He grabbed her, sliding his arms around her and holding her tightly. "I love you enough to let you go, but not to that man—never to him!"

Harman Parnell watched Jena Leigh move down the pathway. He wanted to reach out to her and put his hands around her neck and squeeze the life out of her. The reporter had dared to call him a monster, and she'd have to pay for that. He'd show her what a monster really was. His hands balled into fists, he could almost feel her white neck beneath his fingers. He stepped across the street to follow her, but pulled back into the shadows when he heard a rider passing. He felt rage gathering inside him like a living thing. He would keep his appointment with J. L. Rebel another time. Right now he had another worthless bit of flesh that was a blight on humanity. He would cleanse the world of all women who tormented men with their bodies.

When Jena Leigh returned to the cottage, she found Grace sitting in a rocking chair, her face buried in her hands and her body shaking with sobs.

"What happened?" She went down on her knees and raised Grace's face. "Why are you crying?"

"He loves me. He asked me to be his wife." She wiped tears away with the tips of her fingers. "I love him so much, but how can I defy Mama and marry him?"

Jena Leigh wondered what it would feel like to love a man as much as Grace loved David, and she wondered what it would feel like to have a man love her. "What did David suggest you do?"

Grace reached out and clasped Jena Leigh's fingers. "He would like to have Mama's blessing, but that will never happen. He wants me to go with him to Reverend Scott and be married. He said he'd arrange it—but how can we keep Mama from finding out?"

"I think your David can handle that." Jena Leigh smiled. "Just think of it, an elopement."

Grace looked at her inquiringly. "What do you think I should do?"

"Grace, I can't tell you how to live—no one can, not even your mother. But ask yourself this—what will your life be like if you don't marry David?"

Grace bent her head. "I'll be miserable, and Mama will probably find a way to force me to marry Simon Gault."

"Then you have the answer, don't you?"

Grace nodded. "Yes," she said in a barely audible voice, and then with more force, "*Yes!* I'm going to marry David."

"The two of you must be very careful and private with your plans. If your mother finds out about them beforehand, she'll try to stop you."

"I asked David to come back tomorrow night, so I can give him my answer. Is that all right with you?"

"Of course. What time?"

"The same time he came tonight."

"Very well. But right now you must go home. It wouldn't do for your mother to find you missing and come looking for you. She might get suspicious. You will be careful, won't you?"

"How can I thank you? If you hadn't come into our lives, I would have been forced to marry Mr. Gault."

"Go," Jena Leigh urged, feeling the responsibility of changing the course of a person's life. "Hurry."

When Grace left, Jena Leigh stood at the window and watched her rush down the path. As always when she was feeling lonely, she reached inside the neck of her gown and clasped her pendant, her only tie with her family; she held on to it as if it were a lifeline. To love someone as Grace loved her David must be a wonderful feeling. She frowned. She couldn't imagine loving a man enough to want to spend the rest of her life with him. Wouldn't they get tired of each other eventually?

A sliver of light spilled across Clay's office as he sat at his desk, his head bent over his paperwork. He heard the door to the outer office open and glanced up to see Private Ellison striding toward him. "Evening, Colonel. I came by on the chance you'd still be here."

Clay neatly aligned the stack of papers on his desk while the young man stood at attention. "At ease, Ellison. What have you got to tell me?"

"Well, sir, I followed Miss Rebel like you told me to. And nothing much happened until today. She went into the Lucky Dollar Saloon and stayed quite a while."

Clay frowned. "What did she do there?"

"She talked to a man at one of the back tables. She didn't drink anything, and they didn't hold hands or nothing like that. After a while she left, and I asked the bartender the name of the man she'd been talking to, and he told me it was the owner, Mr. Calhoun."

Clay realized she had been questioning Calhoun about Betsy Wilson. "I think I know what she was doing there. Did she do anything else that was unusual?"

"It was almost dark, and I followed her to her house— at a safe distance, of course. I'd just about decided to leave when I spotted another fellow watching the cottage. I ducked behind some bushes, and he never saw me, but I can tell you he was up to mischief."

"Did you get a good look at him?"

"I'm sorry, sir. He was nothing more than a shadow. Then later a man showed up at her house, and Miss Rebel let him in."

Clay frowned, wondering if it could be her lover. He wouldn't put anything past Miss Rebel. "What happened next?"

"Well, this young woman showed up, and Miss Rebel left her alone with the man." Ellison was proud of himself because he'd recognized the man as a shopkeeper in town. "It was Mr. Taylor. I could see him and the other woman through the window. They were hugging and kissing, and then later Taylor left, and the woman waited for Miss Rebel, and then after a while, she left, too. I watched her walk to the Marsh house and figured she must be Grace Marsh."

"And the unidentified man who was watching the house?"

"I heard him ride away, and then I left. I didn't want to get too close and spook him."

"You have done a good job, Ellison. But I want you to keep following Miss Rebel. Keep your sidearm handy. I don't like the thought of some man watching her."

"Yes, sir. Do you want me to go back there now?"

"No. I think you can wait until tomorrow afternoon. She'll probably be working most of the morning."

After Private Ellison had gone, Clay blew out the lamp and left the office. As he rode back to his apartment, he couldn't get Miss Rebel out of his mind. Taylor had apparently gone there to meet the Marsh girl. And who was the other man—the one who was watching J.L. so closely?

He nudged his mount forward, wishing the little beauty would get out of his head and go bother someone else.

When Clay went to bed, he spent a sleepless night, dreaming that someone was after Miss Rebel, and he couldn't get to her in time to help her. It was almost dawn when he woke, feeling as if he had been in a battle all night.

He ran his hand through his hair and sat up in bed. Someone had to protect that reckless woman before she got herself into real trouble. And it looked like that task had fallen to him.

Chapter Thirteen

Jena Leigh shoved her notes across Dickerson's desk. "I think you'd better read these. If what I suspect is true, we've got a real problem here in Galveston."

She sat down and watched the different emotions that crept across his rugged face as he read her notes. "If we take as truth what you've been told by Chantalle and Mr. Calhoun, there must be a connection between the two deaths." He scratched his head and glanced at her. "I wonder why no one put the two deaths together before now? It seems pretty evident that one man committed both crimes."

"I wish the authorities had taken the first murder seriously; then there might not have been a second one."

Dickerson nodded. "You're a damned good reporter. If you'd been here at the time, you might have made them listen to reason."

She brushed his compliment aside. "Then you agree

with me that something has to be done about this, and quickly?"

"I most certainly do." His expression hardened. "But we have to be careful and protect our story. We certainly can't have the competition getting wind of this."

"But surely we should share this theory with others so we can get the word out for the women of Galveston to be careful. We have to warn them about the danger and advise them to not go out alone—and to be careful of strangers, or anyone in a military uniform, for that matter."

"No, no. Think what you're saying. If we print that, it'll alert the killer and cause chaos in the streets. Imagine our women running away scared every time they catch sight of a blue uniform."

"I hadn't thought of that." She pursed her lips. Considering the trouble she was already in with Colonel Madison, she capitulated. "You're right. That wouldn't be a wise thing to do at all."

"This whole thing has to be handled with delicacy. And if we act too quickly, the criminal might leave town and lie low for a while. Let's see if we can keep him here and flush him out." He smiled and then laughed aloud. "What a story this will make if we solve the crimes."

Jena Leigh sat forward. "I don't understand your reasoning."

He swiveled in his chair as an idea began to grow in his mind. "We need someone—a woman—to draw him out. Someone he'll go after. We'll make our move when he does."

"We can't ask any woman to risk her life, Mr. Dickerson. She'd have to be out of her mind to allow herself to be drawn into such an absurd plan."

"Think about this: so far the killer seems to go after only prostitutes. But what if you plant a little story in the *Daily Galveston* that'll make him mad?" He gave her a guarded look. "I mean *really* mad."

She looked at him as if he'd lost his mind. "What good would that do?" Then it became clear to Jena Leigh what he was suggesting. "You want me to be the bait, don't you?"

He motioned toward her. "You wouldn't really be in danger. I'll see that you're well protected at all times." Excitement rose in his voice as his imagination grew. "Think about the story you could write if we actually caught the maniac! And," he said, watching doubt flicker across her face, "we might be saving another unfortunate woman from meeting an untimely end."

She caught her boss's enthusiasm and nodded eagerly. "We'd have to print something that only the killer would understand. We would have to make sure of that."

Dickerson knew he had her now. "Let's put our heads together and see what we can come up with."

"It will have to be subtle but powerful."

"The way I see it—" Dickerson looked out the door and froze in midsentence. "Well, well, look who's striding toward us with eagle bars shining on his uniform."

Jena Leigh couldn't see who it was from where she was seated. "Who?"

"Look sharp, my girl. We're about to be invaded by

the great man himself. He's in all his glory, right down to his military spurs." Dickerson glanced at his young reporter. "I can only think we owe this visit to you. He wouldn't be coming to see me."

Jena Leigh rose to her feet and almost collided with Col. Clay Madison. He reached out his hand and, with a firm grip on her shoulder, steadied her.

"You are just the two I want to see." He closed the door and moved to the desk. "You would be Mr. Dickerson," he said, extending his hand for a handshake. He nodded at Jena Leigh. "It's Miss Rebel I came to talk to you about, and it's just as well that I find the two of you together."

"What's on your mind, Colonel? It was my understanding that you already cleared up that little matter about J.L.'s editorial the other day."

Jena Leigh could hardly breathe; Colonel Madison seemed to suck all the air out of the room. His presence was so commanding that even Mr. Dickerson, who never showed anyone deference, was clearly impressed. He seated himself behind the desk as if he needed to stake out his territory.

Jena Leigh moved to the far side of the desk and sat on the edge, leaving the only chair for Clay. However, he remained standing and slapped his leather gloves against his hand. "I have reason to believe Miss Rebel may be in a great deal of danger."

Jena Leigh glanced at Dickerson and smiled. "Pay no attention to him—this is the Yankees' notion of how to frighten little girls." She smiled tightly at Clay. "But you don't scare me at all, Colonel."

He stared at her in anger. He'd allowed her to get under his skin again, and that was the last thing he wanted. "I am not making a threat, just stating a fact. Do you know that a man is following you everywhere you go?"

She shook her head. "Why would anyone want to follow me? And how would you know unless you had someone watching me yourself?"

Anger hit him, and he glowered at her. "It doesn't matter how I know. The fact is, someone is following you. And he's also watching your house at night. He was there last night."

Jena Leigh felt a prickle go down her spine, but she pushed the feeling aside, suspicious of his motives. "You are trying to scare me."

"I hope you are frightened, Miss Rebel. One of my soldiers saw the person who was watching you, and he assured me that the man is up to no good."

"I came in contact with one of your men my first day in town, and if you'll pardon me for saying so, I have more to fear from him than any would-be window peeper."

Exasperated by trying to reason with her, Clay turned to her boss. "Surely you understand the significance of what I'm saying. Miss Rebel has certainly attracted notice since arriving in Galveston. And someone is paying her too much attention."

Dickerson nodded, his gaze sliding to Jena Leigh. "Suppose it's our man? Suppose he's already tracking you? That would save us a lot of trouble."

Jena Leigh shook her head. "That would be too much of a coincidence." She spoke to Clay, "This man you say is following me—does he wear a Yankee uniform?"

"I don't know. It was too dark, and Private Ellison couldn't see him clearly. When the man realized he wasn't alone, he quickly left."

She slid off the desk and took two steps that brought her in front of him. "And what was your man doing spying on me?"

He lowered his lashes, choosing his words with care. "We watch all troublemakers. You are at the top of my list."

"I think we need to let the colonel in on what we are planning," Dickerson said, watching Jena Leigh place her hands on her hips. She was about to land herself in trouble again if he didn't stop her. "If we don't tell him, he might get in our way. Especially if he has someone watching you."

"Very well." She folded her arms over her chest. "Tell him."

After Dickerson explained the situation and told him what they intended to do, Clay looked from one to the other as if they'd lost their minds. "You can't be serious! You can't use her for bait. If this man really is the killer, she is already in grave danger."

"I will have her guarded every moment," Dickerson said. "We were going to lure him to her, but if he's already after her, so much the better."

"No." Clay moved to the door and back again. "No, I will not allow it."

"And just what do you think you can do to stop it?" Jena Leigh asked. "If the man is already there, you can't arrest him for merely watching my house. Besides," she said, dropping back onto the edge of the desk, "we don't need your approval."

He leveled his sharp gaze on her. "Oh, but you do. I am the authority here, and you will feel the full force of my office if you proceed with this ludicrous action."

"If he's already following J.L.," Dickerson said, "we can watch him and follow his movements. Maybe prevent another murder."

Clay was silent as he pondered the situation. He could see the plan had merit—still, he didn't like it. "Are you determined to do this thing, Miss Rebel?"

"I am."

"Then I'll allow it under these conditions: Two of my men will guard you while you're at home." He nodded at her boss. "You can have her watched while she's here at work."

"I wouldn't trust your men in my house. Since I believe our killer to be a Yankee, how could I know that one of your men isn't the killer we are after?"

"I'll handpick the men myself."

Dickerson folded his hands on his desk. "I guess we'll have to work together on this—we have no choice." He stared at Clay. "You had better make damned sure she doesn't come to harm. And think of this—if we have too many people watching her, they'll likely stumble over one another and scare away our prey."

Jena Leigh ran her finger down a seam in her leather skirt. "I don't like it."

Clay shrugged. "It's your only choice, Miss Rebel. Take it or leave it."

"All right, all right. But I do this under protest."

"I think the best thing to do is get my man into your house before you return home, since the stalker might well be following you today. He won't think to watch the house if you aren't in it."

Jena Leigh shivered, but she didn't want either man to know how frightened she was. "That poses a problem."

Clay nodded. "Are you expecting that same couple that visited you last night to return?"

She whipped her head around to him. "So you know about that. How dare you invade my privacy! I ... The couple, as you called them, have a very large problem. I'm helping them, and I don't want anyone to interfere."

"My man will be as inconspicuous as possible."

Jena Leigh moved off the desk and walked to the door. Clutching the doorknob, she turned to Clay. "You invited yourself into this, and if you get in my way, I'll invite you out." Without another word to either man, she flung the door open and left.

Both men watched in silence, each lost in his own thoughts.

"That's one stubborn woman," Clay said, lowering himself onto the chair.

"You have no idea," Dickerson agreed. "She is one of the finest reporters I've ever seen, and she knows how to get a story. She was tutored by the best in the business."

"But who will save her from herself?"

"You take an uncommon interest in her," Dickerson remarked, watching the officer suspiciously. "Why is that? And don't tell me it's to keep the peace in Galveston, because I won't believe you."

"I'm damned if I know. I had a nightmare last night and …." He shook his head. "Let's just say she's in danger and needs help from both of us." He crossed his legs and braced his hand on his boot. "And while we're at it—who thought up this foolhardy plan in the first place?"

"It was kind of a joint agreement." Dickerson smiled. "But I'm more interested in why J.L. wandered into your nightmares last night."

"I don't know. But I think the reason she's in danger might be my fault."

"How could it be your fault?"

"You know about the man who roughed her up the day she arrived in Galveston? I brought the man in and questioned him, reprimanded him, then let him go. I remember he told me his name was Wayne McIntyre, and he mentioned the outfit he served with. On investigating the matter, I discovered that he had taken the name, rank, and identity of a dead man."

"So you haven't been idle," Dickerson said, impressed that Colonel Madison had so much information.

"Yesterday," Clay said, "the quartermaster informed me that two of our men's uniforms had been stolen from a clothesline." He looked at Dickerson. "Why would anyone want to steal a uniform unless he wanted to convince others that he was in the military? We are closing in on his identity, but it will take time."

"So you're thinking the man who pestered J.L. the day she arrived might be the murderer?"

"It sounds improbable when you put it that way. But, yes, I believe it's the same man. At any rate, we don't dare take a chance with her life."

"And that's why you had her house watched last night."

"And it's precisely why I'm worried. If he is our man, it's my fault he got away. And I intend to do everything within my power to keep Miss Rebel safe."

In truth, Dickerson was glad to have the help. "Why didn't you tell J.L. that you were investigating the incident? She'd think more kindly of you if she knew you hadn't let the matter drop."

"I see no reason to tell her unless my suspicions are confirmed."

Dickerson was impressed with the officer, damned impressed. "Just let me know what you want us to do."

"If there weren't the possibility that the man is already after her, I wouldn't go along with this madness. Here's the way it's going to be—I will take care of her safety, even during the day. I myself will escort her to and from work. I sure as hell don't want you hiring someone who might bungle the job and get Miss Rebel hurt." His tone hardened. "Do I make myself clear?"

"I understand you, all right, but she won't," the newspaperman said with a smile. "You Yankees don't stand too high in J.L.'s estimation. Especially not you."

"She'd like it even less if the killer got to her," Clay answered with authority.

"I don't need to warn you that you'll have your hands full with her."

"God, she's ... She ... I know it."

Chapter Fourteen

Jena Leigh had just handed her editorial to Steiner and had returned to her desk when a slight woman approached her.

"Excuse me, ma'am," the young woman said shyly, not quite meeting Jena Leigh's eyes. "Are you Miss Rebel?"

"Yes, I am. What can I do for you?"

"My name's Marian Graves, and I work for Chantalle. She asked if you'd mind visiting her."

"Now?"

Marian's eyes flickered, and she lowered them. "She said I was to tell you it's important."

Jena Leigh knew that if Chantalle had sent for her, there must be good reason. "Of course I'll come with you. Let me get my things." She called out to Steiner, "I'll see you in the morning."

Not having been informed that J.L. was not to leave

without an escort, Steiner nodded his head and waved his hand, his attention drawn back to the presses.

Jena Leigh gathered her satchel and her bonnet and found Marian waiting for her just outside the door.

"Chantalle sent her carriage for you. It's covered, so no one has to see me riding with you." Marian lowered her head. "Of course, if you don't want to be seen getting in with me, Chantalle said the carriage was to come back for me."

"Nonsense. Of course I'll ride with you." Jena Leigh frowned at the thought of leaving the woman behind. "But I'm presented with a problem. My horse is in the stable, and I won't be able to get back home without him."

Marian called out to the driver. "Will, please get Miss Rebel's horse."

The huge man jumped from the driver's seat, touched the brim of his hat, and nodded politely. A short time later Jena Leigh's mount had been tied to the back of the carriage, and the two women got inside. Marian looked at Jena Leigh with a shy smile. She had never talked to such a grand lady before, and she didn't know what to say to her.

Jena Leigh was having an equally hard time trying to think of something to say to the young woman. Marian was small and delicate, and Jena Leigh wondered what turn of events had caused her to work at a place like Chantalle's. She was actually startled out of her musings when Marian spoke to her.

"Miss Rebel, I read your column every day."

Constance O'Banyon

"Thank you. I hope you enjoy it."

Marian suddenly reached out and touched Jena Leigh's hand. "I have something I want to tell you. I know it's none of my business, and you may want to tell me so." Her gaze fastened on Jena Leigh's. "Are you a friend of Grace Marsh?"

Jena Leigh was puzzled. "Yes. I am."

"Is she going to marry Simon Gault?"

"Her mother wants her to." Jena Leigh watched the young woman's eyes fill with sadness.

"Then what I heard is true." Marian's grip tightened even more on Jena Leigh's hand. "Please, warn her for me that she must not marry him. He's … he is evil, and she seems so sweet and innocent."

David had also accused Simon Gault of being evil. "Her mother is pushing the marriage."

Marian dropped her hand and settled back against the cushioned seat. "I have often seen Grace Marsh around town. When we meet, she always smiles and nods at me. Not many in this town would do that."

Jena Leigh smiled. "Grace is truly a good person—she always follows her heart."

"I would warn her away from Mr. Gault myself, but I don't dare speak to her in public." She gazed at Jena Leigh worriedly. "I can't tell you anything else, but I would be grieved if she married that villain."

Jena Leigh decided to trust Marian. "Can you keep a secret?"

"Yes, ma'am, I surely can."

She searched Marian's eyes and could detect no cunning, only a real need to help someone who had been kind to her. She felt pity for this girl, who couldn't be much older than Jena Leigh was. "I believe I can trust you, Marian, so I am going to tell you Grace's secret to ease your mind. Put your worries aside—Grace is soon to marry the man she loves."

Sudden tears trailed down Marian's cheek, and she brushed them aside. "Then my prayers have been answered."

"Say nothing to anyone about this. If her mother found out before the wedding, she would find a way to force her to marry Mr. Gault."

"I would die," Marian said earnestly, "before I would betray that sweet lady."

Chantalle was waiting at the door when the carriage arrived, and she escorted Jena Leigh inside. "Thank you for coming so promptly. If you don't mind, follow me to my office so we can talk in private."

Jena Leigh fell into step with the madam. "Has something happened?"

Angie was lounging on one of the red chairs, pretending not to notice the visitor but watching every move she made out of the corner of her eye. Chantalle, knowing Angie very well, didn't trust her and didn't want her slipping upstairs to listen to their conversation.

"Serve drinks to the men in the card room, Angie," Chantalle told her. "Remain with them until my business is concluded."

A pout curved the woman's lips. "You just want me

out of the way because there's a *lady* in the house," she accused, and flounced out of the room.

"Pay no attention to her," Chantalle said as they climbed the stairs. "Angie is never happy unless she's making someone else miserable. I guess we all know someone like her."

Jena Leigh silently agreed as she thought of Mrs. Marsh, who seemed to foster unease in those around her. When they entered the office at the top of the stairs, Chantalle closed the door.

"Please be seated. Would you like a cup of coffee, or perhaps a cup of tea?"

Jena Leigh nodded at the ewer on the marble table. "I'd love a glass of water, if you don't mind. It's so hot—would you mind if I removed my jacket?"

"Please make yourself comfortable." She waited for the reporter to remove the leather jacket that matched her split skirt before handing her a glass of water.

Jena Leigh had drunk half of it when she noticed that Chantalle was staring at her with the most peculiar expression. The madam's face had turned pasty white, and her hand trembled. Jena Leigh handed her back the glass. "Is something wrong? Are you feeling ill?"

"I was just looking at your pendant." Chantalle glanced into the young woman's eyes. "It's very unusual."

"Yes. It is." She offered no more information, because she was reluctant to talk about her personal life with this woman. "Why did you ask me to come here?"

Chantalle was quiet for a moment, her head lowered, trying to make the world stop spinning. When she finally raised her head, she stared into a pair of golden eyes—Whit's eyes. She had come to know Whit very well when he was in Galveston. He had a ring with the same design as the young woman's pendant, but how the pendant came to be in the possession of J. L. Rebel, she couldn't guess. It was clear the reporter didn't want to talk about it with her, and yet Chantalle hated to let the matter go. Whit had said his sisters were both dead, but one of them was still alive and going by the name of Elizabeth Huntington. Could this be Jena Leigh? J.L.— Jena Leigh? Her heart tightened, thinking of the guilt Whit carried with him because he felt responsible for the deaths of both his sisters.

"Mrs. Beauchamp, are you sure you aren't ill?"

She brushed a strand of red hair out of her face with a trembling hand. "I'm just tired. But you will want to know why I sent for you." She leaned her arms against her desk for support. "You asked me to let you know if anything happened, and it has. One of my girls was attacked last night in a dark alleyway."

Jena Leigh sat forward with a sick feeling in the pit of her stomach. "Is she all right?"

"She managed to escape without harm. It was Marian. When she found out I was going to send for you, she asked to be the one to fetch you."

Jena Leigh let out a relieved breath. "Thank God she wasn't hurt. We both know what would have happened to her if she hadn't made her escape."

"Of all my girls, Marian is the most fragile, and yet she managed to get away from her attacker. The reason

I'm not allowing her to tell you about the attack herself is because she can't speak of it without crying. I'm sure she told you nothing about it on the way here."

"No. She didn't. She seems like such a sweet person."

"She is a gentle soul."

"Did she describe the man to you?"

"It was dark, but she could tell he was wearing an army uniform. She didn't see him clearly, but when they were struggling she felt a scar on his face."

Jena Leigh sprang to her feet. "It's him! I'm sure of it. Have you gone to the authorities and told them what happened?"

"No. What good would that do? I told you that when Goldie was killed, they didn't do much about it. I'm afraid for my girls." She raised a worried gaze to Jena Leigh. "What would you advise me to do?" Her eyes kept going to the pendant; she was having a hard time thinking of anything else.

"I can assure you that I'm doing something right now that I hope will lead to the killer's capture. But I can't discuss it with you. I'd advise you to keep your women close, and don't allow them to go anywhere without an escort."

"I've already decided that." Chantalle looked at J.L.'s features, trying to find any resemblance to Whit. But there were no similarities except for the eyes. "You aren't doing anything that puts your own life in danger, are you?" She watched J.L.'s eyes and recognized the flicker of fear that was quickly hidden when her lashes swept down. "You are, aren't you?"

"I can only tell you this much—read my article in to-morrow's paper."

Chantalle felt as if she'd been hit by a fist. "You're trying to lure him out. You want him to come after you, don't you?"

"I can't say any more, but I will be well protected, so there is no need for concern."

"Are you sure whatever you're doing is wise?"

"This man has to be stopped before he kills again."

Chantalle wanted to caution this lovely, brave woman not to put herself in the path of a killer, but she had no right to interfere in J.L.'s life, and she doubted her advice would be welcome. "Please, at least allow Will to take you home in the carriage. It's almost dark, and I don't think you should be out alone. I'll instruct him to remain with you until you are safely inside your house. Lock your doors, and don't open them to anyone."

Jena Leigh smiled. "Yes, ma'am. I'll do that. If it will make you feel any better, I'll confess to having a six-gun beside my bed, and a derringer within reach. And I know how to use them both." She reached for her jacket. "I should leave now."

Chantalle waited while Jena Leigh put on her jacket. "I'll walk you downstairs," she told her. "You can wait by the front door while I fetch Will."

Jena Leigh was nervous while she waited for Mrs. Beauchamp to return. What if someone she knew walked in and saw her here? Loud laughter and male voices came from the room Chantalle had referred to as the card room. She didn't want to think about what was happening in there. She thought about Marian being attacked—the killer was getting bolder. To think she had come face-to-face with him her first day in Galveston. She'd had no way of knowing at the time what a deranged man he was.

She hadn't been afraid of much of anything in her life—but she was afraid now. She glanced outside at the gathering darkness and shivered. Night shadows were lengthening, swallowing the last remnants of daylight. Somewhere out there was a man who preyed on women.

She clutched her pendant in her fist, but it offered her no solace this time—tonight it left her with the same empty feeling she had lived with for years.

Gut-wrenching emptiness.

Chapter Fifteen

Clay paced between the window and the door. When he had arrived at the *Daily Galveston* to escort Miss Rebel home, he had found she'd already left, and the old man who ran the presses couldn't tell him where she'd gone. If this was what Dickerson called taking care of Miss Rebel, he was much remiss in his duty. Anger fed his fear. She knew she was in danger; why would she take such a risk?

He'd come directly to her house to find she hadn't even taken the precaution of locking her door. Pausing at the window, he pulled the curtains aside so he could gaze into the darkness. He ached inside, experiencing an unsettling feeling. He was afraid for her—terrified that something would happen to her, and he wouldn't be able to prevent it. He wanted to shake some sense into her, make her see that she was putting herself in danger.

His breath caught when he heard the sound of a carriage coming down the dirt road. Clay stepped back into the shadows, watching as the carriage drew up in front of the cottage. His jaw tightened when he watched J.L. climb to the ground, untie her horse from the carriage, and secure it to a hitching post. He heard her footsteps as she came up the walkway, and he watched her wave to the driver when she reached the door.

The crescent-shaped moon allowed very little light inside the cottage, and she was no more than a shadow when she stepped inside the room. Clay was so relieved she was safe that he couldn't speak. Silently he watched her remove her bonnet and hang it on a peg.

"Where have you been?" he at last demanded.

Jena Leigh spun around, her heart beating in her throat. She could see only a vague outline of a man, and she edged toward the door with the intention of running to the Marsh house for safety.

"It's only me," Clay bit out, striking a match and lighting a lamp. "But you left your door unlocked—anyone could have come in here."

Jena Leigh's breathing slowly returned to normal as lamplight flickered across the room, and she recognized Colonel Madison. He looked different because he wasn't wearing his uniform. "What are you doing in my house?"

He blew out the match and turned his attention to her. "In case you've forgotten," he replied in an irritated voice, "we decided today that you needed someone to protect you. That's why I'm here."

She moved into the ring of light. "I thought one of your men was going to fill that role."

He watched the light shimmer against her hair, and he had a sudden urge to run his fingers through its silken texture. He wanted to work the braid free and … His thoughts had taken him where he didn't dare go with her. "I was the obvious choice, since you are acquainted with me. I assumed you would feel more comfortable with me in your house than with a stranger."

"You are a stranger."

Before he could answer there was a rap on the door, and she looked undecided for a moment. "As you will recall, I told you I would be expecting a couple, and I don't want them to see you here." She bit her lip worriedly. "They might draw the wrong conclusion. They might think I … that we …"

He nodded in understanding. He'd already searched the house, and he knew all three rooms. "I'll wait in the bedroom." He unfastened his holster and laid his hand on the butt of his gun. "Make certain you know who the caller is before allowing anyone inside the house."

He stepped back into the darkened bedroom, watching while she opened the door. An unexpected emotion hit him full force when he heard a man's voice. He recognized it for what it was.

Jealousy.

Even when he'd found Paula in the arms of his best friend, he hadn't felt this unsettled. He had always considered himself to be the master of his emotions, but they had been running wild since Miss Rebel came into his life. He closed his eyes and leaned against the wall.

That woman was turning his world upside down and his life inside out.

"David, I'm glad you could make it," Jena Leigh said.

"Nothing could have kept me away. Is Grace here?"

"Not yet. She may be having trouble leaving the house. Mrs. Marsh keeps a very close eye on her."

In that moment the back door opened, and Grace entered, her gaze going longingly to David. "Mama went out tonight to visit friends. I said I had a headache, and she let me stay home. She shouldn't be back until after midnight." She moved across the room, and David folded her into his arms.

The shopkeeper glanced over Grace's head at Jena Leigh. "Miss Rebel, how can we ever thank you for helping us?"

"Just seeing the two of you happy will be reward enough for me. But you must be careful," she warned. "Don't do anything rash."

"No, ma'am. I won't. Grace and I are going to make plans tonight." He grinned down at the woman he loved. "Wedding plans."

Grace pressed her face against his chest. "I'm not going to let Mama stop me, David. I will marry you no matter what she says."

Jena Leigh was in a quandary. This time she couldn't leave the lovers alone, since it would be too dangerous for her to go outside by herself. A sudden thought struck her. "David, you'll find a horse tied out front—why don't you and Grace take it to the stable?"

Grace's face lit up. "Ethan drove Mama to the party,

so he won't be there." She took David by the hand. "We've imposed upon J.L.'s hospitality long enough."

Jena Leigh waited until the lovers had left and were safely down the path before she spoke to Colonel Madison, "You can come out now. They have gone."

She swallowed a lump in her throat as she watched him duck his head because he was too tall for the bedroom door. She hadn't realized how tall he was until seeing him in the small cottage. He seemed to take up all the space, and it was hard for her to breathe. He wore a light blue shirt with his army sidearm fastened about the waist of dark trousers. He was even handsomer now than before, if that was possible. His face was tan, his dark hair perfectly groomed. He was well over six feet tall, with broad shoulders and a face that would draw any woman's attention. She didn't know anything about him, really. Was he married, engaged, in love? What kind of woman did he prefer? Hundreds of questions swirled through her mind. And for the first time since she'd met him, she allowed herself to admit that she admired him in spite of their numerous disagreements.

"So," he said, moving to the window to draw the curtains together, "it seems you are a matchmaker." His smile was slow, sardonic. "If I understand the situation correctly, you are helping the daughter defy her mother."

"You know nothing about the situation; therefore, you have no right to comment on it. Grace is going to marry the man she loves rather than the man her mother has chosen for her."

"And who is the man her mother wants her to marry?"

"Simon Gault."

He stared at her a moment before he replied, "Gault is too old for that young woman, and he's not at all what I would call husband material."

"He's lecherous, cruel, and despicable."

"So you give the lovers a place to meet. But what happens when the mother finds out about it, as surely she will?"

"By that time I hope Grace and David will be safely married and out of her clutches."

"How old is your protégée?"

"Grace is twenty."

"Most women are married by her age." He turned to glance at her. "You cannot yet be twenty."

"No, I'm not." She wanted to change the subject, because he'd probably think she was too young to be out on her own if he learned she was only eighteen. "Have you eaten, Colonel?"

"No. I was more concerned about finding you. I rushed here hoping you would be safely home."

She almost smiled. He'd been worried about her. "I can't offer you a full meal, since it's so late. How do you feel about leftover roast?"

"It's my favorite."

"If you'll excuse me then, I'll have it ready in a few moments." She paused in the doorway. "Since you are already acquainted with the place, please make yourself at home."

"Beautiful, and you can cook, too," he said nonchalantly. "You'll make some man a worthy wife."

"I'm not in the market for a husband, thank you. I can take care of myself, and don't need any man," she stated pointedly.

He laughed softly when he saw her eyes sparkle with anger. "Forgive me. I thought every female's goal in life was to acquire a husband."

"That shows what you know. Besides, I learned long ago that no man is interested in a woman like me. And I don't intend to change who I am just to suit someone else's idea of what I should be." Before he could say more, she turned and disappeared into the kitchen.

Clay moved around the room, glancing at the desk, where papers were piled high. He picked up a scarf that had been thrown over a chair and breathed in the exotic aroma he'd come to associate with her. A pair of scuffed brown Western boots had been placed neatly by the door, and he noticed that she had small feet. Everything about her spoke of beauty and grace. She was tall for a woman, but she was delicate and feminine. Clay didn't understand why some man hadn't already taken her for his wife. He was thunderstruck by her quick wit and intelligence. Until now he'd thought of a wife as no more than a decoration on her husband's arm. But to actually meet a woman who cared nothing about fashion, and even less about how a man viewed her, was a refreshing change. How shallow he had been in his thinking. Her beauty was secondary to her intelligence—she would be more than an ornament to the man she married. He would never be bored with her at his side. She would be a companion, an equal.

Constance O'Banyon

Running her scarf through his fingers, he thought about how it would feel to take her to bed. A painful longing stirred deep within him. Her soft smile tore him apart inside. Her often angry words tormented him. He'd promised himself he'd never care about a woman again—but this one was working herself past the barriers he'd erected, and she didn't even like him.

Jena Leigh called from the kitchen, "Supper's ready." She felt her heart pound when Colonel Madison appeared at the kitchen door. What was the matter with her? Why was tonight different from the other times she had been with him?

She pointed to a chair, but he walked around and pulled Jena Leigh's out for her.

"The meal isn't much," she said apologetically, "but I am never home long enough to cook."

He looked at the thinly sliced roast with relish. There were fresh vegetables, cheese, and a loaf of bread. "It looks delicious to me. I haven't had a home-cooked meal in a long time."

She smiled. "I'm not sure this would qualify as home-cooked. Although I did bake the bread. Grace brought me the roast yesterday. I did, however, slice the cheese and vegetables."

Clay filled his plate and took a bite of the roast. "This is delicious. Thank you for feeding me."

Jena Leigh met his probing gaze. "Allow me to apologize for my reaction to you when I first arrived home. You are here to help me, and I sounded ungrateful. I'm not. I was just surprised that you would be the one here."

"Think nothing of it. I should have waited outside until you arrived and not frightened you."

"Why did you come yourself, instead of sending one of your men? And don't tell me again that you came because your man would be a stranger to me."

He silently examined his motives. He had come because he didn't want any other man to be alone with her. But he wouldn't be confessing that. "It's as I told Mr. Dickerson: I feel partly to blame for your predicament. So here I am."

She poured him a cup of coffee. "Would you like to know where I went when I left the office?"

He leaned back, his arm against the chair next to him. "If you want to tell me."

"Mrs. Beauchamp sent a carriage for me." She waited for him to look shocked, but he only arched his brow.

"The two of you seem to be on friendly terms."

"One of her girls was attacked last night but managed to escape unharmed. She didn't see the attacker very clearly, but she says he had a scar on his face. I think we both know who he is." As she spoke, she watched his expression become grim.

"The man I interrogated and released."

"How could you have known? How could any of us have known what he really was?"

"The situation is very serious. Something has to be done about this killer. He's clever and always manages to elude capture. But he can't hide forever."

"Which is why it is so important for me to draw him out."

He was now more concerned than ever for her safety, but he didn't want to inflict his concerns on her—not yet. He would have to watch her closer now, and she wouldn't like that. Thinking he should change the subject, he took a bite of roast and watched her break off a piece of cheese and nibble on it. "That's an unusual pendant you are wearing."

Her hand moved up to touch it. "This and a broken toy ship that I rescued from the ruins of a house is all I have left of my family."

He took a sip of coffee and placed the cup back in the saucer. "You have no family?"

"I don't know where my mother and father are. I can't find my two brothers, and my sister is … is …" She stumbled over the words that were still hard to say aloud. "She died a long time ago."

"So you have no one?"

She looked into his eyes. "I have my career as a reporter."

He wanted to know more about her—he wanted to learn about every aspect of her life. There was sadness in her past, and he could tell it was eating away at her. He had not realized she was alone in the world. What set of circumstances, he wondered, had brought her to such a state?

"My mother still lives in Baltimore," he told her. "But when my brother was old enough, he came to Texas and started a business in Houston. When the war broke out he joined the Confederate Army, and I've lost track of him. So I know something of what you're feeling."

"You and your brother fought on opposite sides in the war?"

"It happened more often than you can imagine. I was involved only in two battles with the Confederates. Each time I prayed that my brother wasn't on the other side of our lines."

They both fell silent as they finished the meal. Jena Leigh sent him to the study while she cleaned the kitchen. When she joined him, he was seated by the window, deep in thought.

"It doesn't look like he's going to come tonight. You can leave now."

He shook his head. "Did I forget to mention I'll be staying with you all night, every night, until he's caught?"

"You can't do that! Think how it would look if anyone found out you were staying the night with me."

"Think how it would be if the madman broke into your house and got his hands on you. I will be staying, so you'd better get used to the idea." He nodded at the ottoman. "I will be very discreet and make sure no one witnesses my coming or going."

"I suppose I have nothing to say about it."

His gaze settled on her. "Nothing whatsoever."

"Don't you care about my reputation?"

"I care. But keeping you safe is my first concern."

"It's hard to believe he could be out there right now." Shivering, she stood, rubbing her hands against her arms.

"After he reads my editorial tomorrow, he'll surely come back."

"I have two of my men watching your house at the moment. If he comes, they'll know it."

She was somehow comforted by his presence. "If you are determined to stay, I'll get you a quilt and a pillow."

He smiled at her, knowing the fight was over. Actually, she'd given in more easily than he'd thought she would. "I would appreciate it."

Jena Leigh loosened her hair and brushed it before blowing out the lamp. Then she sat in the darkness, wondering how her life had brought her to this place. She could go back to Altamesa Springs and forget about Galveston—surely the killer wouldn't follow her there. But she couldn't leave while other women were in danger. She must do everything within her power to find this killer.

But what was she to do about her growing feelings for Colonel Madison? He didn't have to stay with her and keep her safe—he had men who could have stayed in his place. She admired him for wanting to protect her. And she felt something more for him that she couldn't name. She went weak inside when she looked into those silver-blue eyes.

Wearily, she nestled her head into her pillow, doubtful that she'd fall asleep. She didn't even know Colonel Madison's first name, and he still called her Miss Rebel.

What would Irene have thought of this situation?

What would Mrs. Marsh think about a man staying in the cottage with her tenant?

She smiled. Irene would have put the story first and said damn the consequences. Jena Leigh was not quite as adventuresome as Irene had been. But she was determined to stop the killer from striking again.

Clay tossed the pillow on the ottoman and sat down to remove his boots. He removed his gun belt and placed it on the floor where he could easily get to it if he needed to. Fully clothed, he lay back, bracing his arms behind his head. Miss Rebel had made this small cottage her home, and he could feel her warmth in it. He had a real problem with her. First, he had to keep her alive, and second, he had to keep her at a distance.

He closed his eyes and took a deep breath, already sleepy. But he was a light sleeper and would awaken at the least noise. He would guard his charge well tonight, even from himself.

Chapter Sixteen

Angie stood outside Chantalle's office, her ear to the door, her gaze alert so she could detect anyone who might come upstairs. The voices of Chantalle and her hired man, Will, were muffled because they were talking quietly. Leaning closer to the keyhole, Angie caught enough of their conversation to put the pieces together.

"I want you to ride to La Posada as quickly as possible. I don't dare put anything in writing like I did when I sent a messenger to Whit before and the man ended up dead. I'm pretty sure Whit never got my note, or he would have come right away."

Will ran a gnarled hand through his white hair. "I think you're probably right. But I'm confused. Are you talking about his sister, Miss Elizabeth Huntington? Is she back in town?"

"No. This would be the other sister. If he had known about Elizabeth, he'd have come right away. You need to

tell him the one sister is definitely alive, and that I think
the other sister is here right now."

Will nodded his head. "I understand."

She felt fear for Will, because Simon Gault would try
to stop any messenger she sent to Whit if he knew about
it. The dead body of the last man she'd sent to La Posada
had turned up a few weeks ago. There was no doubt in
Chantalle's mind that Simon had been instrumental in
the man's death. There was no point in going to the authorities with what she suspected, because they would
never believe such a fine, upstanding citizen as Simon
Gault would commit murder.

"Be careful and keep your gun handy; is that clear,
Will? Whit has a powerful enemy in Simon Gault. It
seems that for reasons known only to him, Gault will do
anything to keep the Hawk family from being reunited."

"When do you want me to go?"

"Now. Immediately! Repeat to me what I want you to
tell Whit."

As he repeated her words, Chantalle shook her head.

"Will, I'm not sure this second one is really Whit's
sister, but I have reason to believe she is. I don't want to
get Whit's hopes up, only to have them dashed if I'm
wrong."

"I'll tell him that."

"Now," Chantalle said, looking worried, "get your
things together and take our fastest horse. Whit will
know that if I send for him it's important that he waste
no time getting here." She looked kindly at the man

who had served her for so many years. "You must stay at the ranch and rest before you start back."

Angie heard the chair scrape against the wooden floor, and she knew Will was about to come out the door. She raced down the hallway and into her room where she stood in the darkened doorway and watched Will go down the hall to the back stairs. She smiled cunningly. Simon hated Whit Hawk with a passion, and he'd pay dearly for the information she'd just overheard. She grabbed her shawl, slipped it around her shoulders, and tiptoed past Chantalle's office and down the hall-way, taking the same route Will had traveled moments before. She waited in the shadow of the stable, watching the hired man bridle a horse. When he finally rode away, she quickly saddled a horse, hoping Chantalle wouldn't discover she was missing. Chantalle had warned all the girls not to go anywhere alone, but this was im-portant. As her horse galloped toward Simon's house, she was already thinking of ways she could spend the money he'd give her.

Simon Gault poured brandy into a snifter and moved from room to room in his mansion. He examined all the fine things he'd acquired over the years, mentally taking inventory. He stared at the marble fireplace carved with dragons and unicorns—it had once graced the halls of an English castle. A fourteenth-century silk tapes-try that had hung in that same castle now adorned his wall. He stumbled, spilling brandy on the fine rug that had been shipped from the Orient at great expense. He downed the liquor in one swallow. Money was his mistress, and he had plenty of that. There was very little he wanted that he couldn't buy. Grace ... he could buy her. She was afraid of him, but he'd have her for his wife in the end. She was pure and innocent, just the kind of woman he wanted to bear his sons. Maybe he had been too aggressive in his need and frightened her. Maybe he should have showered her with expensive gifts and played the smitten lover. He didn't love her—he was incapable of loving any woman. But he wanted to add her to his collection of fine things.

He heard someone knocking at the front door and cursed under his breath. The servants had all gone to bed hours ago, and he was forced to play the butler. Whoever it was had better have a good reason for coming to his house at this late hour.

He swung the door open, and when he saw Angie standing there, he gripped her arm and pulled her inside, glancing about to make sure no one had seen her arrive. "I told you after the last time you came here that you were never to come to my home again. Apparently you don't listen so well. Do you think I want the good people of this town to see you here? You'd better have a good reason for this intrusion."

Angie giggled and tossed her long black hair, rubbing her body against him. "You fool yourself if you think the people of Galveston don't know about the room you keep at Chantalle's."

He flung her away from him and placed his empty

glass on a low table. "Have you a reason to be here other than to irritate the hell out of me?"

"You did tell me to come to you with any information that might interest you," she said, rubbing her arm where he'd gripped it. She saw that she'd caught his interest. "I have information that you'll pay dearly for."

He despised Angie because he needed her when he wanted a woman. "Get out of here, Angie. You aren't much use to me anymore. Not in any way."

She sauntered up to him, allowing her gown to slip off her shoulder, showing the swell of her breasts. "If you say so."

Simon grabbed her, his fingers digging into her shoulders. In a rage of passion, he shoved her across a fifteenth-century marble-top chest and pushed her gown up past her waist. "You asked for it, and you're going to get it."

Angie had been intimate with Simon many times, and he was always rough with her, but she hadn't minded that. Now, however, he looked at her with hate-filled eyes as he fumbled with his trousers.

"No. Simon, don't."

He struck a forceful blow to her jaw and positioned himself so he could thrust into her. Angie's shoulders were just at the edge of the marble-top chest, and whenever he lunged forward her head banged against the wall, but Simon didn't care. He pounded into her until he was satisfied, which to Angie's relief didn't take very long.

"That's all you're good for, whore," he ground out,

fastening his trousers and turning away from her because she disgusted him. "Now get out of here and don't ever let me see you at my door again. After this business, I'll not be asking for you anymore when I'm at Chantalle's. You no longer please me."

Angie swallowed her hatred of the man. No one had ever treated her with the disrespect that Simon had shown her. He always used her to satisfy his lust and then made her feel like the lowest creature on earth. But she knew better than to believe his threat. Tonight he said he wouldn't want her anymore, but the next time he craved a woman, which he did all too often, he would be asking for her. She shrugged as she slid off the chest and straightened her gown. "Then I don't guess you want to know what I heard about the Hawk family."

He gripped her shoulder and spun her around, his dark eyes murderous. She pried his hand off her shoulder and took a quick step backward. She had seen him angry before, but the mere mention of anyone with the last name of Hawk sent him into a fury that frightened her. His black eyes darkened even more, and he pounded his fists down on the arm of a chair.

"What about the Hawks?"

She moved toward the door, watching him all the while. He'd had too much to drink, and she knew what he was capable of when he was drunk. She'd felt the brunt of his fury many times before, and had the scars to prove it. "I'll talk to you another time." Her voice trembled with fear. "Maybe tomorrow. You were right," she said, edging toward the door. "I should not have come here tonight."

He moved so fast she was taken by surprise. When he grabbed her, pulling her against him, she froze with fear. "Don't play games with me, harlot. If you can tell me anything about Whit or his sister Elizabeth, I'll reward you nicely for your troubles."

She tried to ignore her fear as she stared into those cold, unfeeling eyes. "I overheard Chantalle talking to Will. She sent him to Whit's ranch to tell him his sister is in Galveston."

"What!"

"That's all I heard. I don't know anything else."

"Has Will already left?"

"About an hour ago."

Simon stared at her for a moment. "Chantalle thinks she's outwitted me this time by sending her man out at night. But I won't rest until I have every member of the Hawk family under my control. Are you telling me that the sister from New York has returned?"

"No. It seems this is another sister."

"I don't suppose you know where I can find her?"

"I don't know. Chantalle didn't say where she was."

"You did right in coming here," he admitted, smiling slyly. "Yes, you did right."

His dark eyes had lost none of their hardness, and she was still afraid. "I'll just be going now, Simon."

He took a roll of bills out of his pocket and shoved them into her hand. "I want to know everything you can find out about this new threat—this new sister." He rolled his neck as if he had a crick in it. "Hell, she could be anywhere, and no one can keep secrets as well as Chantalle. Keep your ears and eyes open. I need to find this Hawk woman before Whit arrives in Galveston. I'll make it worthwhile if you get more information for me."

Angie's greed overcame her fear when she watched his fists clench. "I'll do what I can. But it's not easy getting information. Chantalle no longer trusts me."

A fisted hand smashed into his open palm. "Chantalle has just about outlived her usefulness. I haven't forgotten how she went against me to help Whit when he was in trouble." His black gaze settled on Angie, and he watched her cringe. "I'll always find some way to punish those who go against me, or reward those who do what I tell them to."

"I'll just go now," she repeated, moving out of the room into the hallway so she could leave through the back door. "I'll keep a close watch and see if I can find out where the girl is staying. It would be easier if I had a name to go on."

He poured more brandy and took a deep drink. "Her name is either Laura Anne or Jena Leigh," he said, his brain fogged by liquor. "I can't be sure which one is which. I never knew which one Elizabeth was when she was here in Galveston." He was beginning to slur his words. "You see, Elizabeth didn't use her real name, and this one may not either. God put that cursed family on earth to torment me. The offspring of Harold Hawk must be disposed of—all of them!"

Angie was trying to make sense of his rambling. She had never understood why Simon had harbored such malice and hatred for the Hawk family. "How many of them are there?"

"Four. Two brothers and two sisters. And it looks like they are all going to show up here sooner or later." He took another drink. "But don't worry—I'll be ready for them."

"How do you know about them?"

"I have a diary that has all their names in it." He pressed his hands over his eyes to keep the room from spinning. "I thought the daughters were dead. They were supposed to have died in a fire." He stumbled toward the brandy bottle and filled his snifter once more. "Get out, Angie!"

She didn't have to be told twice. She edged past Simon and hurried toward the back door. Simon Gault was becoming a sniveling drunk, and that made him twice as dangerous as before. He had an obsession with the Hawk family, and he was out to destroy every one of them. The only connection she could think of was that he now owned the shipping company that had once belonged to the Hawks.

Glancing down at the money Simon had given her, Angie saw several hundred-dollar bills. With excitement thrumming through her, she stuffed the money into her pocket and mounted her horse. She had to get back to Chantalle's before she was missed.

Simon had promised to reward her if she could find out where the Hawk woman was. And one thing she could say about Simon—he was always generous when she gave him what he wanted. And she always tried to give him what he wanted. She smiled and then laughed aloud. He had certainly rewarded her for the news she'd given him tonight.

Chapter Seventeen

Jena Leigh opened her eyes and heard the sound of thunder rumbling in the distance. Coming fully alert, she listened to rain pounding on the roof and pouring from the storm gutters. She lay there thinking about the night before; then her eyes widened. Colonel Madison was sleeping in the library. Quickly she slid out of bed and pulled on her dressing gown, belting it at the waist. She tiptoed to the door, opening it just enough so that she could see the ottoman where Colonel Madison had slept. The quilt had been neatly folded, and he was nowhere in sight.

She ventured out of the bedroom and into the kitchen, thinking he might be there. He wasn't. But there was a fresh pot of coffee on the back of the stove, and a note propped against the sugar bowl on the table. Dropping onto a chair, she unfolded the piece of paper and stared at his neat, bold handwriting:

*I thought it best to depart early, before anyone
was about. Do not leave the newspaper office today without an escort. I will be back here tonight.
I have learned that you make rash decisions. I do
not want to scour the town looking for you.*

She poured herself a cup of coffee and stared at the
note. That man had taken over her life, and there didn't
seem to be much of anything she could do about it.

Jena Leigh was forced to admit she'd slept like a baby
knowing he was there to protect her. She had never been
alone in a house with a man before, but she had not
worried about his taking unfair advantage of the situation. That was something he would not do.

Taking another sip of coffee, Jena Leigh pondered
her situation. If the truth be told, the colonel had treated
her with the utmost respect—more respect than she'd
shown him. With him, she always seemed to say the
wrong thing and lose her temper. He brought out the
worst in her. She frowned. He was so dictatorial, any
woman would lose her temper with him.

This morning her editorial would be in print, and she
was hoping the killer would see it. She hurried to her
bedroom to dress for the day. When she was ready to
leave, it was still raining, so she grabbed her umbrella
and hurried down the path toward the stable.

Rain peppered the grimy windows as a man bent over
the newspaper reading by faint lamplight. Anger burned
inside him, twisting his stomach in knots. He slammed

his fist down on the rickety table, fury coiling in his brain. J. L. Rebel had figured out who he was. That day they'd met, he should have dragged her behind a building and strangled her. She had to die, and soon. She thought she had outsmarted him, but he'd show her who was the clever one.

He reached for one of the uniform jackets he'd stolen from the Yankee quartermaster. He feared McIntyre's insignia would make him too recognizable. He put on the felt hat and pulled it at an angle that hid the scar on his cheek. Time was running out for him—he had to act fast.

The day was a routine one for Jena Leigh, except for the letter she received from Byron telling her the *Altamesa Springs Gazette* was running smoothly, but that everyone there missed her and wanted her to come back home. In the afternoon, David Taylor came by the office to see her. She was not surprised when he told her that Grace had agreed to marry him, and he had arranged for the ceremony to take place that very night. Both he and Grace wanted Jena Leigh to be at the church to stand up for Grace. And she wouldn't miss it for anything.

At five o'clock sharp, Colonel Madison came strolling into the building, his gaze sweeping across the room until he saw Jena Leigh. Her heart fluttered, and she pressed her hand against her stomach. That man was causing her no end of trouble, and everyone in the office seemed to notice. Her colleagues were staring from him to her. He stalked toward her, his eyes never leaving her face. She sank back into her chair, and he towered over her.

"I half expected you to be gone when I arrived."

"Why would you think that? Do you believe that just because I'm a female I don't have good judgment? "

He shook his head. Everything he said to her always came out wrong. He could hold a conversation with anyone but her—why was that? "Are you ready to leave?"

She pulled on her gloves. "Yes. But there is something I have to do tonight—somewhere I have to be."

"I don't think so."

Tying her bonnet beneath her chin, she nodded. "You don't have the right to order me around. I have a life, and I am perfectly capable of making my own decisions." After her angry words were spoken, she wanted to take them back. He must think she was a shrew, because she always battled with him.

His eyes rested on her upturned face. "Just tell me where you have to be, and I'll go with you."

"At a wedding." She picked up a package from her desk. "I hope you brought a carriage—I don't want this to get wet in the rain."

"I did. You can keep your mount stabled here until tomorrow, can't you?"

"Yes, of course."

A smile transformed his face. "So the lovebirds are going to defy Mama and get married."

"Yes, they are. And I'm going to be there to see it done," she said emphatically. "Nothing you can say will stop me."

He looked thoughtful for a moment. "Do you think they'll mind if I attend their wedding?"

She was astounded. "You would do that?"

"I don't see that I have a choice. We are connected, you and I, Miss Rebel. Until this killer is apprehended, I'm your shadow."

"I don't think they would mind." She bit her lower lip. "But I don't know how either of them would feel about having a Yankee at their wedding. Anyway, it's not my place to invite you."

"If you go, I go." He smiled and then laughed. "I wonder what Mama will do when she finds her little chick has flown the nest?" he ventured.

"I'm wondering how Simon Gault will react when he finds the woman he wants to marry is the wife of another man."

It was still raining when Jena Leigh and Clay arrived at the church. Grace had been watching for her just inside the door, and she rushed to Jena Leigh, clutching her hand. "I was so afraid you weren't going to get here in time."

"Nothing could have kept me away." Jena Leigh walked around Grace and smoothed a wrinkle out of her pink silk gown. "You are a beautiful bride."

Grace's gaze kept going to the Yankee colonel who stood near the door. "I'm sorry, may I introduce you to Colonel Madison?" Jena Leigh said. "He wanted to come with me—I hope you don't mind."

Grace smiled at the handsome officer and offered him her hand. "If you are a friend of J.L.'s, then you are most welcome."

"Thank you," Clay said, glancing at Jena Leigh. "She and I are inseparable."

Jena Leigh wanted to poke her elbow in his ribs, but chose instead to ignore him. "I have something for you," Jena Leigh said, withdrawing a pearl necklace from her reticule and holding it out for Grace's inspection. "After David told me you were to be married today, I had Mr. Steiner take me by the cottage so I could get a few things I thought you might need."

"But ... the pearls are real—I can see they are. Surely you don't mean for me to have them."

Jena Leigh smiled. "That is precisely my intention. Someone who was like a mother to me bought these in Paris. I believe Irene would approve of my giving them to you on this occasion. After all, you were my first friend in Galveston." She fastened them around Grace's neck and turned her around. "This will be your 'something old.' "

"You are so thoughtful, J.L. There was no time for me to prepare anything. I hardly had time to dress in my best new gown and to leave the house before Mama returned from town."

"I have other things for you." She withdrew a blue ribbon from her reticule and tied it in a bow around Grace's wrist. "This is your 'something blue.' " She then unwrapped the package she'd brought with her. "I was almost sure you wouldn't have time to get a veil, so I

213

thought this might do instead." She unfurled a delicately woven shawl and slipped it over Grace's head, then stood back and smiled. "This will be your 'something borrowed.' Now you look like a perfect bride."

Grace was crying as she hugged her friend. "I'm so happy, but what will Mama—"

"No." Jena Leigh put her finger up to Grace's mouth. "Don't even think about anything but the man who is waiting to make you his wife. This is your wedding, and I insist that you have only happy thoughts tonight."

David had been talking quietly with the minister, and he walked down the aisle toward Grace, his eyes shining with pride. "It's all arranged." He bent to kiss Jena Leigh's cheek. "Thank you for everything. We couldn't have done this without your help."

Jena Leigh quickly introduced Colonel Madison to a confused David. Her eyes flashed with mischief. "Since you have no groomsman, he can stand up for you." She watched Clay arch his brow, and she smiled at him. "You will make a fine groomsman."

David took Grace's hand and stared down into her glowing face. "Are you ready to become Mrs. Taylor?"

Her eyes were brimming with tears of happiness, and she could do no more than nod. As the couple walked toward the pulpit, Clay offered Jena Leigh his arm, and they followed.

The solemnness of the occasion hit Jena Leigh as she and Clay stood on either side of the bride and groom. Grace was going to be happy with her gentle giant as a husband. And after tonight, she would be out of the reach of Simon Gault.

As the reverend spoke the age-old words that joined the two lovers, Jena Leigh stared into Colonel Madison's silver-blue eyes, and she could not look away. When the minister said the words *love and cherish*, she imagined herself standing beside the colonel and repeating that she would love him unto death. She tore her gaze from his just as David and Grace were pronounced man and wife.

David's huge hands spanned Grace's tiny waist when he picked her up and swung her around while she giggled with happiness. Jena Leigh felt hot tears cling to her lashes. It was the single most tender moment she'd ever experienced in her life. Grace kissed Jena Leigh's cheek, and then shyly turned to have Clay kiss her forehead and wish her happiness.

"Where will you go tonight?" Jena Leigh asked David.

"We are leaving early in the morning for San Antonio, where we will honeymoon for three days." He looked worried for a moment. "Grace left a letter on her bed for Mrs. Marsh. By now she will probably have read it. She'll have someone searching every church in town looking for us. We are staying the night at my aunt's house. I don't think Mrs. Marsh knows about her. If she happens to seek you out and ask if you know anything about our marriage, I would appreciate it if you told her nothing until we are safely away. Grace will send her a telegram from San Antonio to let her know that we are married."

She pressed his hand. "Be assured that Mrs. Marsh will hear nothing from me about the marriage." She watched David lead his new bride down the steps and hand her into a carriage. Rain was falling, and there was darkness all around them, but Jena Leigh felt her heart lighten. Her little friend had escaped a loveless marriage and was going to find great happiness with her new husband.

She waved to the couple until they disappeared into the driving rain. She felt a strong arm go around her, and an umbrella snap open over her head. "Are you ready to leave now?" Clay asked in a deep tone. "Or would you consider going back into the church and allowing the minister to make you mine?"

She glanced up at him, expecting to see humor in his silver-blue gaze, but instead found him staring at her lips with a serious expression. She could hardly draw a breath when his hand tightened on her arm. For a fleeting moment she wondered what it would be like to be his wife, and warmth spread through her body at the very thought.

A slow smile curved his lips. "You will cause your husband no end of trouble when you do get married." His tone was teasing now, but he thought to himself that he finally knew how it felt to love a woman. The feeling had come to him tonight as he had listened to the words of the marriage ceremony. The emotion was new to him. He'd heard people speak of love, and he'd thought he'd known love with Paula, but he hadn't. What he felt for Jena Leigh humbled him, made him want to be a better man, to be worthy of her. The emotions were raw and unsettling, and he had much to think about.

Jena Leigh managed to smile back at him. "And you will drive your wife to distraction if you ever decide to get married."

He guided her toward the buggy. "We should leave now. From what you've told me about the mama, she'll probably be hot on their heels. It wouldn't do for her to find you here."

She gave him a mischievous glance. "We could always tell her we had just gotten married."

"No one would believe that."

He helped her inside the buggy, then took up the reins. The rain had slackened, and the horse clopped across standing puddles on the cobbled streets.

"I thought anyone with the rank of colonel would have someone to drive him everywhere he went."

"That is true in some cases, but I like my independence." He gave her a sideways glance. "Besides, would you want my driver to know I spend my nights with you?" He flicked the reins, and the horse trotted into the night.

"Two of your men already know," she reminded him.

"I trust those two implicitly. They know why I'm with you, and they will not speak of it to anyone."

"I hope you are right."

"I'm sorry that it has to be this way," he said earnestly.

"I am trying to be as unobtrusive as possible. Unfortunately, there is always the possibility that someone will witness my comings and goings. I hope you see the necessity of my men guarding your cottage."

She did. What she didn't understand was why *he* had chosen to be her protector.

Chapter Eighteen

The rain had stopped by the time they reached the cottage. All was quiet. Jena Leigh looked around for the two guards, but if they were out there, they were well hidden.

"It's late," Clay said, his gaze steady on her. "Go on in the house, and I'll have one of my men take care of the horse and buggy."

She moved to the doorstep and into the cottage, reliving Grace's wedding in her mind. She'd never given much thought to marriage. But the sweetness of the ceremony, and the love Grace and David had for each other had touched her heart.

The quilt and pillow were still on the ottoman for the colonel's use, so she went into the bedroom and dressed for bed. She was weary, but she couldn't stop thinking about the wedding. If she was going to be honest with herself, she'd have to admit that she wanted to belong to someone and have him love her in the way David loved her friend.

She heard Clay enter and prepare for bed. She found she couldn't sleep, so after a while she got out of bed and put on her midnight blue dressing robe. She moved quietly to her bedroom door and slowly opened it. It was dark in the library, and she hoped Colonel Madison was asleep as she tiptoed across the room. Silently she made it to the back door, opened it carefully, and held her breath when the hinges creaked. She waited a moment to see if she had disturbed the colonel. When nothing happened, she stepped out onto the small back porch and settled on the top step.

The storm clouds had moved away, and the air smelled fresh and clean. A pale moon shed little light on the grounds, but light poured out of every window at the Marsh house. Jena Leigh could only imagine her landlady's anger when she'd read Grace's note. She wondered if Mrs. Marsh had brought Simon Gault into the fray. She propped her elbows on her knees and rested her chin on the palm of her hands. It didn't matter what the mother did now—Grace was safely married to David. She dreaded the day Mrs. Marsh would seek her out and ask her questions about Grace and David. When that happened, she intended to be as vague as possible.

Clay was having a hard time falling asleep, because his mind kept wandering to the woman in the next room. The more he learned about her, the more she intrigued him. He couldn't imagine any woman of his acquaintance going to the trouble to help a friend escape an undesirable marriage. She was rash and impetuous and totally adorable. Just for a moment tonight, as the minister had recited the marriage vows, he found himself wishing that he stood in David Taylor's place, and Miss Rebel was at his side. That thought brought him up short. He couldn't seem to stop thinking about her.

He'd heard her bedroom door open and watched her tiptoe across the room. He'd held his breath as weak moonlight shimmered on the unbound hair that fell almost to her waist. His body tightened and ached. He wanted her—he wanted her more than he'd ever wanted any woman. But he was in a position of trust, guarding her; he certainly wasn't there to make love to her.

Clay sat up, buttoned his shirt, and walked barefoot to the door. Carefully, he opened it. She didn't turn around, so he supposed she must be deep in thought. He studied her delicate profile, and the ache inside him deepened. A light breeze tossed her golden hair, and he wanted to take a fistful and bury his face in it. He took a step closer and was hit by the enticing scent of her perfume.

He bent down beside her and touched her shoulder. "Is something the matter?" he inquired.

She swung around so fast, her body collided with his. When his arms went around her to steady her, he could feel the soft curve of her shoulder. She raised her head to look into his eyes, and he was lost. Time ceased to have any meaning. Clay didn't know how long his hand rested on her shoulder, and his body cried out for hers.

"I couldn't sleep," she admitted in a soft tone.

"Neither could I." He wondered if her reason was the same as his. He touched her hair and allowed his fingers to stroke the silken strands. There was so much he wanted to say to her, and yet, he was honor-bound to keep silent.

His hand dropped from her shoulder, and he stood, moving to lean against the porch post and stare at the main house. "It looks like the mother is awake."

"Yes," Jena Leigh agreed, finding her voice. "I can only imagine what is going on in Mrs. Marsh's mind." She had felt the touch of his hand, and she had hoped he'd take her in his arms to say the sweet things a man whispered to his lady love.

Clay glanced down at her. "I was wondering," he said in a deep voice, "if you would allow me to call you by your first name?"

Her full lips parted, and she smiled. "Actually, my first name is Jena Leigh."

"I'm glad to hear it. I could never call you J.L. I just don't see you that way."

"Isn't it strange you are staying in my house, and I don't even know your first name?"

"It's Clay. I cringe every time you call me Colonel."

"Clay," she said, testing the name for the first time. "It suits you." She shivered as a sudden gust of wind swirled about her. "Tell me about yourself."

He smiled. "I will if you will tell me something. Why do I always remember that sweet scent you wear after you have gone?"

Jena Leigh smiled to herself. "Irene had it made especially for me when we were in Paris. The perfumer swore she could put anyone's personality in a bottle. It is called simply 'Jena Leigh.'"

He thought the woman in Paris had captured her personality very well with the haunting scent. "We shouldn't be out here—the killer could be hiding behind any of those hedges." He took her hand and helped her to her feet, leading her toward the door. "Besides, you're cold. Let's go inside, and I'll tell you whatever you want to know about my life."

His clasp on her hand loosened as soon as they stepped inside. "Shall I light a lamp, Col … Clay?"

There was very little light in the room; she was merely a shadow. "I don't think that would be a good idea. You don't want to attract anyone's attention, not even Grace's mother. If she sees you are awake, she might trot down here to question you about her daughter."

"You're right, of course." She seated herself on a chair, and he dropped down on the ottoman so he could be near her.

"Tell me about your home and your family. Let's talk about anything and everything so I don't have to think about the man who hunts me, or what is happening at the main house tonight."

He was quiet for a moment, as if he were gathering his thoughts. "I'm from Baltimore, Maryland. I'm a lawyer by trade. My father died seven years ago, but my mother is still living in Baltimore."

"And you have only one brother?"

He hesitated for a moment. "Yes, his name is Mark. Actually, my mother came from Texas when she married my father. Mark and I grew up on her stories, and we learned to love the state, looking at it through her eyes. As I told you before, Mark always said he was moving to Texas as soon as he was old enough, and he did. He started a freight business in Houston. After the war ended Mark didn't return to his business, so I fear the worst." He shifted his gaze to her. "Tell me about you."

"My story is very unlike yours. I once had a family. I don't know where my mother or my father are for reasons I'd rather not talk about. I had two brothers and a sister. The four of us were taken to an orphanage in El Paso by our uncle. Both my brothers left when they were old enough to look for our father. I never saw either of them again. We once lived in Galveston, so I returned to our roots, hoping they would do the same, and we could be reunited. So far I have not located either of my brothers."

"And your sister? How did she die?"

Her voice trembled. "In a fire that consumed the orphanage. I relive that sadness over and over in my dreams."

He moved forward, took her hand, and drew her slowly onto the ottoman with him, feeling her anguish. "Have you any other family that you know of?"

"No one."

He could only imagine how lonely she must be at times. He pushed down his growing desire and concentrated on being a comfort to her. She allowed him to pull her against his chest and laid her head there. It was no wonder she was such a strong person—she had to be.

"What did you do after the orphanage burned?"

"Have you ever heard of Irene Prescott?"

"I've heard you mention her." He rested his cheek on the top of her head. "But then, I'm new to Texas, so I don't know many people here."

"She owned the newspaper in Altamesa Springs, Texas. After the fire, she took me to live with her. She taught me all I know about the newspaper business. Irene was respected and honored for her many accomplishments. She took me to Europe, Africa, and Asia. She made my life full and happy, and yet, there is always an emptiness inside me that will never be filled."

He closed his eyes, his arms tightening around her. "So you think you have to take on the whole world by yourself."

She raised her head, and he could hear the smile in her voice. "No, not the whole world. Just your department of the Union Army."

"And that is the truth. You have given me no end of trouble."

She laid her head back against his chest, not wanting to move. It felt right that she should be in his arms. For a long time neither of them spoke. She felt his hand sweep up her back and move to her arm.

"Why have you never married?" she asked.

"I almost did once. But luckily I escaped just in time." He'd never been able to jest about his relationship with Paula, but now telling Jena Leigh about it seemed to erase the distastefulness from his mind. "How about you? Do you have any old loves in your past?"

"No. Men don't like me in that way."

He'd heard her say that before, and the comment astounded him now as it had then. Didn't she know how beautiful and exciting she was? He'd seen men staring at her in his office. If she was in a room with forty beautiful women, men would still stare at her. "Why would you say that?"

"To quote Mrs. Marsh, 'Men don't like bookish women. Men don't like women who are as smart as they are.' "

His body shook with laughter. "I suspect Mrs. Marsh suffers from never having read a book herself."

Jena Leigh felt his hand slide up and down her arm, and she wanted to stay where she was for the rest of her life. She turned her face the merest bit and pressed her lips against the rough texture of his shirt. She went weak all over, and thought he must surely have felt her body tremble.

"Clay, do you like women who can think for themselves and don't need to have a man telling them how to live their lives?"

He rested his chin on the top of her head. "I haven't really thought about it. I have always supposed women think mostly of the latest fashions, sewing, dancing, and finding a wealthy husband."

"Then you wouldn't like me very much, if that is what you expect of a woman." She started counting off on her fingers, an endearing trait he adored about her. "Number one, I don't care anything at all about the latest fashions although Irene made sure I had a fine wardrobe. Number two, I don't sew, embroider, or do silk screens. Number three, though I do like to dance, no man has ever taken me to a dance. And lastly, I don't need a man with money—Irene left me with more money than I will spend in my lifetime."

"So no man has pursued you for your wealth?"

"I'm afraid not. I made up my mind a long time ago that no man would ever want me as his wife."

He touched his lips to her forehead; he couldn't help himself. "You are exactly the kind of woman I would want if I were looking for a wife."

Her heart swelled, and she felt funny inside. "Truly?"

"Absolutely."

"You don't mind a woman who can think for herself?"

"Not if she's you, Jena Leigh." He hadn't meant to say it, but it was what he felt.

"I don't understand." She was allowing him to hold her in his arms, and they were talking about their respective lives, and yet his words struck at her heart, and she was confused.

He raised her chin. "Sweetheart, I think you were created for me."

She swallowed once, and then twice before moving forward and pressing her lips against his mouth. For a moment he was startled and didn't move. Then his hand moved to the back of her head, holding her so he could deepen the kiss.

Swirls of light burst in Jena Leigh's mind. She had never felt so alive, and it frightened her. Heat crept through her body, and she pressed herself closer to him. She felt his hand glide up her arm to lightly touch her breast, and she melted inside. Fire, heat, desire burst through her as his tongue slid into her mouth, tangled with hers, and then darted in and out in an exotic dance. She was aware that he'd untied her robe; his hand moved beneath her gown.

"Ohh," she moaned as he bent his head and pressed his lips against her exposed nipple.

Suddenly she realized what was happening, and she pulled away from him, shaking her head.

His hand moved over her breast, and his voice was deep and trembling. "No one has ever touched you like this, have they?"

She closed her eyes, reveling in the feel of his hand on her skin. "No, never."

He pulled her gown together with trembling fingers and raised his head as if he were conversing with the ceiling. "I should have known the first day we met, you were going to cause me nothing but trouble. I shouldn't have touched you." He stood up, taking her with him.

"Go to bed, Jena Leigh. And try to get some sleep. It's but a few hours until dawn."

She didn't want to leave him, and she was hurt that he was sending her away; nevertheless, she fled to the bedroom and closed the door. Climbing onto her bed, she touched her breast where his lips had touched. Although she'd never experienced the emotion before, she knew that what Clay had awakened in her was lust. She had kissed him first and then welcomed his touch. But he was probably blaming himself for what had happened between them.

Instead of being distressed, she smiled. He had been affected as well. She'd heard his sharp intake of breath, and his voice had deepened after he had touched her intimately. She'd heard him groan and felt his hands tremble.

Jena Leigh lay back on the pillow, her body needing something she didn't understand. But she did understand why Clay had sent her away. He was an honorable man, and he'd done the right thing. Whatever had happened between them tonight had taken her totally by surprise. Clay had said she had been created for him, and she believed it to be true as far as it went—he meant for lovemaking, but she wanted him for the rest of her life.

Clay ran his hand through his hair and swore under his breath. He'd taken advantage of her innocence. Even now, he wanted to go into that bedroom and take her in his arms and finish what he'd started. He walked to the window and pulled the curtain aside, seeing nothing but darkness. He wanted Jena Leigh in every way a man could want a woman. He wanted to take care of her and to have the right to take her naked into his bed. He wanted her to have his name, and he wanted no other man to touch her as he had tonight.

He braced his hand against the window frame and lowered his head. How could he remain in this house and not want to touch her? Even now his heart was beating so fast he could hardly breathe. Well, he damn sure wasn't going to let any other man stay here with her. She was dangerous. He would just have to control his desire. But how could he when his lips had touched her sweet breasts, and he'd felt her yield in his arms?

Suddenly he caught sight of movement on the porch. He backed away from the window, dropped down, and grabbed his gun. Had he locked the door when they came back inside? He didn't think so. He heard the door handle rattle, and he eased back into the shadows and cocked his gun.

The door creaked open, and he saw the faint outline of a man. "Make one move and you're a dead man," Clay warned.

The intruder was taken by surprise and leaped backward, taking flight into the dark shadows. Clay fired twice in rapid succession, not sure if he'd hit anything until he heard a cry of pain. Running outside, Clay wondered if he was going to find a dead body. He heard the man running through the hedge, but he didn't dare pursue him and leave Jena Leigh unprotected. When he reached the bottom step, he almost stumbled over a body lying in the shadow of the porch. It was Private Tipton. Bending down, Clay placed his hand at the young private's throat and discovered he was dead.

Anger exploded inside him—the madman had just made it personal for the United States Army. Jena Leigh appeared beside him with her gun in hand. When she saw the fallen soldier, she went down on her knees, but Clay pulled her away. "He's dead."

"Oh." Her trembling hand went out to him. "I am so sorry."

Private Ellison came running around from the front yard and knelt down beside his fallen comrade. "That villain must be the very devil himself if he was able to slip up on Tipton." There was sadness in his tone. "I'll take care of him, sir."

Clay drew Jena Leigh closer to him. "I need to get her undercover in case the man doubles back."

Jena Leigh shook her head, feeling responsible for the tragedy. "Are you sure he's dead?"

"Without a doubt. And I want you safely in the house." Clay guided her up the steps. "One of the first things you need to understand, Jena Leigh, is that an animal is at its most dangerous when wounded."

She paused to stare into the darkness. "This young soldier died to save me."

"That was his job," Clay reminded her. But he was not as unaffected by the death as his impersonal statement might have suggested. His anger was growing by the moment, and he was determined to find the madman.

Constance O'Banyon

"I need to do something," she said, going back toward the steps.

He grabbed her arm, realizing for the first time that she wore only her thin nightgown, but so far Private Ellison hadn't noticed. "Unfortunately there is nothing either of us can do," he said, lifting her in his arms. "Never do this again," he reprimanded. "If you hear someone breaking into the house, remain in your bedroom with your gun ready." His jaw tightened. "And don't come out in your nightgown."

She nodded, hooking her arms around his neck and letting the gun dangle from her fingers. He carried her inside, placing her on her feet. "Remain here while I help Private Ellison. Keep your gun nearby. I won't be long."

She paced the floor when he left. After what seemed like forever, he called out to her before he reentered the house, "Jena Leigh, it's me."

When he appeared beside her, she turned into his arms, her body trembling. "I'm so very sorry."

His arms tightened around her. "To think the man was so close to you."

She raised her head, needing his comfort. Without meaning to, she pressed her lips to his. He vaguely heard her gun hit the floor, and he felt her softness pressed against him.

"Don't do that," he said, tearing his lips from hers. "Don't you know what you're doing to me?"

She stroked her hand down his cheek and moved for-

232

ward. "I think so." In an effort to forget about the young soldier's death, she let her mouth seek comfort from his.

Clay forgot to lock the door; he forgot his resolve never to touch her again—every rational thought he'd ever had went out of his head. Desire hit him so hard, he couldn't get close enough to her softness. He still had sense enough to toss the guns onto a chair. Then he placed her on the ottoman and followed her down.

"Jena Leigh, sweetheart," he said before his mouth took possession of hers in a masterful way, pressing, lightly touching, and then deepening the kiss.

Nothing mattered to Jena Leigh except the touch of his mouth on hers. She wore only her thin nightgown, and he slowly eased it up past her hips, pressing his thighs against hers. Her eyes flew open when she felt the swell of him, and her bones melted. "Clay. I want—"

His mouth sealed whatever she had been saying in a kiss so tender she felt tears in her eyes. She had been born for this moment. Born to be his.

Chapter Nineteen

His lips brushed her ear, across her forehead, then to her mouth. "I need you," he whispered. "You need me, too."

Clay slid his hand up Jena Leigh's leg, and she almost came out of her skin. "To think I didn't like you when we first met," she whispered, her eyes wide. "I never knew it could be like this. Is it wrong, what I feel with you?"

Her innocent question was like a dash of water in his face. With aching regret, he smoothed her gown down over her legs and sat up. "Yes, it is wrong, Jena Leigh— wrong of me, not you." He stood up and turned his back to her, fearing that the sight of her would weaken his resolve to do the right thing. "You did nothing wrong—it was me."

She slid off the ottoman and touched his shoulder. "Irene taught me what to do in almost every aspect of life, but she never explained about the feelings between a man and woman. I know what happened between us was not all your fault. I am the one who kissed you first."

He turned to her. "I'm here to protect you." He looked into her confused eyes. "But I stepped across the line, and I shouldn't have. Do you know anything about love-making, Jena Leigh?"

"I'm not really sure, but I think I do." She frowned. "Since I met you, I have begun to wonder how it would feel if you kissed me."

She was like no woman he'd ever known. She was honest with her feelings, and so fresh and innocent. "Jena Leigh, I can't seem to keep my hands off you," he told her. "Tonight I almost took your virginity."

She shook her head in denial. "Clay, how can you take what is freely given?"

He took a deep breath, and she could see the battle he was waging with himself. "Jena Leigh, don't talk like that. I'm trying to hold on to my honor."

"You would be dishonored if you made love to me?"

"Yes."

"I suppose I understand how you feel."

He closed his eyes and tried to recapture his composure.

"How *do* you feel about me, Clay?"

He didn't dare look at her. "When I'm not with you, I find that time passes slowly. Why do you suppose that is?"

She shook her head. "I don't know. But it's the same

235

with me. Even when we are on opposite sides of an argument, I feel pleasure in being near you."

"You know what almost happened between us." His voice was deep, the tone commanding. "You do, don't you?"

"I know that love should happen to a woman only if she's married."

He closed his eyes for a moment and then moved away from her. "We aren't talking about love here, Jena Leigh, because love is a lifelong commitment. We're talking about lust, want, need. There is a difference."

Every word he spoke pierced her heart like a sharp knife. "And those things are what you feel for me, aren't they?" She dreaded hearing what he had to say, but she waited breathlessly for him to speak.

"I don't think I'll answer that right now. We are both too close to the edge."

She took a step toward her bedroom, but she didn't want to leave him in spite of his response. "I think I know what your answer would be."

He moved to her, took her chin, and tilted it up to him. "The question is, can I trust myself to guard you now that I've tasted those sweet lips?"

"I trust you." She pushed his hand away and crossed her arms over her breasts, feeling exposed for the first time because of the transparency of her nightgown. "You must be thinking that I set out to tempt you like one of the women at Chantalle's. That's what you think I did, isn't it?"

"No. Of course not." He pushed her toward her bedroom door, needing to put distance between them. "But Jena Leigh, you should never allow a man to do the things to you that I did tonight."

She stopped at the door and glanced back at him, feeling wounded and rejected. "How could you think I would allow any other man to take such liberties?"

Despite his resolve to keep his distance from her, he wanted to take her in his arms because joy swelled in his heart. She had just admitted that he was special to her. In truth, he was almost as confused as she was. These feelings were as new to him as they were to her. But he could not speak of what was in his heart. He needed time to understand what was happening between them. For now he was responsible for her safety—and that must be foremost in his mind. But it wasn't. He drew her into his arms for one last kiss.

She felt his arms around her, tender yet unyielding. She sucked in her breath when he leaned nearer. She thought he was going to kiss her, but instead he blew softly on her lips, and they opened in surprise. His gaze settled on her parted lips, and then he dipped his head, brushing his mouth against hers.

"Good night, Jena Leigh."

"You won't let anyone get close to you, will you, Clay? Are you always going to live your life on your own terms and turn your back on anyone who challenges you?" She turned toward her bedroom, not knowing she'd hit a sore spot with him.

With a quick stride he went after her, grabbed her by the shoulder, and spun her around, his fingers biting into her tender flesh. "What in the hell do you mean by that?"

"I mean you don't want any woman to disturb your well-ordered life."

"You are exactly right," he said, dropping his hand from her arm.

"Will you be gone when I wake up, like you were yesterday morning?"

"No. I'll be here because I'll be taking you to work. You left your horse in the stable at the *Daily Galveston,* remember?"

"Again, I'm so sorry about the young soldier who lost his life tonight. Please let me know when the funeral services will be held so I can attend."

He could do no more than whisper, "Thank you. I'll let you know."

She nodded and entered her bedroom, closing the door behind her. Clay stood by the window, trying to clear his mind. He stood there until the first glow of sunlight touched the eastern sky. He could hardly bear to think about the evil that had come close to Jena Leigh in the night. He knew the man would come again if his wound wasn't fatal. What would have happened if Clay hadn't been with her?

One thing was for sure: Clay was going to put a guard on Jena Leigh during the day as well as at night. Escorting her to and from the office was not enough to keep her safe.

* * *

Jena Leigh sat beside Clay as he drove her to work. He was coldly polite this morning, so she said very little to him. But they were both thinking about the young man who had lost his life during the night.

Clay saw that her hair had been braided and coiled at the nape of her neck, and she was even wearing her eyeglasses. "Do you really need those?" he asked.

"Sometimes. To hide behind," she answered. And they fell into silence once more.

When they arrived at the newspaper office, Clay helped her down from the buggy, releasing her hand the moment her foot touched the ground. In an impersonal manner he informed her that he would be sending a guard to protect her here at work. He acted as if nothing had happened between them the night before. She saw regret in his eyes. She knew he was resolved never to let it happen again.

"I won't be staying with you tonight," he announced in a clipped tone. "But someone will be watching your house."

"He got past your guards last night," she reminded him.

"I can assure you it won't happen again."

She met his gaze but couldn't read anything in his eyes. "You are staying away because of what happened between us." She turned and walked into the building without a backward glance. Her heart was breaking. Clay was exactly the right man for her. He was the one she'd dreamed about but thought she'd never find.

* * *

Though it was Saturday, Jena Leigh had an article to finish. She was trying to concentrate on her work, but it wasn't easy with all the commotion going on around her. True to his word, Clay had sent a guard to stand outside the newspaper office. Mr. Dickerson had informed her that the soldier had orders to follow her if she left the building. Earlier, her boss had been visited by two of the local authorities, who had wanted to know how the newspaper had connected the two murders. Mr. Dickerson had given them a description of the man, and that same description was also being published in today's edition.

No matter how she tried, Jena Leigh couldn't get Clay out of her mind. She frowned when her lead pencil broke and reached for another. Irene had once told her that the pencil would one day be obsolete with the new typewriting machine becoming so popular. Although Jena Leigh knew how to use the machine, she still preferred a pencil.

Bob Steiner interrupted her thoughts. When she glanced up at him and smiled, he handed her a letter. "This just came for you. There is no return address." He winked and said in a teasing voice, "Could it be from a secret admirer?"

"If he were a secret, then I wouldn't know about him, would I?" she laughed as she opened the envelope.

Steiner watched her face whiten and her hands tremble. "Is something the matter?"

She swayed as she stood. "I have to show this to Mr.

Dickerson right away." She hurried toward the editor's office with Steiner trailing behind, wondering what was the matter.

Dickerson could tell by the stricken look on Jena Leigh's face that something was wrong. He took the letter from her trembling hands and read aloud, " 'Next time you won't be so lucky. You and Colonel Madison are both marked for death. No one can stop me.' " He crumpled the paper in his fist and reached for Jena Leigh's hand, guiding her to a chair. "Something has to be done about this man. He can't go around terrorizing Galveston forever. I'm sending you home, and the guard will go with you. Don't let anyone into your house whom you don't know. And keep your gun nearby."

She nodded. "You will warn Colonel Madison about the letter?"

"Right away." His voice was gentle. "You have done everything that was expected of you to catch this madman; now we have to let those in power do the rest. It's too dangerous for you to come to work until he's caught."

She nodded, knowing he was right.

He led her out of his office. "Get your belongings and take a week off. I want you to be safe, and we can't protect you here with so many people coming and going all day."

Again she nodded—she was incapable of anything else.

Jena Leigh was pulling on her gloves when she heard a commotion at the front of the building. "I don't care if

241

she is busy," Mrs. Marsh said, pushing past Steiner. "I'm going to talk to her right now."

Jena Leigh had known she'd have to face Grace's mother sooner or later—she just wished it could be later. "How are you, Mrs. Marsh?" she asked, nodding to Steiner that she was capable of talking to her distraught landlady.

"Can we speak in private?" Mrs. Marsh whispered, her gaze sweeping to a quiet corner at the other side of the room.

Jena Leigh shook her head and motioned to her desk. "No one will bother us here. Why don't you sit in my chair?"

The poor woman was so overwrought she could hardly speak without crying, and Jena Leigh felt a spark of pity for her. After all, Mrs. Marsh's dreams of a socially brilliant marriage for her daughter had been shattered. "Can I get you something—perhaps a glass of water?"

Mrs. Marsh dabbed at her eyes with her handkerchief. "No, nothing. I need to ask you if you've seen my Grace?"

Jena Leigh felt the need to dance around the truth without telling an untruth. "Isn't she at home?"

The woman shook her head, her curls bobbing. "She's committed such an atrocity—she's run off and married that shiftless storekeeper."

Jena Leigh was glad the landlady didn't suspect her of helping her daughter elope. "You are talking about Mr. Taylor."

"Yes. That's him. She will live in poverty with that man. As the wife of Mr. Gault she could have had everything that mattered."

"Love?"

"You already know my views on that subject," Mrs. Marsh said in a disgusted tone. "Love can never set Grace up in a fine house with servants, silk gowns, and satin slippers."

"Perhaps material gain was more your dream than Grace's," Jena Leigh suggested.

The landlady shot Jena Leigh a sharp glance. "You young girls are all alike, thinking of a man like some hero out of a book. Well, I can tell you they aren't. God knows, I discovered that when I married Grace's father. I can also tell you that love doesn't put food on the table."

"And a loveless marriage to a man you fear is no way to live either. You do know Grace was frightened of Mr. Gault, don't you, Mrs. Marsh?"

The landlady waved that aside. "Mr. Gault would have brought her around after they were married."

Jena Leigh knew she was accomplishing nothing by trying to reason with the woman. "I have met Mr. Taylor, and I found him to be a man of honor, with great prospects for the future. I know he has tender feelings for your daughter. Could you not be happy for them?"

"Humph. He'll have my daughter working behind the counter like a common trollop."

"Have you told Mr. Gault?"

"No. But I must. I'm going to see him as soon as I

leave here." She lowered her head. "So much going on with Grace running off to marry that man—and a killer stalking women." She raised her head and looked at Jena Leigh. "Did you hear gunshots last night?"

Jena Leigh nodded her head. "Now that you mentioned it, I do recall hearing some kind of explosion. What do you suppose it was?"

Mrs. Marsh slowly got to her feet. "Who can say? Be careful and make sure you lock your doors at night, and don't sleep with a window open," she warned. "With Yankees tramping through our streets, there's no telling what will happen." She nodded to the door. "You even have one outside this office, asking personal questions before he'll let anyone enter. Why is that?"

"As you say, you can't be too careful, Mrs. Marsh. With a madman preying on women, my boss is taking every precaution."

"These are troubled times," she stated with disgust. "I'll go visit Mr. Gault now. Lord only knows how he's going to take the news. Poor man—he is so partial to Grace."

Jena Leigh couldn't help feeling pity for the woman, even though she wanted wealth for her daughter rather than a man who loved her. Perhaps Mrs. Marsh would accept David in time. Jena Leigh hoped for Grace's sake that that would be the case.

Chapter Twenty

Dusk was settling over the land, and Jena Leigh paced the floor, needing something to do. For two days she'd been confined to the house. She couldn't find enough to do to keep from being bored. She had cleaned the house, scrubbing the floors on her hands and knees. She had dusted all the books on the shelves, and she continued to write articles, which Steiner picked up each day and took to Mr. Dickerson. She doubted she'd written anything halfway intelligent under such circumstances.

Although she'd never caught sight of them, Mr. Dickerson had told her that two soldiers from the adjutant general's office were keeping watch on her house. She'd heard nothing from Clay since that morning he'd taken her to work. She had no regrets about what had happened between the two of them. Irene had taught her to be honest about her feelings, and she had shown Clay how she felt about him. She'd had a lot of time to think about the two of them, and had come to the conclusion that Clay didn't have any deep feelings for her.

She sighed. Everywhere she turned she walked into trouble. The one bright spot in her life at the moment was knowing that Grace and David were happy. It didn't really bother her that she hadn't been entirely honest with Mrs. Marsh about her daughter.

She dropped onto the ottoman and picked up a book she'd been trying to read all afternoon. It took her several minutes to realize she hadn't comprehended one word she'd read. She slammed the book down. That settled it—tomorrow she was going back to work, no matter what anyone said to the contrary. She couldn't stand much more of this being idle. She listed in her mind the tasks that awaited her at the newspaper. But she was yanked out of her musing when she heard a heavy rap on the door.

"Jena Leigh, it's me," Clay said. "Open the door."

She rushed forward. He was there! No matter what the reason, she would see him. When she opened the door, she fought the need to walk into his arms. The dying rays of the sun reflected off the double row of brass buttons on his uniform. With his black hat under his arm and the softness in his silver-blue eyes, he looked so handsome it took her breath away.

"Have you caught the man yet?" she asked, hoping that was why he had come.

"Not yet. But we found out his identity. Do you mind if I come in?"

Uh-oh, she thought. He was being very polite, send-

ing her the message that he wanted only to talk to her,
and that she shouldn't try to get close to him in any way.
She stepped aside. "Please do."

When he was seated, she sat down opposite him.
"Who is he?"

"He once served in the Confederate Army. He deserted from his unit in Gettysburg, and his real name is
Harman Parnell. He killed a man and a woman in Virginia, where he's wanted by the law, and took the man's
identity. He pretended to be Sergeant McIntyre of the
Union Army."

"Why would he take another man's identity?"

"No one seems to know." His gaze swept over her.
"Now that we know who he is, we may be better able to
find him."

"Maybe, but he seems cunning and able to avoid
detection."

He looked into her eyes. "I've sent my men away," he
announced, tossing his leather gloves on the ottoman.
"I'll be staying with you tonight."

"Oh. I didn't expect you would—"

He held up his hand. "I know what you're thinking,
and I don't blame you. I also know all the reasons I
shouldn't be here, but none of them matter—I had to
come. I've spent the last two nights walking the floor,
so I might as well be here." He looked thoroughly disgusted with himself. "I couldn't spend another night
worrying about you."

She chose to misunderstand and smiled. "You take
your duties very seriously, Colonel."

He reached for her, pulling her to him. "To hell with duty. I had to see you."

She ran her tongue over her lips, because her throat had just gone dry. "You'll have to help me understand what you mean, because I'm not quite sure." She knew how she felt—Clay was the only man in the world for her—but she needed to know if he felt the same way about her.

He touched her cheek. "How can I make you understand when I don't understand myself?" His fingers moved through her hair, removing pins and unbinding the golden curls that fell down her shoulders like gleaming satin. "I want you to be mine, Jena Leigh."

With a sinking heart, she demanded, "Define 'mine.' "

His gaze settled on her mouth. "I want all of you. Everything you have to give."

She pulled back, trying to sound casual when she asked, "You are asking me to marry you?"

He shook his head. "I'm not sure."

Her voice had an edge to it. "Then there can be only one other explanation: You want to make love to me and then walk away when it's over."

He stood, pacing to the window, staring out, and rubbing the back of his neck. "It was a mistake for me to come here."

"Perhaps it was." Her attempt to appear calm was spoiled by the tears that gathered behind her eyes. "I'm not promiscuous, Clay. I never could be."

It had been a long time since he'd allowed himself to trust a woman, but he did trust Jena Leigh. She was like a breath of spring air; she was beautiful of heart and face. If there was another woman in the world like her, he'd yet to meet her. He wanted to be with Jena Leigh, touch her mind, feel the softness of her skin, make love to her.

"I know you aren't, Jena Leigh. I've known it from the start."

He was struggling with his feelings for her, and his uncertainty made her angry. If he loved her, why didn't he just say so? And if he didn't, she wanted him to leave. "Go home, Clay. I can take care of myself."

He turned around and pinned her with a hard glance. "You haven't even been in Galveston a month, and already you have aided Grace Marsh in defying her mother, you have a killer after you, and you are on speaking terms with Madam Chantalle. Is that what you call taking care of yourself?"

She tossed her head and said bitingly, "You forgot to mention I've stirred your interest. I'm sure that's no small accomplishment."

"I'm not leaving."

"Fine. Suit yourself. I hope you grow accustomed to sleeping on the ottoman."

"Jena Leigh ... I have so much to say to you. But I have never felt like I needed to share my thoughts with a woman before now, and I find it difficult."

"You mean sharing your genius with a lesser being," she stated testily.

"No. That's not what I meant, and you know it. I once thought I loved a woman, but obviously I didn't, because my heart did not seem to be involved at all. I didn't miss her when she was no longer in my life. She had only wounded my pride. It's not the same with you."

"What's that supposed to mean?"

He sat down on a chair and rested his head on the back of it, staring at the ceiling. "I had some bad news today."

She went to him, hearing pain in his voice. "What has happened?"

"I found out where my brother is.... He died at one of the battles in Charlottesville. I received his death certificate this afternoon." He drew in a shaky breath. "I don't know how my mother is going to take Mark's death."

She went down on her knees and took both his hands in hers. "Oh, Clay, how dreadful for you." Tears clung to her lashes. "I know this won't help, but I understand your sorrow. I experienced it when I saw my sister die."

His grip tightened on her hands, and he pulled her onto his lap. Her arms slid around his shoulders, and he held her tightly. "Talk to me, Jena Leigh. Explain how you lived through such a loss."

"I had someone who helped me through the grieving. And," she said, pulling back and looking into his eyes, "you have me."

He bent forward, touching his lips to her eyelids and tasting the saltiness of her tears. He couldn't ever remember anyone crying for him, and he was overwhelmed with feelings he couldn't control. She was young, and yet, there was a world of knowledge and kindness in this one small, beautiful woman. "Forgetfulness," he breathed as his head descended, and his mouth covered hers in a long, drugging kiss. He wanted to lose himself with her, in her, and forget for a while.

"Let me comfort you, Clay," she whispered when he raised his mouth from hers. "Let me help you get through this horrible night."

Clay had come directly to Jena Leigh as soon as he received the letter. He needed her warmth, needed to bask in her sweetness. He needed her, and the intensity in his voice conveyed that need. "I want you to belong to me." He watched understanding brighten her eyes, and her compassion struck at his heart.

Jena Leigh watched the growing tenderness in Clay's gaze and slid off his lap, taking his hand, indicating that he should stand. "For tonight, I shall bring you comfort."

Reason told him to stop while there was still time; desire pushed him over the edge. There was no going back to sanity. He pulled her to him, his lips finding hers. He felt her body quiver when he pried her lips apart with his tongue and plunged inside the warmth of her mouth. He gripped her by the waist and pulled her tighter against him, needing to feel all of her.

Tenderness softened her heart. She wanted to give herself to him so he could forget, if only for a short time, what had happened to his brother. She could imagine nothing worse than learning that either Whit or Drew was dead.

Clay lifted her into his arms and carried her to the

bedroom. Her feet had hardly touched the floor before he unbuttoned her blouse and pushed it off her shoulders. "Sweet, sweet Jena Leigh," he whispered. "I need you."

Her fingers slid into his dark hair, and she looked into his eyes. "Love me, Clay."

Groaning, he buried his face in her silken hair. Then, with gentleness driving his emotions, he touched his mouth to hers in utter reverence. She was the shrine at which he'd come to worship.

Intensified sensations churned inside Jena Leigh, and she frantically pressed her body tighter against his. She felt the swell of him against her thigh, and her knees almost buckled. His kisses became deeper, more demanding, and she gave him everything she had. With a soft moan, she experienced a mind-destroying sweetness as he bent his head, his lips brushing against her nipple, teasing, his tongue swirling until it hardened in the heat of his mouth. Endless moments later he moved on to give the other nipple the same attention.

"Clay," she breathed, burying her hands in his hair and throwing her head back to give him unlimited access. She protested when he moved away, but it was only to remove his gun belt and jacket. He kicked out of his boots and came back to her with his shirt half-unbuttoned.

Her fingers were shaking as she finished unbuttoning his shirt. She heard his intake of breath when she moved her hand over his bare chest.

"You touch me all the way to my heart, Jena Leigh."

She imagined men would say anything when they were making love to a woman; it didn't really mean their hearts were involved. But that didn't matter—not with him. He slowly undressed her while his lips stole her breath away and her desire swelled. She watched him unbutton his trousers and slide them to the floor while she removed the rest of her clothing.

In the glow of moonlight he stepped away from her, allowing his eyes to feast on her soft curves. The heat in his gaze was so intense that it took her by surprise. He lifted her onto the bed and bent to recapture her lips, his hot mouth grinding against hers, his hands running over her back and drawing her to him.

"You are the most beautiful sight I've ever seen," he muttered thickly.

Jena Leigh stared in fascination, her breath catching in her throat as he slid up her body, his hard muscles molding to her softness. He was beautiful, and she ached from wanting him—all of him.

He kissed her hotly, caressed her gently, and made her heart beat so fast it felt as if it were going to tear right out of her body. His hands tangled in her hair, and he lifted her head, his tongue erotically sliding in and out of her mouth, setting the pace for what was to come.

Clay stroked his hand down her back and across her hip, drawing her closer, tighter to his body. He wanted her to feel what he was feeling. He slid her legs apart and moved into position, wanting to bury himself deep inside, to dominate, to make her cry out in want and need. He reminded himself it was her first time, and he knew there would be pain. His mouth took hers, and his hand stroked down her stomach and slid between her thighs. He touched her cautiously and intimately, and her hips rocked off the bed. Her arms locked around his shoulders as she buried her face against his neck, feeling the pulse beat wildly there.

His finger slid into her, and he found her hot, moist, and ready to receive him. He probed farther into her, and she gasped with earth-shaking pleasure.

Jena Leigh felt the gentle invasion, and it opened a world of aching need for her. Not knowing what she was supposed to do, she took his face in both hands and pressed her lips against his mouth.

He tore his mouth away. She was breaking down barriers inside him, twisting his guts, fanning his desire out of control. How would he bear it when he finally took her? he wondered, kissing her neck, brushing his mouth across her breasts, first one and then the other.

"Clay," she pleaded, clutching at his arms. "Please make the ache stop."

He groaned, and his breath caught in his throat. "I will, sweetheart—I know what you are feeling. But I must go slow—you are new at this."

She pressed her face against his shoulder, wishing the constant ache could be sated. Would it ever be? She didn't know.

He moved lower, his mouth brushing against her stomach, and she gripped the headboard and clung to it while his mouth stroked across her.

With gentleness, he moved back to cradle her face in

his hands, wanting to see her expression when he entered her. Soft moonlight fell across the bed and caught the feverish glow in her eyes.

"Look at me," he whispered gruffly.

Their gazes were fused as he pushed against her moistness and eased inside, resisting the urge to drive deeper. He watched her eyes widen and soften, and he knew that image would be burned into his mind for all time. With a deep groan, he covered her mouth with his. He pressed farther inside her, then stopped when he came to the barrier of her virginity. For a moment he felt heavy guilt for taking what was not yet his to take, but that wouldn't stop him. Not now that her velvet softness was closing around him and powerful quakes shook his body. He pushed quickly and took her cry of pain into his mouth with a kiss.

For a moment, neither of them moved as he waited for her pain to pass. Then his tongue started an erotic dance in her mouth that matched the gentleness with which he introduced her to his body.

She moaned, closed her eyes, and lifted her hips to meet his thrusts. Her fingers clawed at his back, and she cried out from sheer joy.

Clay stared into eyes that were losing their innocence, and he took greedily of her sweetness.

Jena Leigh, remembering the loss Clay had suffered today, touched her lips to his mouth, bringing a quick darkening to his eyes. His strokes became deeper and more forceful, and she welcomed the waves of pleasure that poured over her. She didn't know where he was taking her, but she went willingly.

Her heart swelled with love, and she cuddled his head, feeling his breath against her breasts. She wanted the moment to go on forever. She wanted to give him peace, love—she wanted to be everything he'd ever need in a woman.

"Jena Leigh," he murmured in her ear. "Sweet, sweet Jena Leigh."

A sharp intake of breath robbed her of every other thought as her body tingled, ached, and exploded. His lips went to her mouth, and he stroked deeper still. She felt him tremble and then pour life-giving seed into her body.

She lay there in wonder as his lashes lowered over his eyes, and his full weight pressed her into the mattress. Silence ensued as he rolled over and placed her on top of him while he was still inside her. His hand swept gently up and down her back. He brushed her hair off her forehead and felt a slight scar there.

"What happened here?" he asked, tenderly kissing it.

"I was in a fire when I was a child."

He rested his mouth there as if he could erase the memory, for he knew it must have been the same fire that had killed her sister. And she sighed contentedly, still feeling him buried inside her.

For a while they were content to hold each other, to relive the wonder of what had happened between them. Her fingers smoothed across his broad shoulders; his hands gripped her waist as he hardened once more, driv-

ing deeper inside her. "This has never happened before," he said more to himself than her. But Jena Leigh
didn't hear him. She was meeting his thrusts and crying
tears of joy because she had given the man she loved
everything he wanted. When their passions were satisfied once more, they needed no words between them.
Sometime during their lovemaking, Jena Leigh knew
they had become one.

At last he spoke, but it was hardly above a whisper. "I
guess you're going to have to marry me."

"I placed no condition on what happened between us
tonight," she said, not wanting him to feel guilt or obligation. "You didn't take my virginity, Clay. I gave it to
you."

He turned sideways and molded her to him. "That
didn't come out right; it was a poor attempt at asking
you to marry me."

He was startled when she giggled.

"If that was a proposal of marriage, it doesn't appear
that you put much thought into it."

He frowned, remembering the eloquent proposal he'd
offered Paula, but his heart had not been involved back
then. If Jena Leigh only knew how much he wanted and
needed her, she would understand why he was tongue-
tied. "That was my clumsy way of telling you I want you
with me for the rest of our lives. I want the right to make
love to you all day and all night. I want to wake up with
you beside me every morning."

"Do not feel guilt," she said, pushing his tousled hair
out of his face. "I don't."

He closed his eyes. "Guilt is the one thing I should feel that I don't. You are everything I could want in a wife. I want you to marry me."

"Let me look into your eyes," she said, raising herself up on her elbow.

He smiled slightly and met her gaze. "What do you see in my eyes?"

"I don't know. I wish I did."

"I am a man of truth, Jena Leigh. I do not lightly ask a woman to marry me. But I'm asking you."

"But you gave your heart once before."

"Not my heart—she never had my heart. Say you will marry me."

"How soon would it be?"

He stared down at the firm breasts that were pressed against him, and he wanted her again. "Soon. Very soon."

She laid her head against his shoulder. "Don't let the passions of the moment push you into making a mistake."

He ran his hand through her hair and pressed a kiss on her forehead. "I'm a selfish being, Jena Leigh. I want you, and I'll take everything you give me and ask for more."

Love … he didn't mention love. "Do you think I can make you happy?"

His body shook with laughter, and he hugged her to him. "There is no other woman like you, Jena Leigh. You will definitely make me happy. The question is, will I be able to attend to my duties if I know you are at home waiting for me?"

She sighed, wanting more than anything to be waiting at home for him to come to her at the end of each day. Clay might not know it, but he needed her. She was willing to do whatever it took to make him happy, even at the expense of her own bruised heart. "I will marry you."

He hadn't realized he'd stopped breathing until his chest tightened. "I will endeavor to make you happy, Jena Leigh. And my fondest wish is to make all your dreams come true."

Her dearest dream was to win his heart. She thought she had a good chance of succeeding, and would take every opportunity that came her way to make him love her. "I promise to be your wife, but there are a few conditions," she said, touching his cheek.

He smiled, knowing she was going to go into her finger counting. "And what are those?"

"Number one," she said, "I promised Noah Dickerson I would work for him for six months. I must be allowed to keep that promise."

"I agree."

"Number two, I can't change who I am, Clay."

"Jena Leigh, I don't want to change who you are. I'm proud of your accomplishments, and I would never ask you to sacrifice your occupation for my sake."

Joy burst from her heart. Mrs. Marsh had been wrong when she had told Jena Leigh she'd never find a man who would accept her for who she was. Clay had.

"And the other conditions?" he prodded, his hand smoothing across her hips, drawing her tighter against him.

"Number three, I will continue to search for my two brothers."

He thought of Mark and experienced a deep sense of loss. "I understand and agree with that." He stared at her lips, which were swollen from his kisses. "Is there anything else?"

She arched her brow and lowered her mouth to within inches of his. "Number four, make me a mother. Give me a child."

Clay's heart throbbed in his chest, and he swelled with need for her. "Come here, my little bride-to-be, although I think we should wait until we are married before I grant your last wish."

The night closed in around them, and he made love to her tenderly, knowing she would be sore in the morning. She met his thrusts, gripped his arms, trembled from the intensity of his lovemaking.

Later, when she slept in his arms, Clay felt a light-heartedness he'd never before experienced. He also felt a growing possessiveness—she was his, and he dared anyone to try to harm her. He'd bring to bear the full power of his office to protect her from the madman who stalked her.

Parnell was out there somewhere—he could feel it. His arms tightened on her. "Jena Leigh," he whispered. "My heart and soul."

Chapter Twenty-one

It was not yet daylight when Jena Leigh opened her eyes. Clay's head was beside hers on the pillow, and she turned to face him. She belonged to him—the marriage vows had not yet been spoken, but she was his nonetheless. She studied his face. Dark hair fell across his forehead, and she gently pushed it aside. His features were so perfect they could have been chiseled out of stone—but he was warm, hot-blooded, and very male. She felt him stir and quickly closed her eyes and pretended to be asleep.

She could feel his gaze on her. He touched her cheek and then touched the corner of her mouth with his lips, and her eyes flew open to find him laughing at her.

He gathered her close. "So you pretend to be asleep, do you?"

Joy sang in her veins. "Just like you."

His gaze swept over her face. "I can't seem to take my eyes off you—or my hands." He lifted her delicate hand, studied it for a moment, and then pressed a kiss on her wrist. "Did you know you're perfect?"

She laughed and cuddled closer to him. "Wait until you know me a little better, and you'll change your mind. Trouble seems to follow me everywhere I go." She looked at him, smiling. "But you already know that."

He pressed her hand against his cheek. "Yes. I do." A grin curved his mouth. "But you now have me to stand between you and trouble."

Jena Leigh was overwhelmed by a flood of feelings. She had never had what he offered. Irene had been her friend and mentor, but that wasn't the same as belonging to someone. "Do you want to talk about your brother?" she asked, sliding into his arms and laying her head against his chest. "I would like to know about Mark."

"And I would like to tell you about him. Mark was two years older than I. He never seemed to mind that I trailed after him as a boy, or that I wanted to imitate everything he did. We had both grown up on our mother's wonderful tales of Texas, and we both swore we would come here to live one day. Mark left Maryland for Houston when he was twenty-one. I saw him only one time after he left, and that was when he came home to Baltimore for a short visit. He'd been happy in Houston and had even met a woman he wanted to marry."

Jena Leigh pressed her cheek against his. "I know how you feel. Only someone who has lived through that kind of loss can understand."

His arms went around her. "In this we are alike. I pray that you find both your brothers. I would not have you suffer another loss."

"Clay, I know this is little comfort to you, but I have learned from experience that when you lose a loved one, the pain lessens with the passing of time. You will always have your memories of Mark, and that is what will keep him alive in your heart."

He rubbed his thumb across her lip. "So sweet."

They both fell silent, locked in their thoughts of those they had loved and lost. Jena Leigh was beginning to lose hope of ever finding her brothers. She raised her head and looked into shimmering silver-blue eyes. Clay understood exactly what she was thinking and feeling. They had known each other for such a short while, and most of that time she'd been angry with him. Now she wondered how she had ever lived without him.

"How do you feel about short engagements and long marriages?" he asked, pressing his cheek to hers.

"I'm very partial to long marriages. But I don't know about short engagements. Everyone knows we just met. What will they think?"

"They will think you swept me off my feet." He nestled his cheek to hers. "They will think you have put me under a spell, which you have."

"Have I now? I must investigate my powers and find out how I bound a man such as you to me in such a short period of time."

He touched his mouth to her neck. "How about a

month from today?" he suggested. "Do you think that is too soon?"

She shook her head. "You already sleep in my bed. Should you not hasten to make an honest woman out of me?"

He laughed, delighted with his child bride. "I will keep you in my bed for days after I put that ring on your finger."

"Where shall we live, Clay?" She was ready to place her life in his keeping. "I don't think we should live here with Mrs. Marsh so nearby. Perhaps we could manage for a time until we found something we both like."

"And my one room is certainly not suitable for you. Would you like to go shopping for a house?"

She smiled, her face brightening. "Yes, I would!" She ran her hand across his stubbled cheek. She couldn't seem to stop touching him. "I've never felt the growth of a man's beard before."

He smiled. "I'm glad to hear that. I will shave for you, little Miss Inquisitive." He sat up, and she pulled him back down beside her.

"I have money, Clay."

He laughed and rolled her onto her back. "A beautiful wife, and she has money. What a fortunate man I am." He brushed his mouth against her breast. "I am a wealthy man, Jena Leigh. Sadly, I just inherited my brother's wealth to add to my own."

She slid her hand down his waist and arched her lower body, firing his blood. "Sweetheart," he said, closing his eyes. "I want to make love to you."

She melted against him and wound her arms around his neck. "Engaged one moment and making love the next. I'm sure we are jumping the gun."

He grinned, overcome with joy that she had consented to be his wife. "Just this last time," he murmured, sliding inside her. "Then I will wait until you are mine, if that is your wish."

She closed her eyes, feeling him inside her, burning his brand on her, taking her heart. She was already his. She probably had been since her first glimpse into those magnificent eyes. "Yes," she said, closing her eyes, meeting his thrust, her breath trapped in her throat.

After their bodies had been satisfied, he turned her to him. "What did you mean when you said yes?"

She touched her lips near his ear and whispered, "I meant it would be all the sweeter if we wait until our wedding night."

He brushed her hair out of her face and smiled. "Even now I want you. It will be sweet torture to wait. But I will do it."

She glanced at the window and judged the hour to be late. "I'm going to work today."

He pulled back. "No. I want you to stay here, where you will be safe."

She frowned. "But he knows where I live. He knows where I work. What is the difference?"

Clay gave her a guarded look, knowing how stubborn she could be when her mind was set on something. "My men can better guard you here. I'll have one watching the front door, and the other watching the back of the cottage. Parnell will not slip past them this time. I cannot be sure of that if you are out in public." He pulled her tightly against him. "I couldn't bear it if anything happened to you."

Jena Leigh nodded. "If you think it's best."

He laughed as he sat up. "This is the first time you have let me have my way." He watched a teasing light brighten her eyes.

"No, it isn't." She slid out of her side of bed and pulled on her robe. "You had your way with me all night. And this morning."

He laughed, experiencing a surge of great happiness. When this little beauty had come storming into his life, he had never guessed that she would bring him so much pleasure and contentment.

Jena Leigh had never been happier. Clay had told her he'd come back in the early afternoon so they could discuss wedding plans. Her life was about to go in a different direction, and she couldn't wait. All she could think about was making Clay happy and being a good wife to him.

She went to the wardrobe to look for something suitable to wear for her wedding. She had brought only her sensible gowns, skirts, and blouses with her. Everything was brown, gray, or dark blue—nothing appropriate for a wedding gown.

She was startled when someone knocked at the back door. Glancing out the window, she saw it was Ethan. When she opened the door she saw a stirring near the hedge, and one of Clay's men stepped out, his rifle aimed at the unsuspecting Ethan. She waved to the guard to let him know there was nothing to fear, fortunately without drawing poor Ethan's attention.

Mrs. March's handyman removed his cap. "Begging your pardon, ma'am; this package came for you just a little while ago. A man brought it to the stable, of all things. Don't know why he didn't deliver it to you or at least to the big house."

Jena Leigh took the package from him and turned it over—there was nothing written on it. She smiled, thinking it might be something from Clay. "Thank you, Ethan," she said, watching him put his cap on and go back down the path, whistling as he went.

She stepped inside and quickly untied the twine, tearing away the brown paper and opening the small box she found there. At first she was confused when she saw the pearls she'd given Grace as a wedding present. Perhaps Grace hadn't understood that she'd meant for her to keep them. There was a note in the bottom of the box, and she unfolded it. A loud gasp escaped her lips, and she began to tremble with fear as she read:

> *You know who these belong to. I have her, and I intend to stamp out her life if you don't do exactly like I tell you. I have included a map for you to follow, and you are to come to Cameroon as soon as possible. You are being watched, and I will know if you tell anyone. Come at once—come alone, or your friend dies.*

Tears gathered in Jena Leigh's eyes as she examined the pearls. There was no doubt they were the ones she'd given Grace. The killer could not have gotten the pearls unless he had Grace. She pressed her hand to her heart, knowing he would not hesitate to kill her friend.

But what should she do?

With trembling hands she spread the map out and studied it. She knew exactly where the place was. Cameroon, Texas, was a ghost town that had been deserted and had fallen into ruin when the railroad had bypassed it some years back. Jena Leigh knew she no choice but to do as Parnell instructed. She ran into her bedroom, stripped off her skirt and blouse, and dressed in a leather riding skirt and boots. Picking up her six-gun, she made sure it was loaded and stuck it in her waistband. Opening a black velvet case, she took the derringer that had been Irene's. It would shoot only once, but she might need it. Making sure it was loaded, she clicked the safety and slid it inside her boot.

She had to think of a way to get past the guards posted outside, and that wouldn't be easy. She paced the floor, knowing time was precious; Grace must be so frightened. A sudden idea struck her, and she went into the library, gathered an armload of books, and carried them outside. "I need to take these to Mrs. Marsh," she told Private Ellison, who stepped into the path at her approach. He was young and attentive to his duty, and he'd already been reprimanded by the colonel for not watching her closely enough the night his companion was murdered. She had to lie to him, and she hoped he would believe her. "I shouldn't be long."

"I'll go with you," he said, walking in her direction.

"No," she said, shaking her head. "My landlady must not see you. She's very nervous and mustn't know about my trouble."

He looked hesitant and then nodded. He didn't see any harm in her going to visit her landlady. He walked around the other side of the hedge and watched her go down the path until she turned near the pond; then he could no longer see her.

When Jena Leigh was out of sight, she stacked the books on a wooden bench and hurried toward the stable. She found Ethan inside, who knew nothing about her trouble. He would not try to prevent her from leaving.

"You want me to saddle the horse for you, Miss Rebel?"

"Yes, please." She was frantic, but Ethan must not suspect or see how distressed she was. "I may be away overnight. If anyone asks, please tell them not to worry."

He tightened the cinch and handed her the reins. "I'll do that, ma'am."

Her gaze swept the dark corners of the stable. Whoever had given Ethan the package could still be lurking about, listening to her every word.

"Have a care today, ma'am. It looks like fog is rolling in."

"I will. Thank you." She jammed her boot into the stirrup and mounted. With a jab of her heels, she sent Buttermilk out of the stable past the driveway and onto the busy boulevard. She hurried past laden freight wagons that clogged the roadway. The sun was beating down on her, and she wished she had taken time to fill a canteen. She had a long way to go before dark, and she was already thirsty.

Clay. What would he think when he came to the cottage and found her gone? She knew she was riding into danger, but she would never forgive herself if anything happened to Grace. Within an hour, she was galloping across open country toward Cameroon.

Chapter Twenty-two

By the time Jena Leigh neared Cameroon, heavy fog had rolled in from the gulf, shrouding the land in a heavy mist. She had to look down at the ground to follow wagon tracks that had been cut deeply over time, leaving lasting scars upon the land. She hoped the mare would be surefooted enough not to stumble on the uneven path. There was an eerie, unnatural feeling in the air. She knew the deserted town was just ahead, and she knew a killer was waiting there for her.

It was cold and bleak as she dismounted and tied the reins to a tree branch, thinking it might be better if she went in on foot, giving her the element of surprise. She clutched her gun and felt more at ease with it in her hand. Her foot struck something solid, and she glanced down at a flat tombstone lying on its side. She was in a graveyard. Bending low, she dodged through broken markers and followed a path overgrown with weeds.

The fog might actually work to her advantage, because Parnell couldn't see her any more than she could see him. But it was unsettling and frightening to think he might be within arm's length of her. Her bet was that Parnell hadn't planned on fog today. Or was it already night? It was difficult to tell what time of day it was because of the murkiness.

She could barely make out the shape of a building just ahead. When she reached it, she braced her hand against a porch post. As quietly as she could, she stepped over warped boards and splintered railings. She felt along the structure until she found a doorway—the door had rotted away long ago. When she stepped inside, her vision was somewhat better. A dented potbellied stove stood in the corner, and rusted stovepipe crunched beneath her boots. She paused, thinking she'd heard something. But maybe it was just her imagination. It was easy to see that the building had been a schoolhouse; there were several desks with missing legs, and a chalkboard that had fallen off the wall long ago. It was somehow sad to think of how many dreams had been started in this room, and she wondered how many of those dreams had been realized.

She resisted the urge to call out for Grace, knowing it would only alert Parnell to her presence. Carefully she retraced her steps, going back out onto the porch, taking great care to step over missing planks. If anything the fog was thicker now, and she was beginning to lose all sense of direction. She went down the steps noiselessly, taking them one at a time. Carefully she stepped inside another building, and it took her a moment for her eyes to adjust to the shadows. There was a horse in one of the stalls, no doubt Parnell's mount. She glanced about and saw a hayloft; off to her left was a rusted bellows and an overturned anvil. This had once been the blacksmith's shop. Quietly she backed out the door and leaned up against the rickety wall—she heard the wood groan. She jumped out of the way as several warped boards tumbled to the ground.

She knew Parnell would have heard the noise and would come to investigate. Reacting quickly, she ran forward blindly, panic taking over her reason. She should never have come without help. She gasped when she rounded a corner and found her path blocked by a building. As she tried to move across the wooden walkway, her boots crunched against rusted metal. She felt along a window frame, and chipped paint flaked off in her hand.

Jena Leigh edged along a second building until she finally found the door. She grasped the doorknob, and it opened with surprising ease. This building was different from all the others. It smelled of onions and the rancid odor of leftover food. Someone had been living in here—probably Parnell. She stood stock-still, allowing her eyes to become accustomed to the dark. This was undoubtedly the den of the killer, and she needed to get her bearings. He'd probably been living here all along, and that was why no one could catch him. If Grace was alive, she was probably in this place. Jena Leigh could

Constance O'Banyon

barely make out the shape of a bedroll in the corner, and a uniform jacket that hung from a peg.

Calling on all her courage, she took another step inside and almost jumped out of her skin when the door swung shut behind her. She could make out the vague outline of a curved counter and a staircase that led to the second floor, so she suspected the place had once been a hotel.

Her hand tightened on the handle of her gun while she stood quietly for a long moment, listening—it seemed an eternity as she stared in the half-light while fear and dread ruled her mind. She could hear heavy breathing coming from a dark corner, and she pointed the gun in that direction. Terror such as she'd never known enveloped her. It seemed her blood turned to ice, and she could not move.

Clay waved to Private Simmons and then knocked on Jena Leigh's door. He couldn't wait to see her, to hold her in his arms. He hadn't been able to concentrate on anything but her all day. When there was no answer, dread settled over him, and he called to Simmons, "Has Miss Rebel left the house?"

"Not by this way, sir. You might ask Ellison if she went out the back door."

Clay walked around the house and was immediately met by Private Ellison, who was aiming his rifle at him. When the young private saw who it was, he lowered his gun. "Sorry, sir. I didn't know it was you. And you said we was to challenge everyone we met."

274

"You did right, Private. Has Miss Rebel left the house?"

"Yes, sir. About two hours ago. She had a stack of books with her—said she was taking them to her landlady."

That didn't sound right to Clay, because he knew the landlady didn't read. In irritation he walked down the path toward Mrs. Marsh's house. Jena Leigh knew it was dangerous to— He stopped abruptly. There on the bench he saw the books where she'd placed them—she certainly hadn't meant to take them to her landlady. Something wasn't right here. He hurried to the main house and knocked on the door. When the maid answered, she informed Clay that Miss Rebel hadn't been there at all, and that Mrs. Marsh had gone to a friend's house for the day.

Worried, he rushed back down the path and opened the door to the cottage. "Jena Leigh!"

There was no answer, so he stepped farther inside. He saw the pearls on the table and a letter. When he picked it up, a map fell to the floor. Picked it up, studied it, then read the letter and ran outside. "Ellison, saddle your horse; you'll be coming with me! Have Simmons go to Taylor's store and give him this letter."

The young recruit looked startled. "Is something wrong, sir?"

Clay hurried around the house and mounted his horse. Although he had never been to Cameroon, or even heard of the town, he'd already memorized the map Jena Leigh had left behind.

"Hurry. We haven't a moment to lose."

His horse was fresh, and he rode full-out, dodging wagons and buggies as he went. He was angry at Jena Leigh for falling into Parnell's plan. He wanted to shake her, and he wanted to hold her in his arms and know that she was all right. When they reached the outskirts of Galveston, Ellison was having a hard time keeping up with him.

As he crossed the long bridge that took him west, he knew he had reached the turnoff, as the map had indicated. Thick fog engulfed the two riders like a heavy shroud, but Clay did not slow his pace. Ellison had told him that Jena Leigh had been gone for over two hours. God help him, he doubted he would be able to reach her in time.

He was battling anger at her for being so reckless, and fear that he would not reach her in time to save her from the madman who held her friend Grace captive.

Chapter Twenty-three

Jena Leigh heard a muffled whimper and took a step forward. "Grace?"

There was a louder whimper, and she ran toward the sound. Her hand reached out in the near dark and connected with warm flesh. If it wasn't Grace, it was some other woman. She fumbled in the dark and removed the gag that had been tied about the woman's mouth, then bent down beside the chair where the captive sat and clamped her hand over her mouth.

"Don't make a noise," she whispered next to the woman's ear. "But if you are Grace, nod." She felt the nod, and relief washed over her. After several tries, she was able to work loose the ropes that bound Grace to the chair.

"Is Mr. Parnell around here somewhere?"

Grace whispered, "Yes. He went out just a moment ago." She grasped J.L.'s hand. "Help me, please! Let's leave now before he gets back," she pleaded.

Jena Leigh wasn't so sure that was a good idea. When Parnell returned, he would probably have to use the door, and she would be waiting for him with her gun drawn. But if they went outside he would have the advantage, because he could come at them from any direction, and they might not see him until it was too late. "Do exactly what I tell you, Grace. I'm going to get us out of this, I promise."

"He—" A sob tore from her throat. "He was going to kill me." Grace was trembling, clutching J.L.'s hand. "He'll kill us both when he gets back."

"Hush. Don't say another word. Sit back down in the chair with your hands behind you as if you were still bound. When he comes through that door, I want him to think you are alone. Do you understand?"

"Yes," Grace whispered, reluctant to sit back in the chair when what she really wanted to do was run into the night. J.L. touched her shoulder, and the gesture had a calming effect on her. Grace trusted her, so she sat back down and allowed J.L. to retie the gag.

Jena Leigh gripped her gun. "I don't know how my aim is, but I won't let him get close to you before I fire. Try to be brave for a little longer."

Grace muttered something, but Jena Leigh couldn't understand her with the gag across her mouth. She only hoped that when the time came, her aim would be true. Most probably she'd only get one shot, and she had to make it count.

"Shh," Jena Leigh whispered in a trembling voice. "Don't make a sound. I believe I hear him coming."

Both women froze when they heard the heavy tread just outside the door. Jena Leigh quickly stepped back into the shadows, where the banister curved upward. "Courage, Grace. Have courage."

The door was suddenly flung open, and Jena Leigh could see the vague outline of a man.

"Well, Grace, pretty one, your friend came for you, after all. I wasn't sure she would. But she's hiding out there somewhere, and I can't see a damned thing in this fog."

Jena Leigh could only imagine Grace's terror, because she herself was so frightened her mouth went dry. She tightened her hand on the gun and waited for just the right moment. Herman Parnell was deadly evil, and her hand wavered as she raised the gun. She knew she had to wound him mortally with the first shot.

She pulled back the trigger, and the sound seemed to echo around the room. Parnell heard it, and without pausing to think he lumbered toward her. Jena Leigh aimed at him, but she had already hesitated too long, and he loomed over her. He reached out and struck her a stunning blow across the face, and she went down to her knees. She cried out as her gun slid from her hand and across the floor, out of reach.

"So I have you at last." He reached for her, thrusting his hands under her arms and dangling her so her feet couldn't touch the floor. "I have dreamed of this moment, J. L. Rebel." His breath was foul, and she could smell the sweat on his body. She almost gagged.

"What?" he asked, slamming her against the wall.

"No begging and pleading for your life?" He pressed his body against hers. "I've watched you sashay around knowing every man in town was watching you, and you liking it. You're just like all the rest of your kind, and you'll end up dead just like the others did."

Jena Leigh was being closely regarded by dark, hate-filled eyes. Pain exploded in her head when he slammed her against the wall yet again. Knowing she had to do something quickly or she and Grace would both die at Parnell's hand, she pleaded, "Please put me down." She had to be able to reach the derringer in her boot. "I'm sick. Do you want me to throw up all over you?"

His laugh was pure evil and sent a shiver down her back. "Well, now, honey, we can't have that, can we? I'm going to put you down until you feel better. A woman shouldn't feel sick when she's about to die." He dropped her as if she were a rag doll, and she hit the floor hard, her neck snapping back against the banister. Pain exploded in her head. She doubled over, bending her head and made a choking sound, and all the while her hand inched toward her boot and the derringer. In one smooth motion she retrieved the gun, slowly rose, and pointed it at his face. She saw doubt flicker in his cold, dark eyes, and then they widened with disbelief. She clicked off the safety and pulled the trigger.

When the gun went off she heard Grace scream, and for a moment she thought she'd missed him altogether, because he was still on his feet. But she watched him sway and then topple forward, landing on her and taking her to the floor. Parnell was a big man, and she couldn't move with his full weight on her.

"Grace, help me." It took her a moment to realize the sticky substance she felt on her arm was Parnell's blood. She panicked, and she couldn't breathe. "Get him off me!"

Grace was there, tugging on Parnell's arm while Jena Leigh shoved against his chest. At last they were able to roll him off her, and Jena Leigh scrambled to her feet. She cried out in a horrified voice, "I have his blood on me. Help me, Grace! I need to wash my hands!" Jena Leigh knew she was half out of her mind with fear, but she couldn't seem to control her panic. And at the moment the most important thing to her was to wash his blood off her.

"Just a moment," Grace told her, striking a match and lighting a lamp.

In the flickering light Jena Leigh located her six-gun, which had slid under a chair, and pointed it at Parnell. Her body shook as she saw the gaping hole in his forehead. "He's dead," she said as a feeling of calm settled over her. "He'll never hurt anyone again."

Grace brought the lamp closer. "Are you sure?"

Jena Leigh nodded. "Quite sure." She wavered and reached out to grasp the banister to keep from falling. She was fighting against the nausea that hit her. Her head felt like it was splitting, but she saw no reason to tell Grace. They had to escape this terrible place.

"Are you all right, Grace? Did he hurt you in any way?" she asked, running her hand over her own face and cringing when it came away covered with the dead man's blood.

"He treated me roughly, but he didn't really hurt me—not like he did you. But I was so afraid until you came." Grace set the lamp on the counter and slid to her knees. "You killed him, J.L. I could never have been as brave as you were."

Jena Leigh took a deep breath. "Yes. I've done murder. But there was no other way. He had to be stopped."

"I thought he was going to kill you, J.L. When I heard the gunfire, I thought he'd shot you."

Amid the blood and the horror of what had happened, the two friends clasped each other's hands. "If you hadn't come for me, he would have killed me—he said he would."

Jena Leigh closed her eyes as another wave of nausea swept over her. "Is there water here? I can't stand his blood on me."

Grace led her forward and poured water into a pan for her. "It's all over your blouse."

"I don't care about that. I just have to wash my hands and face." She rubbed her face vigorously, then dunked her hands in the water and scrubbed and scrubbed. Then Grace poured clean water over her hands, and she washed them some more.

Grace had some of the blood on her hands, too, and she dampened the cloth and wiped them clean. "It was brave of you to come for me, J.L."

She turned to Grace. "You are my friend. I had to come."

They hugged each other, and then Jena Leigh moved away and blew out the lamp. "Let's get away from here. I'll take his horse. I left Buttermilk tied on the other side of the graveyard."

"Yes," Grace replied, casting a last look at the dead man and grasping J.L.'s arm. Now that it was over, she couldn't seem to stop crying. "Let's go home. I want to see David." She wiped tears from her cheeks. "He must be so worried by now."

Miraculously, a strong northerly wind had blown the fog back toward the gulf, and they were able to walk down the weed-choked street in the light of a brilliant sunset. While Jena Leigh saddled the dead man's horse, she asked, "How did he capture you?"

Grace rubbed her hands up and down her arms. "We had just come home from San Antonio the day before. David had finished the house he was building for us, and I was unpacking and getting settled for most of the day. It was nearing dark, and I wanted to meet David so we could walk home together. I was so proud of the new curtains I'd hung in the bedroom, and I wanted him to see them. As I crossed the Strand I heard footsteps behind me, but I had no idea that someone was following me. Suddenly a stranger grabbed my arm, clamped his hand over my mouth, and pushed me into an alley. He gagged me, tied my hands, and put me on his horse. I was so afraid. I don't even know how long I've been his captive. I'm still afraid, even though I know he's dead."

"You had every right to be afraid of him."

"J.L., he told me he'd been watching you since the

first day you came to town. He said he knew your habits, and who your friends were. He made me take my pearls off and hand them to him. He said when you got them, you'd know I was his captive. He saw you give me the pearls the night David and I were married." She shook her head. "Can you imagine him watching you like that?" Her body trembled, and cold crept into her bones. "He put me in front of him on his horse and brought me here. It was so dark I didn't know where we were. He tied me up and gagged me, and then rode off, and I didn't see him again until just before you came. I'll probably have nightmares about what happened here for the rest of my life."

"No, you won't. You'll curl up in the arms of that man who loves you and have only happy dreams."

"The funny part in all this is he never paid any attention to me. Hardly talked to me unless it was about you. I think he was so deranged, he didn't even see me as a person."

Jena Leigh could see Grace trembling, and she touched her shoulder. "He can't hurt you anymore," she said, taking Grace's hand. "Parnell has killed three women that we know of—we were lucky to get away with our lives."

Grace's mouth flew open. "Is he the one you wrote about in your newspaper articles?"

Jena Leigh led the horse toward the graveyard, walking fast. "Yes. That was him. Now, let's get away from here. As it is, we won't reach Galveston until morning."

Grace glanced back at the place that had been her

prison. A sudden gust of wind rocked and twisted the broken sign that hung over the hotel, and she shivered.

Her hair was tangled and matted, and she knew her face was streaked with dirt, but she was too weary to care. It hurt her to see J.L.'s jaw red and swollen from the blows Parnell had delivered to her face. And she imagined J.L. had a knot on her head where she'd fallen against the banister. "What will we do if we meet some other unseemly person on the road?" Grace asked nervously.

Jena Leigh mounted the horse and checked her gun to make sure it would fire in the event she needed it again. "No one would want to tangle with me tonight. If trouble comes, I'll shoot first and ask questions later."

Grace actually laughed. "Pity the poor fool who ever tries to get in your way. You are the bravest person I've ever met."

Jena Leigh didn't feel brave. She felt scared and sick.

The fog had been driven back out to sea, and night was falling. But the sky was clear, and the moon shed its light on the roadway. Clay stared straight ahead, looking neither to his left nor his right. The town couldn't be more than two miles ahead if the map was accurate.

He was thinking of all the things he wanted to say to Jena Leigh when he saw her. She was in real danger, and he couldn't understand why she hadn't asked for his help. It seemed no one could curb her recklessness, not even him. He had told her he didn't want her to change but, at the same time, he didn't want her to court danger without a thought to her own safety. He loved her, but he couldn't face each day wondering what new trouble she was going to get herself into.

He couldn't even allow himself to contemplate that she might already be dead. With Ellison keeping pace beside him, their horses thundered on through the night.

He had to get to her in time—he just had to. Anger grew in him with a force that surprised him, and that anger was directed at Jena Leigh. Why was she always so careless with her life?

The horse Jena Leigh was riding soon developed a limp, and she had to dismount and lead the animal. "Apparently Parnell didn't take very good care of his horse," she said, sighing. "You can go on if you want to. I'm going to have to walk this animal into town."

Grace dismounted beside her. "I won't leave you. We go together, or we don't go at all."

Jena Leigh smiled. Grace had found her courage after her long, frightening ordeal. It was possible her friend could even face down her mother if the need arose. "Just think of it," Jena Leigh said, wrapping the reins around her hand, "you are partly responsible for ending the terror in Galveston. Women can now walk the streets without fear."

"It wasn't me who was responsible. We both know I would be dead if it weren't for you."

A chill wind made Jena Leigh shiver. She wasn't feeling very well, and each step was an effort. "We may be cold, tired, hungry, and thirsty but we're alive," she said, forcing a smile for Grace's sake. The pounding in her head was worse, and she was slightly dizzy. She had to reach Galveston as soon as possible.

She gripped the side of the saddle and took a deep breath. Every step she took shot pains through her neck and head.

"Let's walk faster," she said to Grace.

Chapter Twenty-four

Jena Leigh was growing sicker and found herself leaning heavily against the horse so she could keep going forward. Finally she stopped and laid her throbbing head against the horse's neck. She felt light-headed.

"Grace, I'm going to have to rest a bit. I don't think I can't take another step."

Grace came to her with concern. "It's no wonder, after what you've been through. Let's get off the road and find a place where you can rest for a while."

Jena Leigh nodded, afraid she was going to lose consciousness. She stumbled and almost fell until Grace caught her around the waist and helped her down a shallow ravine.

"The ground is soft here—lie down. Rest a bit. Your hands are as cold as ice."

Jena Leigh licked her trembling lips. "If you hear a rider coming, stop whoever it is, but keep the gun with you at all times and don't hesitate to use it if you need to."

Grace knew something was dreadfully wrong with Jena Leigh. "You rest. I'll take care of you this time."

Jena Leigh tried to raise her arm, but it was just too much trouble. "I think I'm going to pass out. Maybe you should ride on into town."

"No. I've already said I won't leave you. We stay together. You took quite a blow to your head. You may have a concussion."

But Jena Leigh didn't hear her, because darkness had enveloped her in a shadowy world.

Clay's horse was tiring, but he jabbed his spurs into the animal's flanks and raced on through the night. He couldn't allow himself to think about what was happening to Jena Leigh. If he did, he'd lose his mind.

Suddenly a shadowy figure stepped into the road ahead of him, waving frantically. He pulled up his mount and the animal reared, missing the woman by inches as Clay jerked back on the reins.

"Please, you have to help us!"

Clay dismounted. "Grace, what has happened? Where is Jena Leigh?"

"Thank God it's you, Colonel Madison. I don't know anyone by the name of Jena Leigh," she said in confusion and fear. "But J.L. is very ill. You have to help her."

"Where is she?"

Grace tugged on his arm and led him down the ravine

while Ellison remained with the horses. "You have to do something to help her!"

Clay went down on his knees beside Jena Leigh, his heart missing a beat when he saw that her white shirt was covered with dried blood. "Was she shot?" he asked, frantically ripping her blouse open to see if there was a gunshot wound.

Grace pushed his hand away and pulled Jena Leigh's blouse together. "The blood you see is not hers. She shot that man, and it's his blood."

"Thank God," he said, lifting her gently in his arms. He had truly thought he'd find her dead body, and he couldn't seem to grasp the fact that she was still alive. For a long moment he stared into her pale face, and his mouth thinned when he saw that her jaw was swollen. "What happened to her?"

"He ... the man struck her several times, and she fell, hitting her head."

Anger assailed him at the thought of anyone hitting Jena Leigh. Clay wondered for the first time if Grace had been injured. "Are you hurt?" he asked.

"No. Just scared. But let's get her to a doctor as soon as possible."

Clay made a quick decision. "I'll take one of your horses since it will be fresher than mine. Grace, Private Ellison will escort you home. I have little doubt that you will probably meet your distraught husband somewhere along the road."

"Take my horse. The other one is lame," she told him.

Clay handed Jena Leigh to Private Ellison, who

handed her back to him once he was mounted. Without a word he spurred the horse forward and was soon lost from sight, disappearing around a curve in the road.

It seemed an endless journey back to Galveston, but Jena Leigh didn't once regain consciousness. She did moan softly, and he held her close. "You are safe, sweetheart. I have you now."

Jena Leigh awoke to sunlight streaming across her bed and a stranger in a Yankee uniform bending over her. "I'm Dr. Grayson, ma'am," he said in answer to her confused look. "I'm here at Colonel Madison's request."

The doctor had white hair and an equally white mustache. His blue eyes were filled with concern. The last thing she remembered was lying down on the roadside. "How did I"—she licked her dry lips—"get here?"

"All your questions will be answered in due time. For now, I need you to tell me how many fingers I'm holding up."

She attempted to turn her head, but pain stopped her. "You are holding up two fingers."

He smiled. "That's right."

"What's wrong with me?"

"You have a concussion. You'll need to remain in bed for a while. I'll probably let you get up in a day or two, but only for an hour at a time."

"Who brought me home?"

The doctor smiled, snapping his bag shut. "I think I'll just let someone else tell you. I've hardly been able to keep Colonel Madison out of the room." He patted her hand. "I'll see you in the morning."

She watched the doctor leave and closed her eyes against the bright light that filtered through the gap in the curtains. She heard the door open, and Clay entered, dressed in all the splendor of his military regalia. She wanted to reach out to him, but something in his stiff manner stopped her. She wanted him to come closer so she could touch him and know he was real. But he lingered near the door.

"The doctor tells me you will make a complete recovery."

There was no warmth in his voice, and he seemed to avoid looking into her eyes. She understood he was angry with her because she had gone alone to rescue Grace. "It was horrible, Clay."

He nodded. "Grace told us all about your adventure."

"I can't begin to tell you how frightened I was."

His eyes narrowed. "And yet you went knowing there could be dire consequences."

She heard the reprimand in his tone. "I had to."

"That's the trouble with you, Jena Leigh," he said, looking past her to the window. "You will always have to go beyond what is expected of you."

It seemed to her that he was being unreasonably critical. "I make no apology for what I did. If I had waited for help, it might have been too late for Grace."

His gaze swung back to her. "Didn't it occur to you that you could have at least taken one of my men with you and sent the other one to tell me where you'd gone?"

"I couldn't. If you read the note, you know Parnell warned me against bringing anyone with me. I couldn't take a chance—he might have been watching me—and he would have killed Grace if I hadn't gone."

"Grace told me all the details. You are damned lucky you aren't dead."

She frowned. "I know that. But I doubt you would have done any different under the same circumstances."

He shook his head. "I don't know any woman who would have acted so foolishly. You court danger, Jena Leigh."

"You found me, didn't you?"

"Only after the danger had passed." He looked into her eyes. "Nothing I can ever do or say will change you, and I can't live on the edge, wondering every day if you are going to get yourself killed."

His words were like a sword in her heart. She knew he was letting her go, setting her free. "You once told me you wouldn't want me to change, that you accepted me as I am."

"That was before I knew to what lengths you'd go to get a story. You will probably be glad to know the whole town talks of nothing else but your bravery and daring."

Her eyes widened. "You think I did that because I … because I wanted some kind of glory?"

"Didn't you? You found and destroyed, single-handedly, the terror who walked the streets of Galveston."

"I would like you to leave now. I don't want to talk to you anymore."

Constance O'Banyon

Clay nodded coldly. "When you are feeling better, there are things that need to be said between us."

Jena Leigh had thought she'd found in Clay the one man who would love her for herself. How could he misjudge her motives for going after the killer? "I have nothing more to say to you. There is no need for you to come back." She watched his eyes close briefly and knew she'd hurt him. "If you think so little of me as to believe I was motivated by a desire for notoriety rather than fear for a friend's life, then you don't know me at all. I don't want to see you again. Not ever."

Clay stood for a long moment, staring into her eyes. Then he nodded and went out the door, leaving Jena Leigh bereft. What she had wanted was for him to hold her, to chase away the black shadows that lurked at the edge of her mind.

She turned her head into the pillow and cried bitter tears. Clay's love for her hadn't been strong enough to withstand the first trial. Mrs. Marsh had been right after all—no man would ever want her for his wife.

Later in the evening Grace sat at Jena Leigh's bedside, telling her all the news. "You are quite the talk of the town. Mr. Dickerson has been here, wanting to know all the details. I sent him away, of course, and told him you weren't up to talking about what happened."

Jena Leigh managed to smile. "He smells a story. If he comes again, tell him he'll have a firsthand account and trump all the other newspapers in town as soon as I'm able."

"Mama came by and wanted to talk to you. I told her no." Grace smiled. "She said you were quite the bravest young woman she'd ever known. And, J.L., she allowed me to introduce her to David, and she shook his hand. For Mama, that's a resounding endorsement.

"Of course, you know Colonel Madison was here. Before he came in to see you, he was pacing the floor." Grace tilted her head and looked into Jena Leigh's eyes. "I think he's smitten with you."

Jena Leigh found herself getting sleepy, and she closed her eyes. "Don't leave me just yet, Grace." Tears clung to her eyelashes. "Stay until I fall asleep."

This was the first emotional weakness Grace had ever seen in J.L., and it broke her heart. "I will be right here. Sleep now." Her friend's eyes fluttered shut, and Grace took a deep breath. The swelling on J.L's jaw had gone down some, but the doctor had found a big lump on her head, the reason for her concussion. If Grace had been blessed with a sister, she could not have loved her more than J.L.

"I'll watch over you tonight just as you watched over me."

Chapter Twenty-five

Three days had passed since Jena Leigh had been brought home. In all that time, Clay did not come to visit. She ached for him, needed him. She had told him she didn't want to see him again, but she didn't mean it. She's spoken only out of hurt and anger.

On the fourth day, it became clear to her that he hadn't loved her enough to weather the first crisis in their relationship, and she wondered how he could so easily have turned his back on her. If he really loved her, he would not stay away.

Grace had found a woman willing to help Jena Leigh while she recuperated. Mrs. Livingston, a widow whom Grace had secretly christened Dragon Spawn, was matronly and cranky. The elderly woman's hair was as white as snow, and she had it braided and wound on top of her head. Her blue eyes could spark with defiance or soften with concern. She was a woman who said what was on her mind, and, in that way, she was not unlike Irene.

The first two days Mrs. Livingston would allow Jena Leigh to get out of bed for only an hour at a time, as the doctor had ordered. Yesterday she had allowed Jena Leigh to walk down the path as far as the fountain.

Jena Leigh was lounging on the ottoman, and Mrs. Livingston had just brought her the mail.

"You can be up for most of today," Mrs. Livingston told her. "But you are not to do anything strenuous, or it's back to bed with you."

"I will do as you say."

"You may as well know I've had to send Mr. Dickerson away for the last three days. I won't have him here talking business until the doctor says you are well enough. I have also limited your landlady's visits and will allow her to remain for only fifteen minutes at a time."

Jena Leigh was grateful for that. She glanced about the room at the flowers from many citizens of Galveston, most of whom Jena Leigh had never met. "I'm embarrassed that everyone has made so much out of what happened. All I want to do is to forget about it."

Her caretaker glanced up from folding the laundry. "What you did was brave; there is no denying that."

"I wasn't brave—I was terrified." Secretly, Jena Leigh had been working on her article, and had decided to let David take it to Mr. Livingston when he and Grace came to visit.

When Mrs. Livingston left the room, Jena Leigh read several cards that wished her a speedy recovery and praised her courage. She laughed when she read one from a man proposing marriage. She picked up a letter in a pink envelope and smiled. It was from Chantalle. She opened it and began to read.

> *Dear Miss Rebel,*
>
> *I hope your convalescence is almost over, and you are soon up and about. I have been concerned about you and wanted to visit, but we both know that would not be wise. Take to heart my best wishes for your continued recovery. I hope you will number me among your friends, although you need not acknowledge me if we should meet in public. I will always wish you the best of health.*

She stared at the letter for a moment, thinking how kind it was of Mrs. Beauchamp to be concerned about her. But for the madam to ask to be her friend came as a surprise. That wasn't possible. She could only imagine Mrs. Livingston's reaction if Chantalle should come to call at the cottage.

She reached for another letter and held it to her heart when she saw it was from Clay. She swallowed past the lump in her throat, reluctant to open it. A letter was a cold and heartless way to say good-bye—she was already quite sure what he had written.

> *Jena Leigh,*
>
> *Grace keeps me informed of your recovery, and she says you are doing well. I hope you will soon be well enough to take up your life again. I*

*wanted to inform you that I am pulling Private El-
lison and Private Simmons off guard duty at your
house, since there is no longer a reason to keep
them there. I continue to pray for your good health.*

It was signed simply, *Clay*.

Jena Leigh had already convinced herself that he
hadn't really loved her. She wondered why he hadn't
understood that Grace would now be dead if she hadn't
gone to Cameroon.

Mrs. Livingston appeared with her lunch tray and
placed it on a low table, then seated herself on a nearby
chair and wiped her hands on her apron. "I'll be going
home today."

"You will?"

"You don't need me now. You're getting along mighty
fine. Helen Wilson's time is coming upon her, and she'll
need me to corral her other kids when the new one
arrives."

Jena Leigh smiled. "I've grown accustomed to you
dictating my life."

The older woman returned her smile. "You don't
need looking after. You'll be all right. I took your measure and knew your worth the first day I laid eyes on
you."

"I will miss you."

"You've not seen the last of me. I'll see you about
town." She looked uncomfortable for a moment. "I
need to say something personal to you, and you can tell
me to mind my own business if you are of a mind to."

Jena Leigh was curious. She couldn't imagine telling Mrs. Livingston to mind her own business.

"It's about that Yankee officer. I don't hold much with Yankees, but I've heard he's got a hard job on his hands, trying to keep down riots and make the citizens of Galveston and his people get along. Everyone I talk to about him says he's fair."

"That's probably true."

"You know, Jena Leigh, you really hurt him. I was here when he came out of your room, and he looked like a broken man. I don't know what went on between the two of you, but that man's got it as bad as I've ever seen."

Jena Leigh frowned. "Got what bad, Mrs. Livingston?"

"The lovesickness. Haven't you ever heard of that?"

She took a breath, then let it out slowly. "You are mistaken about him. He has no feelings for me."

"Then why has Private Ellison hung around and kept asking how you're doing so he can report to his colonel?"

"He'll be leaving today." She nodded at the letter in her hand. "Clay is pulling him off guard duty here."

"So you don't think this Yankee cares about you?"

"I thought he did—but I was mistaken. He will find another to take my place soon enough."

The wise blue eyes settled on Jena Leigh. "I'd say he's a man who'll give his heart to only one woman in his lifetime. And I think you're that woman."

"But he—"

"Let me finish. I want this said before I leave. I know

people—I can sometimes read what's in a person's heart. He will never turn to another woman, because he'll never get over you."

"You don't know him. He has complete discipline over his feelings."

Mrs. Livingston stood. "I've said my piece and given you something to ponder. Think long and hard before you turn your back on him."

Jena Leigh lowered her head, not wanting the older woman to see her tears. "I have nothing to think about."

"I suspect he was angry because you took such a chance with your life; am I right?"

"He was angry."

"That's what I thought. There he was thinking you were dead, and him trying to get to you and not able to—that would make any man mad, any man with gumption."

Jena Leigh lay back on the pillow. "Are you packed?" she asked, changing the subject.

"I packed last night, so I'll just be saying good-bye for now." She patted Jena Leigh's hand, but Jena Leigh reached up and hugged her.

"Take care of yourself, Mrs. Livingston."

"And you mind that you don't go off looking for any more trouble."

After Mrs. Livingston had gone, the house seemed strangely empty. Jena Leigh lay on the ottoman, watching shadows creep across the landscape. Mrs. Livingston had said Clay would love only one woman, but she was wrong. Clay had been engaged to a woman back in Maryland, and that marriage had never taken place either. Jena Leigh was the one whose heart would never heal.

Jena Leigh walked into the office of the *Daily Galveston* and was immediately surrounded by her fellow workers, who welcomed her back with enthusiasm. Dickerson stood in the doorway of his office, his arms crossed over his chest.

"It's about time you got back to work." He glanced down at her leather satchel. "Have you got anything for me in there?"

She walked into his office, and the others came to stand at the door so they could hear what she had to say. She withdrew the article she had been working on for the last few days and handed it across the desk to her boss. Everyone fell silent as he read with relish.

At last he raised his head and grinned. "This is exactly what I wanted from you. Our competitors might as well not even go to press today, because tomorrow everyone will be buying copies of our newspaper so they can read your story."

The article was passed around, and everyone read it. Steiner grinned. "It'll be a pleasure to set the type for this one. Just think, one of our own reporters single-handedly rid Galveston of a killer."

"Mr. Steiner," Jena Leigh told him, knowing how he would sometimes embellish when he was typesetting, "I want this story to run just the way I wrote it. Grace was the one who suffered the most at the killer's hands. And I want the town to understand that nothing happened to her except that she was scared for her life and tied up a long time. And I want people to know I would not have survived without her help."

The older man turned and smiled at her. "You know, J.L., I don't think you realize how grateful this town is to you. I hear tell that the city officials are going to honor you in some way."

She felt her face go pale, and she looked at her boss. "May I talk to you privately, Mr. Dickerson?"

He nodded. "Close the door and sit down."

She chose to stand. "I know when I first started working for you, I gave my word I'd stay for six months." She met his gaze. "Are you going to hold me to that?"

He was quiet for a moment while he considered. He'd been expecting this, so her question hadn't come as any surprise. "You've been through a lot, and I understand your wanting to leave Galveston for a while."

"I certainly don't want any city officials to honor me—that's just not my way."

"I'll tell you what I'm going to do," he said, not ready to completely relinquish the best reporter he'd ever had. "I'll let you go if you'll promise to send me an article once a month."

She smiled and held out her hand, and he shook it firmly. "I promise."

"You're going back to Altamesa Springs, aren't you?"

"For a while. Just long enough to settle my affairs there. Then I thought I might travel abroad. I want to revisit some of the places Irene took me when I was younger."

He gave her a lopsided grin. "I don't care how far you go, as long as mail will reach me once a month."

She picked up her satchel and tucked it under her arm. "And would you do something for me?"

"Anything."

"Run a small notice once a week for me." She handed him a sheet of paper. "I have it written out for you."

He nodded and then read it aloud. " 'Jena Leigh Hawk is inquiring whether anyone knows the whereabouts of her brothers, Whit or Drew Hawk. If you have knowledge of either of these men, please contact the editor, Mr. Dickerson, of the *Daily Galveston*.'

"You still think they might be out there somewhere?"

"I have all but given up hope."

The usual sparkle was missing from Jena Leigh's eyes; he wanted to see her happy and spitting fire, like she had been the day he'd met her. This little gal had touched everyone she'd come in contact with, and he was going to miss her. "Starting today, I'll run it every day for a month, and after that once a month. You never know; one or both of them might show up here in Galveston and read it for themselves."

Chapter Twenty-six

Jena Leigh had already said a tearful good-bye to Grace. They promised to write each other often. Jena Leigh didn't intend to lose touch with the best friend she'd ever known. Even though she gave the landlady an extra month's rent, Mrs. Marsh wasn't happy when Jena Leigh told her she'd be leaving. Her trunks were almost packed, all except for a few items she'd saved for last. Her heart was heavy, and she wished she could see Clay just one more time. She would have liked to have said good-bye, but she was afraid she'd break down in front of him.

As she stood at the back door watching the morning sun slant across the beautiful grounds, she already felt a sense of loss. She loved this estate. She walked outside and looked about her, needing to imprint every bush and tree on her mind. She had truly enjoyed living in her little cottage. She had found love there—and lost it.

She still had two hours before Ethan would be driving her to the train depot, so she had time to walk down the path for the last time. She paused near a pink rose-bush to pluck a small bud, thinking that when she reached Altamesa Springs she would press the flower in a book. Soon the leaves would be turning colors at home. Not here, though, because it was eternally summer in Galveston. She wanted to keep her memories of this place, especially the ones of lying in Clay's arms. She'd always remember the touch of his hands on her skin, and how she'd felt when he'd kissed her.

Jena Leigh shook her head. She hadn't wanted her last memories of Galveston to be sad, but maybe that was the way of it.

She retraced her steps to the cottage, going over in her mind last-minute details to make sure she hadn't forgotten anything. She'd sent a letter to Chantalle, telling her she was leaving. Jean Leigh almost wished she had gone to the madam in person to say good-bye.

She stepped into the coolness of the cottage and stared about the library. She picked up a book and slid it into the shelf. Her heart ached as she went into the bedroom to finish packing. She had just closed the last trunk when she heard a knock on the front door. She went to answer it, thinking it would be Ethan arriving to load her trunks.

It was Clay.

She raised her gaze no farther than his chin. "I'm surprised to see you."

"Are you?"

"I believe we have already said our good-byes."

"I don't recall that we did. I have been waiting for you."

She looked confused when she saw the haunted look in his eyes. "Why?"

"Were you going to leave Galveston without letting me know?"

"Yes."

"May I come in?"

She nodded and stepped back so he could enter. "I don't have very long. The train leaves in less than two hours."

He ducked his head and stepped inside. "We can't leave it like this, Jena Leigh. Grace told me you were going back to Altamesa Springs, and that you might be going abroad from there."

She stared at the brass buttons on his uniform. "There is nothing more we have to say to each other. It was all said."

He moved across the room and back again. "I was angry and said things to hurt you. I was afraid I was going to lose you if you continued to—"

"If I continued to be who I am? You said you accepted me, but you didn't."

He closed his eyes, and then focused on the curtain, which was waving in a breeze blowing through the window. "I haven't slept. I can't eat. I can't do my job. All I can think about is you." He reached out and took her hand. "I need you."

She eased her hand out of his grip and stepped away from him. "I don't understand your kind of need, Clay."

He stepped next to her and gripped her shoulders, turning her to face him. "Then let me tell you about my needs. I need to be with you. I need the right to keep you safe so nothing evil can ever come near you. I need to hold you while I fall asleep at night and feel you close to me." His hand moved down her cheek to rest at her throat. "I've already asked you to be my wife, and nothing has changed, as far as I'm concerned."

She was quaking inside. She wanted to throw herself in his arms, but she dared not. "I believe when two people love each other, they can change something about themselves if it is important to the other one—but I do not believe love should try to change the basic traits that make them who they are."

"Jena Leigh, can you ever forgive me? I was out of my mind with worry. I thought that if I found you dead, I wouldn't want to live anymore either."

"Don't ask me to decide something so important before I've had time to think about it. I know I love you, and, in your way, I think you love me. But I could not endure a marriage in which I would have to behave like someone I'm not. Do you understand?"

He swallowed. "I understand I hurt you. If you need more time to get to know me, I have all the time in the world. But at least give me a chance to prove myself. Don't leave."

She was quiet for a moment. "I have to go, Clay."

"No. No, you don't. For what we have together, for what we shared, give me a few days to convince you we belong with each other."

"First you have to decide whether you can accept me for who I am."

He gathered her close to his heart. "My only fear is that I can't convince you that I love your spirit—it speaks to mine." He tilted her chin upward. "Will you give me another chance?"

She could only nod, because her heart was in her throat. His lips were gentle as they settled on hers. He was careful not to stir their passions. First he would prove to her that she was exactly the woman he wanted.

When he raised his head, he gazed into glittering golden eyes. "Whatever there is between us, it's very powerful, sweetheart. I don't think either one of us can walk away from it."

She stiffened. "I wasn't walking away, Clay. I was running."

"Stay with me and be my wife."

"We have a lot to consider."

"You love me, Jena Leigh."

"There was never any question of that."

"I wish I had more time to spend with you this morning," he said regretfully. "But I'm meeting with General Ross before he sails for Washington. May I return this afternoon, and will you still be here?"

He seemed unsure and nervous. She'd never seen him when he wasn't confident and assured. "I will be waiting for you."

Reluctantly he released her hand, and she walked to the door with him. Before he could take his leave, a buggy stopped in front of the cottage. "That will be

Ethan. I need to tell him I won't be leaving today, after all."

Mrs. Marsh's handyman was climbing out of the seat when Jena Leigh approached him. "I've decided to stay for another few days. If you don't mind, please let Mrs. Marsh know I'll be needing the cottage for a little longer."

Ethan grinned, looking from the Yankee to Jena Leigh. "The missus will be glad to hear you're staying. She's grown right partial to you." He climbed back into the buggy and drove away, leaving an astonished Jena Leigh staring after him. "Mrs. Marsh is partial to me?"

Clay's laughed as he thought of Jena Leigh's endearing qualities, which she was not even aware of. "You could make a dog love his fleas, Jena Leigh."

"Oh, could I?" She gazed past him to a wisteria bush that was in full bloom. "I do love this place. I don't know why, but it seems like home to me."

"It's because I made love to you here," he said, drawing her close. Clay studied her face for a moment, then brushed a quick kiss across her lips before mounting his horse. "Think about us today, Jena Leigh."

How could she think of anything else? "I will."

He was controlling his prancing black stallion with the pressure of his knees. "Don't shut me out, sweetheart. Wait until I return this afternoon, so I can convince you how much I love you."

"Until this afternoon," she agreed, watching him ride away. When she'd awoken that morning, she had been devastated. Now she had hope. He had come to her—

he'd said he loved her, and he wanted her to be his wife. But could she trust their feelings for each other? There was more to marriage than making love. There had to be trust, understanding, and patience.

She bit her lip. She had not been patient with him, she realized. She was so confused.

Chapter Twenty-seven

Jena Leigh spent the rest of the day trying to decide what she should do. In the early afternoon Mrs. Marsh sent Ethan to ask her to come for tea.

A short time later Jena Leigh knocked on the front door, and a smiling Mrs. Marsh met her. "My dear, I can't tell you how delighted I am that you aren't leaving, after all. Your wonderful young man was here, and I must say, I was charmed by him—even if he is a Yankee." She bent forward and whispered, "He is quite wealthy, you know."

Jena Leigh followed Mrs. Marsh into the parlor, where tea had already been laid out on a low table. Henrietta Marsh poured a cup of tea and added cream to Jena Leigh's, knowing that was the way she liked it. "You sly thing, you," she commented, "never letting on that you had caught yourself such a worthy husband."

Jena Leigh took a sip of tea, wondering how Mrs. Marsh could know about her and Clay. She was sure

Grace would never have told her. "I have not agreed to marry Colonel Madison," she said, watching the landlady's face whiten.

"But he told me you were getting married. And if you haven't yet agreed to marry him, you should snap him up right away." She offered Jena Leigh a sandwich from a platter. "He is quite the gentleman, and you will never want for anything. He wasted no time in convincing me to sell him my house and grounds because he said you liked them."

Jena Leigh had just taken a bite of the sandwich and almost choked. "I ... What do you mean?" she asked when she could catch her breath.

"Oh, dear, I hope I haven't spoken out of turn and spoiled the colonel's surprise. I believe he meant it as a wedding present."

Jena Leigh was frantic. "When did he buy your house?"

"A week ago he came to me and asked to purchase it, and I agreed. I thought you should know what lengths he went to just to make you happy."

Jena Leigh took another sip of tea to steady herself. "I had no idea." She was confused because Clay had bought the house even not knowing whether she would marry him. What could it mean?

"Marry him, my dear. You never know when another woman will sink her claws into him. And you aren't going to have very many chances to get a man like him, J.L."

Jena Leigh smiled inwardly. There was continuity to

Henrietta Marsh's personality—she always considered wealth as a road map to happiness. Jena Leigh took another sip of tea, more confused than ever. "What made you decide to sell this place?"

"It's quite simple—I can't afford to keep it up. I have decided to take most of the money from the sale and put it in an account for Grace. I had already asked her if she wanted me to keep this place, and she doesn't. So there you have my reasons."

"But where will you live?" Jena Leigh asked, hoping the woman didn't intend to live with Grace and cause trouble between the newlyweds.

"My sister, Dorothy, is a widow, as I am, and she's been begging me for years to move in with her. She lives down Rio Rosa way and has a very fine house and several servants. I will be quite content to stay there with her."

Jena Leigh spent the rest of her visit in a daze. Clay hadn't turned his back on her if he'd bought the house during her illness. Despite their misunderstanding, he had still wanted to marry her—even after she had sent him away.

There was much to think about. She had hurt him—she saw that now. How could she not have seen how desperate he'd been after her encounter with Parnell? She had been thoughtless of his feelings.

For over an hour Jena Leigh walked the floor, waiting for Clay. It was she who owed him an apology, not the other way around.

* * *

It was early afternoon when Clay arrived. Jena Leigh met him at the door and invited him inside.

"Did you conclude your business?"

"I did. And I tendered my resignation while I was at it."

She searched his eyes. "You don't want to remain in the army?"

He shook his head. "My tour of duty will not be over for another two years, but afterward I have decided to settle here in Galveston." He watched her face as he asked, "You are going to remain here, aren't you?"

"Do you think I should?"

He clasped her hand and his gaze fused with hers. "Jena Leigh, have I ruined it between us? Do you want me to get down on my knees? If you ask it of me, I'll do it."

A cry escaped her lips, and she leaned into his arms and felt them close tightly around her. "Oh, Clay, I was so wrong. I am sorry I put you through such torture. I have been thinking how devastated I would be if you were the one in danger." She pressed her cheek against his. "But I can't say I would react any differently if the same situation were presented to me again."

He drew her tighter against him. "Then I'll just have to make certain you never have to make that choice." He raised her chin. "Will you be my wife, Jena Leigh? Will you take me on and make me into the man you want me to be?"

"Clay," she said, burying her face against his jacket.

"I will never want to change you. I love you just as you are."

He tilted her chin, and his mouth descended slowly. Her arms slid around his waist, and she surrendered the last bit of doubt that lingered in her mind.

He broke off the kiss and held her face between his hands. "Sweetheart, you have had me in despair for days. If you don't marry me, I fear I'm a lost man."

She smiled. "I've never known a man as self-assured and arrogant as you. No woman could tame you completely, and I wouldn't want you too docile."

"Then you will marry me?" She could hear the doubt in his tone. "Will you, Jena Leigh?"

"Just let anyone try to stop me," she said with a gleam in her eyes.

She felt his chest rise and fall. "I want to take you into that bedroom and make love to you right now." He stepped away from her and stared down at the toe of his shiny black boot. "But I will wait until we are husband and wife, as we agreed before."

"I don't want to wait anymore," she said, standing on tiptoe and pressing her mouth against his.

With a groan, he backed her into a wall and pressed his body against her. "Don't tempt me. It wouldn't take much for me to pick you up and bury myself inside you." He pulled away from her. "I came here this morning not sure whether you would even speak to me. I wouldn't have known you were leaving Galveston if Grace hadn't told me." He smiled as he took her hand. "She has this idea that we belong together."

"Grace is right. We do belong together."

Clay was the first to hear a rider approach. A horse whinnied, and there was the jingling of spurs as someone dismounted. Clay fastened his holster and stepped to the door, his hand on the handle of his gun. He watched as a tall stranger walked with long strides toward the cottage. "Stay inside, Jena Leigh, and I'll send this man on his way."

She was hesitant, because she believed the threat to her had passed with the death of Parnell, but Clay was obviously still being cautious. He stepped out the door, and she heard him speak.

"What can I do for you, stranger?"

"I was told a Miss Hawk lives here. Jena Leigh Hawk."

The man's voice stirred memories in Jena Leigh's mind. She knew it from somewhere.

She was afraid to hope.

She went to the window and pulled the curtain aside, staring at the dark-haired man. He was tall—as tall as Clay—and there was something strikingly familiar about him. She caught a glimpse of his eyes, and her heart stopped. Every day when she looked in the mirror, she saw the same-color eyes staring back at her. Racing across the room, she wrenched the door open and stood beside Clay, still afraid to hope. "I'm Jena Leigh."

Whitford Hawk took a quick step toward his sister. It was true—she was alive! She hadn't died in the fire at the orphanage, as he'd been told so many years ago. He held his arms out to her, and she didn't hesitate to run to him. His arms closed around her, and he kissed her cheek; he gripped her hand; he stared into eyes so like his own.

"It's really you." His eyes were swimming with tears. "At long last, the road has brought you back to me."

Her tears dampened Whit's shirt, but Jena Leigh didn't care. Her brother was here, and everything was going to be all right now. "Oh, Whit, I thought I'd never find you."

He hugged her even tighter. "They told me you and Laura Anne had died in the fire, and I believed it."

She pulled back, touching his dear face. "How did you find me?"

"Chantalle saw your pendant; she knew about my ring, so she put the pieces together and sent Will to the ranch to get me. I just spoke to her this morning."

She linked her arm through his. "Have you found Drew?"

"No. But I know where Laura Anne is."

A painful cry escaped her throat. "I know. I saw her die in the fire." She laid her head on his shoulder while her body trembled with sobs. "It was so horrible."

Whit gripped her arms and made her look at him. "Laura Anne isn't dead, Jena Leigh. According to Chantalle she was here in Galveston just a few short weeks ago. I don't know all the particulars yet, but Chantalle tells me she's married and in New York with her husband."

"Laura Anne alive! Oh, God, this is the best day of my life!"

Whit smiled that old smile she remembered so well, and her heart burst with happiness.

"You can't imagine how fast I rode to get here." He laughed and swung her around. "Who ever would have guessed that tiny little girl who once trailed after me would turn out to be such a beauty?"

Jena Leigh's heart was still plagued by doubt. "Are you really sure about Laura Anne? I saw fire all around her." She gripped his arm. "Please tell me she's alive!"

Whit's arms went around her, and he rocked her comfortingly. "She is. But she lost her memory, Jena Leigh. According to Chantalle, she doesn't remember anything that happened to her before the fire."

Jena Leigh saw Clay over Whit's shoulder, and she turned to him. "Clay, I told you that I was looking for my brothers. This is my oldest brother, Whit Hawk."

"Hawk? I never knew that was your last name," Clay said to her.

Whit turned to the officer and shook his hand, looking at him carefully. "I think we've met before," he said, sizing him up with penetrating eyes. "Aren't you with the adjutant general's office?"

Clay was happy that Jena Leigh had found two members of her family. He looked at Whit, and a vague memory stirred to life. "Of course, I remember you now. You came to my office inquiring about your brother."

"That's right," Whit said. "And you mentioned at that time you were looking for your brother as well."

Clay lowered his gaze, and pain stabbed at his heart.

"My brother is dead." He met Whit's gaze. "He died in battle at Charlottesville."

Jena Leigh moved toward Clay, and took his hand while Whit looked on with astonishment. There was more between those two than met the eye, and he wanted to know what it was—but the matter would wait until later. "I know how you feel, Colonel, because I have lived with that possibility every day."

Clay drew in his breath, feeling the pain of loss. "I had suspected for some time that my brother hadn't survived the war. But seeing the death certificate was … difficult."

Whit remembered the day he'd gone to the colonel's office looking for word of Drew, and how understanding the colonel had been. "Please accept my sympathies. I'm sorry," he said, gripping Clay's hand in a firm shake.

"Come into the house and visit while I make supper," Jena Leigh said, opening the door. "I'll call you when it's ready." She was so happy, she couldn't help laughing. "Promise me that if I leave the two of you alone, you won't start the war all over again."

Clay and Whit watched her enter the house; then Whit turned to the colonel. "I haven't seen my sister since we were young, but I'm still her brother, and I think I'm within my rights in asking why she seems so partial to you."

Clay stood eye-to-eye with Whit. "Jena Leigh might want to be the one to tell you, but since you've asked, there is more than mere friendship between us."

"How much more?"

"I've asked her to marry me, and she has accepted."

Whit turned to watch the last streak of color disappear from the eastern horizon. "Maybe you'd better explain to me how you came to know my sister."

After dinner, the three of them sat in the library. Jena Leigh wanted to know all about Whit's life since he'd left El Paso. She was delighted to learn that she had a sister-in-law. "Why didn't you bring Jackie with you?" Jena Leigh asked. "I would love to know her."

"Because I didn't want to get her hopes up in case it wasn't you." He smiled warmly. "She'll be happy to meet you."

Clay watched the brother and sister become reacquainted. He watched Whit tease her, and Jena Leigh poke her finger in Whit's chest when she was trying to make a point. He was happy for her. She had been alone for so long, and now she had a family. Since the hour was late, and the brother and sister had many things to talk about, Clay stood, excusing himself. "I must be going." He nodded at Whit. "I will be seeing you tomorrow."

"I'm not so sure of that," Whit said, watching Jena Leigh's face. "I'm going to try to convince my sister to go home with me. If she agrees, we'll leave early in the morning."

Clay's gaze went to Jena Leigh. "Will you be leaving with him?" He waited, holding his breath for her answer.

She shook her head and looked at her brother. "I

can't go with you, Whit. Clay and I have wedding plans to make." In truth, as much as she wanted to be with her brother and to meet her new sister-in-law, she couldn't imagine a day without seeing Clay.

"Is that your final word on the subject, Jena Leigh?" her brother asked. "I would like to take you with me when I leave."

"We will talk about this later. Right now I'm going to walk outside with Clay, so I can tell him good night."

Whit nodded in understanding.

When Jena Leigh and Clay stood near his horse, he looped the reins around his hand. "Are you sure you won't be leaving with him?"

She heard the worry in his tone. "Do you want me to stay?"

He reached for her and pulled her to him. "I don't want you to be anywhere where I can't reach you."

She looked into his eyes. "Then I shall remain in Galveston." She smiled up at him. "You haven't yet told me about the house you bought me."

A smile played on his lips. "So Mrs. Marsh let the cat out of the bag?"

"She did."

"I know how you love the house and grounds. And I wanted to give you something you could always have."

She raised her head and watched the way the moonlight reflected in his eyes. "I would live with you anywhere, but I do love this place. Thank you."

He gathered her close, his breath stirring against her ear. "I want to be with you."

"I know. It won't be long until we will never be parted."

He touched his lips to the side of hers. "I want to kiss you until you beg me to stop."

She moved back and looked at him. "Then do it."

His laughter rang out. "You are the most delightful creature I've ever known. I can only imagine how you are going to unsettle my world after I've made you my wife."

"Then you'd better run now," she said, smiling.

"It's too late for me. Go inside and be with your brother. We'll make our plans later."

There was so much she wanted to say to Clay, but it could wait. "When will I see you?"

He touched her cheek, and then leaned forward and brushed his mouth against hers. "Tomorrow."

She watched him ride away, already wishing him back. She sensed a loneliness in him tonight that was deep and painful. He might have felt left out when she and Whit were reliving old memories. When she was his wife, she was determined that he'd never feel lonely.

Brother and sister talked through the night, catching up on the years they had missed. She learned about Whit's wife, Jackie. He told her what he'd discovered about Laura Anne, and she told him about growing up with Irene to guide her.

He smiled at her. "Do you know I've read your columns many times without any inkling that J. L. Rebel was my baby sister?"

"I'm not a baby anymore."

"No, I can see that you're not."

She frowned. "I have been considering what I should do with the newspaper and the house in Altamesa Springs, because I will never live there again."

"What do you think you should do?"

"Byron Arnold has been a loyal employee for many years. I think I should make it possible for him to buy the newspaper. I will keep the house because I can't bear to part with it just now. It holds so many memories for me."

Silence fell over the room as each was lost in thought. At last Whit spoke. "Do you love that Yankee?"

"More than I could have ever imagined. He is a truly good man." She leaned her head back on the chair cushion. "Very few men would accept me as I am." She smiled at him. "You know, Mrs. Kingsley taught me to think for myself, and then Irene furthered the notion that I should be independent, so I'm hopeless."

He watched her for a moment. "Chantalle told me about your misadventure. It seems to me you didn't use good judgment, Jena Leigh. Thank God you are all right."

"You share the same view as Clay." She looked at the dear face of the man who had shaped her life and had always been there to comfort her when she was young. "You don't need to worry—Clay will take good care of me."

He held his arms out toward her. "So I find my sister, only to lose her again."

She rested her head on his shoulder. "We will never lose each other again." She pulled back so she could see his face. "We have so much to do. We have to contact Laura Anne, and we still haven't found Drew."

He nodded. "I'm worried about Drew, Jena Leigh. It's as if the earth opened up and swallowed him. I know if he were alive, he'd find his way back here to Galveston."

"We mustn't lose hope. I thought Laura Anne was dead, but she's not."

"And now we have each other," Whit said. "As long as there are at least two of us, we are a family."

Chapter Twenty-eight

Whit rose early and went into the kitchen to make coffee. He walked outside, taking special interest in everything, since Jena Leigh had told him Clay had bought the estate.

He was watching a seabird soar overhead when he heard Clay's voice. "So you are an early riser, too."

Whit glanced at the man who was going to marry his sister. His uniform set him apart from most other soldiers because of the winged eagles on his shoulders. He nodded. "You have to get up early when you live on a ranch."

"I'd like to see a working ranch. My mother grew up on one here in Texas."

"So," Whit said, "you are half Texan."

"I guess you could say that—although I've never thought of it that way."

"My sister tells me your home is in Baltimore. Although you bought this estate for her, do you intend to take her to Baltimore to live?"

"I don't think you know how hard she has searched for her family. I would never take her away from you now. We will settle here, if that is what she wants, and I believe it is."

Whit nodded. "I'm just beginning to like you, Yankee."

"And on which side did you fight in the war?" Clay asked.

"Neither. Even though you won, I'll always feel both sides lost in the conflict. It was a war that should never have been fought."

"On that I agree."

"Jena Leigh tells me you are to be married soon."

Clay stood near a rail fence and propped his boot on the bottom rung. "I hope it's very soon."

"My sister loves you."

Silver-blue eyes met golden in understanding. "I count myself the luckiest man in the world."

"If you don't mind, I would like to be at the wedding, and Jackie would want to be here as well."

"I'm sure Jena Leigh wouldn't have it any other way."

"I'll be leaving today. I trust you to keep my sister safe while I'm gone."

Clay frowned. "Do you think she is in any kind of danger?"

"Keep an eye on Simon Gault. He seems to have a grudge against me. He's just the kind of man who would take that grudge out on my sister."

"Be assured I will not let him anywhere near her."

"And I'd like to have a definite date for the wedding before I leave."

"I was going to ask Jena Leigh if we could set the date for the fifteenth. That's when my three-week furlough begins."

"Let's go ask her. I'm hungry—how about you?"

Jena Leigh had just come from the *Daily Galveston,* where she'd informed Mr. Dickerson that she wouldn't be leaving town, after all, but she still wanted to write only one column a month. She'd never considered giving up her job as a reporter, but now all she wanted to be was Clay's wife. She was about to step into the street when a man riding a huge black horse blocked her path.

She glanced up. "Mr. Gault."

"Miss Rebel."

"Let me pass, please."

He dismounted and stood beside her. "I'll have a word with you."

She found him as distasteful as ever. When he reached for her arm, she moved away from him. "Talk fast then, Mr. Gault, because I have things I need to do."

"I just want to ask you one thing."

"You can ask, but I don't feel obligated to answer."

Anger thrummed through him, but he smiled. "Did you have anything to do with Grace marrying that shopkeeper?"

She looked into his cold black eyes. "Grace merely

married the man she loved. She certainly never loved you."

Gripping her arm, he moved so quickly she didn't have time to react. "If I ever find out you interfered in my life in any way, it'll be the worse for you."

Clay had just come out of the *Daily Galveston,* where he'd been looking for Jena Leigh. When he saw her with Simon Gault, he hurried to her side. Taking Jena Leigh by the hand and pulling her near, he saw the relief in her eyes. "Mr. Gault, isn't it?"

Simon nodded, his heavy gaze settling on Clay. "I was just asking Miss Rebel a question."

She moved closer to Clay. "Take me home."

Simon watched them walk away, holding on to his fury by a mere thread. Instinct told him that woman reporter had somehow intervened in his plans to marry Grace. But if Colonel Madison was her friend, he'd have to tread lightly. He certainly didn't want to tangle with a man in that officer's position.

Jena Leigh glanced in the mirror at her sister-in-law's reflection just behind her. Jackie had midnight blue eyes, and her red hair curled at the sides of her delicate cheekbones. Although Jena Leigh had met her only the day before, she felt as if she'd always known her. She seemed just the right wife for her brother, and it was easy to see that Whit adored his fiery little redhead.

Jackie straightened Jena Leigh's veil and stepped back to look at her. "You are lovely. I see so much of your brother in you."

Jena Leigh turned around and took Jackie's hand. "I can tell you have made Whit happy."

"He will never be completely happy until he knows what happened to Drew, and you can all be reunited with Laura Anne."

Jena Leigh sighed. "I think that's true for both of us."

The wedding was taking place in the enormous parlor of General and Mrs. Ross's home, and Jena Leigh could hear the murmur of voices all the way upstairs.

Grace came into the bedroom where Jena Leigh was dressing and closed the door behind her. "I never saw so many Yankees in one place in my life," she remarked. She walked around Jena Leigh and nodded in approval. "Mrs. Livingston is a wonder. The gown is beautiful, and she made it in just a little over a week."

Jena Leigh pressed her hand against her heart, and joy sang through her body. Grace smiled and held a velvet box out to her. "This is your 'something old.' "

Jena Leigh opened the case and smiled. "It's lovely." She lifted the chain with a simple pearl dangling from a nest of small diamonds. "You can't mean for me to keep this."

"Oh, yes, I do. My mother bought it for me on my twelfth birthday. And to quote a friend of mine, 'I would never give you anything I didn't treasure myself.' " While Grace was fastening the necklace, Whit entered.

"Everyone has gathered." He offered his arm to Jena Leigh. "Shall we go?"

Clay, in full dress uniform, stood beside General Ross, his gaze on the lovely vision descending the stairs on her brother's arm, while Grace and Jackie, both wearing pale yellow gowns, led the way.

"She's a rare beauty, Clay," the general said loudly enough to be heard above the army band that was playing the bridal song.

"Thank you, sir." The woman he loved was coming toward him wearing satin and lace and looking so beautiful it took his breath away. "I agree with you."

Whit relinquished Jena Leigh to Clay, who looked into her eyes and mouthed the words, *I love you.*

The age-old vows were spoken by the bride and groom, and Clay slid a ring on Jena Leigh's finger. Jena Leigh blinked as the army chaplain announced that they were man and wife. Clay drew her into his arms and kissed her, holding her just a little longer than necessary.

Afterward, in an atmosphere of merriment, everyone feasted at the general's long table. Many toasts were offered to Colonel and Mrs. Madison, but none more poignant than the one offered by the bride's brother. With champagne in hand, Whit raised his glass. "May the bride and groom always be as happy as they are tonight." He looked into his sister's eyes. "And may their road often lead them to my table."

Whit drew Jena Leigh aside and held her for a moment. "Don't forget you and Clay are coming to *La Posada* in two weeks."

She pressed her cheek to his. "I won't forget. Your being here has made this a perfect day for me."

Jena Leigh suddenly found herself surrounded by friends, family, and many people she was meeting for the first time. Later, the newlyweds walked down the porch steps beneath the arched sabers of the guard of honor. As Clay lifted Jena Leigh into General Ross's carriage, which was being driven by a smiling Private Ellison, she glanced at her brother, and he smiled and nodded.

Clay's hand clasped hers. "Happy?"

She laid her head against his shoulder. "Very happy."

He was quiet for a moment, and she thought it was because he didn't want to say anything that could be overheard by Private Ellison. At last he whispered, "You came bounding into my life, upsetting my orderly world and making me the happiest of men."

Everyone in Galveston seemed to be watching the grand carriage as it passed by, so Clay could do no more than hold Jena Leigh's hand. They passed a corner of the Strand, and Madam Chantalle nodded to them. On an impulse, Jena Leigh removed a rose from her bouquet and tossed it to her. She watched as the woman caught it in midair and tucked it into her gown, smiling.

They turned from the boulevard onto a dirt road, and Clay's arms slid around Jena Leigh's shoulders. "When you were coming down the stairs to me today, I knew I would never see anything more beautiful."

"We're here, sir," Private Ellison said, halting the team of matching blacks in front of the cottage.

Clay helped Jena Leigh down and returned Private Ellison's salute. Taking his new wife's hand, he scooped her into his arms and carried her over the threshold. "We will have to make do with the cottage until the house has been vacated and then renovated to your liking," he told her, just before he kicked the door shut and brought his mouth down on hers.

Instead of setting her on her feet, he carried her to the bedroom. Jena Leigh's heart was beating like a wild thing.

"There were times when I thought this moment would never come," he said, his voice low and husky.

"You are going to have to help me undress," she said, knowing it was customary for the bride to go to her new husband adorned in her dressing gown—but nothing had been customary between them since the day they'd met.

"With the greatest of pleasure."

She could feel his hands trembling as he undid the tiny buttons at her back. When the white creation slid to the floor and pooled around Jena Leigh's feet, he turned her around, his gaze sweeping over her. He unhooked her hooped skirt, and she stepped out of it.

Boldly she unbuckled the belt that held his saber, and removed his scarlet sash. Clothing was flung aside indiscriminately, and he reached for her, bringing her naked body against his. For a moment they stood locked in each other's arms as their bodies became reacquainted. Her soft curves nestled just right against his hard muscles. She raised her head and saw the glitter in his eyes.

"I want you so badly. In the past weeks we have hardly had a moment alone together," he murmured in her ear. "I want tonight to be memorable for you."

She arched her brow. "We are alone now." Her hand

swept down his chest and paused at his waist. "And every day I've known you is memorable."

He lifted her in his arms and laid her on the bed. Then he went down to her, his mouth hovering above hers, his eyes intense. "Jena Leigh." It was whispered like a prayer. "My wife."

His hand swept over her breasts. "I've been going out of my mind trying to prove to you that I could wait until tonight." He moved back and looked at her. "Were you impressed?"

She giggled. "Very impressed, husband." She buried her fingers in his hair. "Now, are you going to kiss me?"

He readily obliged her. Jena Leigh closed her eyes when his hand moved across her stomach and went lower. "As I remember," she said, gasping when he spread her legs and gently massaged between them, making her hips come off the mattress, "I was similarly tortured, because I wanted to be alone with you." She couldn't think clearly when his finger slid into her warmth and his mouth covered hers.

She twisted and turned, gasping as he gave her pleasure, tormenting her until she was ready to beg him to make love to her. Her fingers sifted through his hair, and she held him to her breast as his tongue swirled across her nipples. When he slid between her parted thighs but paused at her hot, damp entrance, she was almost mindless. "Love me, Clay," she pleaded. "Now," she said in desperation.

He thrust slowly into her, and she closed her eyes, a tear escaping her lashes. Their bodies became one when he gave Jena Leigh everything she wanted and more. She felt his hot arousal glide inside her. She heard his groan and felt his body tremble, and she secretly smiled because she could so easily stir this powerful man's desires.

"I love you," she said against his ear.

His mouth took hers, and he silenced a groan when he plunged deep into her warmth. Her arms held him close as he brought them both to total satisfaction.

Afterward, as the night turned toward morning, he held her in his arms while he slept. Her lips brushed against his cheek. They had been perfect together—he was her life, her heart.

Though her mind would still seek answers about Drew and Laura Anne, she was home with this man who had brought her out of the darkness into the light.

"I love you," she whispered.

He drew her closer and molded her against him. Even in his sleep, he held on to her.

The first shards of light fell across the room, and he opened his eyes, smiled and touched his lips to hers.

Jena Leigh had seen her future in the depths of Clay's silver-blue eyes. At last she belonged to someone, and her home would be wherever he dwelled.

Epilogue

It was a pristine day with seagulls circling over the water as Simon stood on his dock watching cargo being loaded into the hull of one of his ships. It always made his chest swell with pride when a vessel with his name on it sailed away for distant ports. A shadow fell in front of him, and he glanced at Bruce Carlton, his longtime henchman.

"I don't need your sour face to spoil a perfect day."

"Then you don't want to see the morning newspaper."

Simon summed Bruce up in only one word: *irritating*. He was a slight man with thinning gray hair, and he had an annoying habit of taking his handkerchief out of his pocket and shining his glasses. He did so now, and Simon clamped his teeth together. "I suppose you are going to show me what you're talking about?"

Bruce took the newspaper from under his arm and unfolded it, pointing to a particular item. "This is what

Constance O'Banyon

you've been wanting to find out." Bruce watched his boss's eyes darken with anger and hatred.

Simon grabbed the newspaper from his assistant, his jaw tightening as he read the article. There was a picture of J. L. Rebel in a wedding gown. He glanced down the page. "She's married to Colonel Madison. So? What if she is?"

"Don't look at the picture, Simon. Read the article."

" 'Jena Leigh Hawk became the bride of—' What the hell!"

Bruce grinned. "I thought that would get your attention. And it seems Whit was at the wedding, too."

"Bring the buggy around front and drive me to Chantalle's place. You can bet she knows all about this. I'll get rid of all the Hawks if it's the last thing I ever do."

Bruce smiled to himself. So far Simon had allowed two members of the Hawk family to slip through his fingers, and here was a third one showing up to plague him. Bruce knew more about Simon's dealings than anyone, but he'd never understood his boss's hatred for the Hawk family. It all had something to do with Simon's shipping business, which had once belonged to Harold Hawk.

His steps were hurried as he went for the buggy. His boss was not an easy man to work for, and as his employee, Bruce had done unspeakable deeds for Simon. He'd go on doing them as long as he was well paid.

Simon was silent as he climbed into the buggy, but as Bruce guided the team down the boulevard, he could feel the malice emanating from his boss. One day there would be a final conflict between Simon and the Hawk family, and only one of them could win. He was betting on the Hawks. If that family knew what he knew, they would bring Simon down so fast and hard, it would cause a storm surge.

When the buggy stopped, Simon got out. "Wait for me," he ordered sharply. Before today, Simon had never arrived at Chantalle's by the front entrance, but now he was too angry to care what anyone thought. When he reached the door, he shoved it open, searched the front room, and then went into the card room. Angie was there, sitting on some cattleman's lap while he fondled her openly. "Where's your boss lady?"

Angie slid off the man's lap. "Can I do anything for you, Simon?"

"Go back to your cowhand. I don't want anything from you except the answer to my question."

Angie was troubled. "Chantalle is in her office, or she was an hour ago."

Anger drove Simon's steps as he climbed the stairs. Chantalle's office door was open, and she watched him approach with a slight smile on her face. She waited silently as he flopped down in a stuffed chair. "You knew all along who she was, didn't you?"

"Who?"

"Don't play games with me, Chantalle. You know very well what I'm talking about."

Chantalle rolled her chair closer to her desk while she studied Simon's face. "You must be desperate if you chose to come to my front door. Don't you care anymore if the good people of Galveston see you visiting my place?"

"Jena Leigh Hawk. That's what I'm talking about."

Chantalle laughed. "Oh, you mean Jena Leigh Madison."

"How long have you known she was in town?"

"For a while." She picked up a wilted rose that she had put in a vase of water, and held it to her nose. "You don't dare touch her now. The man she's married to would rip your guts out if you came anywhere near her. And I intend to tell him that you are a threat to his wife, if Whit hasn't already told him. You'd better be very sure you don't do anything that will point a finger at you. In fact, if I were you, I'd guard the colonel's lady from harm, because if anything happens to her, a whirlwind will be stirred up."

"What are you talking about?"

"Colonel Madison. Would you dare touch a hair on the head of his wife?"

Simon's face whitened. "Dammit," he swore. "I should have suspected when I first met that reporter that she was Jena Leigh."

Chantalle leaned forward and fixed Simon with a hard glare. "Unless you want the whole Union Army crawling down your neck, you'd better leave her alone."

Simon shot out of the chair. "Someday, Chantalle, you are going to push me too far."

"No. Someday you are going to push the Hawk family too far. Get out, Simon."

"With pleasure," he said, heading for the door.

She heard his heavy tread on the stairs, and moments later the front door slammed. Jena Leigh was safe from Simon. He wouldn't dare do anything to hurt her now. Chantalle's gaze turned to the window, and she frowned. Where was the other brother? Perhaps dead—she hoped not. She cared a great deal about what happened to the Hawk family.

Chantalle would keep her vigil. She knew Simon was still a threat—not only to the family, but to her as well. He would strike again, and she would be watching him when he did.

HAWK'S PRIZE

Don't miss the
final book in the
Hawk Crest saga—
Coming
November 2006!

Elaine Barbieri

Drew is the last of the four siblings to return to Galveston, the first to admit he is in over his head. Stranded in a high-priced bordello because of a wounded leg, Drew finds himself being nursed by a woman of mystery. Sensual lady of the night or innocent angel of mercy, she keeps her identity secret. But as he is reunited with his brother and sisters, and the wrongs of the past are righted, one thing becomes clear: Tricia Lee Shepherd is the other half of his soul, the only person who can make his future shine bright.

THE MOON
AND THE STARS
CONSTANCE O'BANYON

Caroline Richmond started running on her wedding day—the same day her husband died. Her solitary life is filled with fear of her malicious brother-in-law always one step behind her. She thought she'd found a shred of peace in Texas. But when a mysterious bounty hunter comes to town, she knows the wrath in his amber eyes is meant only for her. He finds a way to be everywhere she is, making her nerves hum in a way she thought she'd conquered.

Wade Renault came out of retirement for one reason: to see a deceptive murderess brought to justice. But when he meets the accused woman, he senses more panic than treachery. She lives too simply, she seems too honest and scared. Someone had deceived him, but he will wait to get her right where he wants her, beneath...*The Moon and the Stars.*
